AMONG THE
BEASTS & BRIARS

AMONG THE BEASTS & BRIARS

ASHLEY POSTON

BALZER + BRAY

An Imprint of HarperCollins*Publishers*

Balzer + Bray is an imprint of HarperCollins Publishers.

Among the Beasts & Briars
Copyright © 2020 by Ashley Poston
Map illustration © 2020 by Maxime Plasse
All rights reserved. Printed in the United States of America.
No part of this book may be used or reproduced in any manner whatsoever
without written permission except in the case of brief quotations embodied
in critical articles and reviews. For information address HarperCollins
Children's Books, a division of HarperCollins Publishers, 195 Broadway,
New York, NY 10007.
www.epicreads.com

ISBN 978-0-06-284736-2

Typography by Corina Lupp
20 21 22 23 24   PC/LSCC   10 9 8 7 6 5 4 3 2

First Edition

To my Oma,
who could make flowers bloom

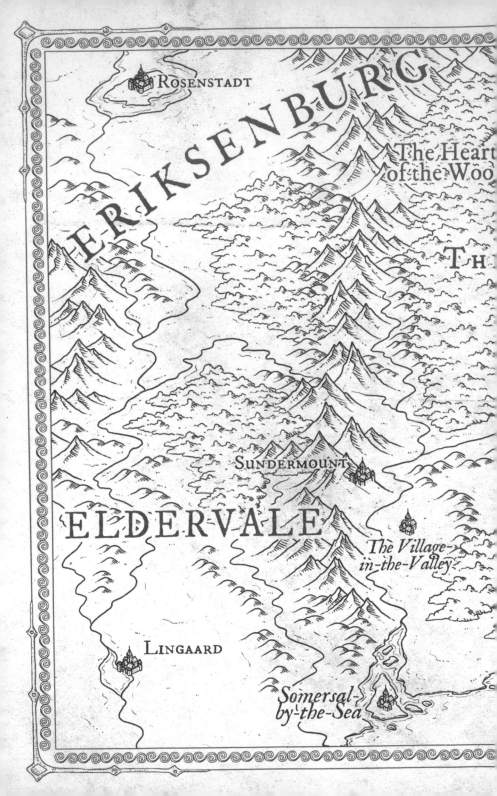

A map of
VAIYL

VORYN

WILDWOOD

ALORIYA

NOR

Levina River

Saferine Sea

PLASSE
2020

IT IS SAID *that the first king of Aloriya was born with fire in his blood. It was a time when the cursed wood that bordered Aloriya snarled and snapped at the edges of the kingdom, the same cursed wood that had been plaguing the people of Aloriya for as long as anyone could remember, but he was not afraid. He razed a path through the cursed wood to the magical city of Voryn and struck a bargain with the Lady of the Wilds. What he asked for was simple—that Aloriya be protected from the monsters who lurked in the forest she commanded.*

It is said the Lady took pity on the king, for he did brave her cursed wood, and gifted him a crown that would protect his people; but because she feared his magic, she made him

1

promise that neither he nor any Aloriyan would ever return to her city. The forest on the edge of Aloriya would be forbidden to all its people. He agreed.

For three hundred years, Aloriya flourished. The crown was passed from father to son, from king to heir, and there were no monsters, no famines, no plagues, no wars.

And the city of Voryn, deep in the forbidden wood, fell to legend.

It is said that the Lady of the Wilds gifted King Sunder a glorious crown.

It is a lie.

❦ 1 ❧

THE VILLAGE-IN-THE-VALLEY

Cerys

THE WILDWOOD CAME for us the day the king died.

At first it was only a few spots on an orchid, small black rotten dots that few would even notice. I didn't think anything of it. It hadn't looked like any disease I could remember; still, I simply bit my first finger until I could taste blood on my tongue, then pressed a droplet into the heart of the dying flower.

It bloomed once again, pale blue petals unfurling, growing to the size of my palm. I needed a bouquet to give Lady Ganara for that evening's coronation, after all. A little blood never hurt anything, and no one was ever the wiser, anyway. I slid the bloom back into the vase, beside baby's breath and a few sprigs of bluebells. Papa told me to only use my *talent*, for lack of a better word, sparingly. A gardener's daughter with blood that could raise entire forests? Only the royal family had magic in their blood. What would Aloriya think if they knew I had a touch of magic, too? Even if my power was small, I was quite sure I would be the talk of the town. And not in the good way.

"Morning, Sprout!" Papa greeted me, coming in through the front of the shop. He knocked the dirt off his boots at the door and hung up his coat. "It's a beautiful day for a coronation!"

"Don't jinx it," I replied, making a tag for the bouque— *Lady Ganara*, I wrote in my tight, neat cursive.

Papa belted a laugh. "What could go wrong? The sky's bright, the sun's out, and there's spring in the air—I can taste it."

"Mm-hmm. Watch it start raining the moment Wen says her vows. 'Oh, I would be *delighted* to accept this crown . . . after the monsoon,'" I said in the princess—soon-to-be queen—of Aloriya's crisp accent, grabbing the crown of daisies I'd made yesterday from the counter and placing it on my head. I mocked the royal wave to all the flowers in the shop. "Why, thank you for coming! I am *delighted* to ruin all your fine clothes this evening."

Papa laughed louder as he escaped into the kitchen just off from the shop. He clanked around in the cabinets to find a cup and poured himself some coffee. He smelled like soil and freshly clipped flowers already, in dirty brown overalls and hard work boots, chewing on a stem of mint. His sun-browned skin was spotted with age, but his gray eyes were bright—like mine. "I got a feeling I won't be comin' back into the village today. It's a riot up at the castle. The seneschal's about to lose her head, she's so stressed."

"Poor Weiss. I feel for her."

"I don't," Papa groused, coming back to lean on the kitchen doorframe, into the small flower shop at the front of the house. The shop itself was part of our house. Papa and I lived upstairs, but the kitchen was downstairs, and out the rear door were the gardens where we grew most of our flowers. "The old crone yelled at me again this morning."

"Probably for trampling muddy boots all over the castle again."

"That was one time, and it was an emergency."

I snorted. What my father deemed an emergency was showing King Merrick four-leaf clovers, or roses I'd accidentally bled on that turned strange shades of purple. I highly doubted it was an actual *emergency*. The late king had been Papa's best friend—one of the reasons that Princess Anwen was mine. He had been in the room when the king took his final breath two nights ago, and we barely had time to mourn his passing, as the kingdom was to be inherited by his children—

Child, I corrected myself. Because there were no longer two.

Papa seemed to be reminiscing about the same thing. "It feels like it didn't happen. Like he's still here. I keep forgetting."

7

"I know," I replied softly.

He stood quietly for a moment longer and then blinked his wet eyes and cleared his throat. "Well! No use dawdling; we've got work to do." He hooked his thumbs into the loops of his overalls and came around the front of the counter. He took a look at the bouquets ready to be picked up and paused on Lady Ganara's. "Kingsteeth, those are some beautiful blue orchids." Papa bent in to smell them—and winced.

While magic couldn't be seen, it did have a distinct scent that lingered for a while where it had been worked. The smell was like that of the Wildwood—like a sunlit forest just after heavy rain. Orchids did not smell like that. He leveled a stern look at me. "Cerys . . ."

"I know. I doubt she'll notice, though. Last night the flowers were fine, but this morning they were speckled with these weird black spots."

"What kind of spots?"

"Rot, it looked like? It was strange—but I fixed them. I just used a drop. I don't see what the big deal is. It's just magic, like Wen and her family have."

Papa's lips thinned into a line, and he took my hands in his, turning them over to see the wound on my finger. "You need to be careful. Our town, our village, they love you so much. I'm not worried about how they'd react to you having magic. But there is magic . . . and then there are curses."

"And mine's a curse, I know."

He squeezed my hands tightly. "The Wilds touched you, but they didn't keep you."

I glanced away.

Papa let go of my hand. "Maybe add a few more sprigs of baby's breath to cover up the scent—and then close up shop at noon and bring the last half dozen rose bouquets with you to the castle when you come."

"Don't forget your garden keys," I reminded him as he turned toward the front door.

He snapped his fingers and retreated back to get them from the hook in the kitchen. As he passed by the counter again, he planted a kiss on my forehead. "What would I do without you, Sprout?"

"Forget your head."

He laughed. "I'll see you in a bloom."

"In a bloom," I agreed, and watched him as he left through the front door and started out of the village on foot. He would catch a ride with one of the guards at the bottom of the Sundermount, and they would take him the rest of the way up the mountain to the castle.

The castle of Aloriya was perched at the edge of the wood, among the peaks of the Lavender Mountains. The spires stretched like shafts of broken bone toward the stars. It was much prettier at night, when all the windows were golden and warm, driving away the coldness that clung to it in the daytime, lit up like a body that had finally found its soul.

After Papa was well on his way to the castle, I slipped out of my apron, poured myself the last bit of coffee from the press, and stepped out back into the garden. It was a quarter to eight in the morning; the shop didn't officially open until eight o'clock. My finger was still bleeding a little, so I ran it across the doorframe, and from it moss grew in a thick green patch, like a swipe of paint across the weathered wood.

I sat down on the stone bench outside the door and leaned back against the house.

The gardens were small, but what they lacked in space they made up for in colors—leaves of green and kaleidoscopes of flowers bloomed on stems and in the latticework creeping up the house, having taken decades to climb. Roses thrived in the side gardens, and strange star-shaped flowers clustered in the corners of the yard where my mother had planted some foreign Wildwood seeds. Papa and I didn't sell those—they might have just been flowers, or they could have been cursed, and while we didn't want to lose the memory of my mother, we also couldn't risk any part of the Wildwood spreading.

The village knew my mother came from outside Aloriya— something that didn't exactly help my dating prospects. There were only so many young people in the Village-in-the-Valley, and I'd gone to grade school with almost every single one of them; we all knew each other's stories—where we came from, what we wanted to be someday, who we wanted to marry— but no one was as whispered about as I was, the girl whose

10

mother had been an outsider. Then, later, the girl whose mother got lost in the wood. The pickings were slim to begin with, and I honestly didn't have time for the ones who "could overlook my oddities."

It also didn't help that most of the village thought that my best friend was a stupid fox that wouldn't stay away from me, no matter how many times I tried to shoo him off. I had rescued him from a hunter's trap near the wood two years ago, and since then, he apparently thought we were inseparable.

"Can you *stop* nosing through the baker's garbage?" I scolded the little jerk as he slunk out from underneath the bench, a hunk of some sort of pastry in his mouth. "One of these days Mrs. Cavenshire's going to catch you."

The fox didn't seem to care. He never cared. He just kept going through the baker's trash, then would hide in our garden, hoping that I'd keep away the hounds when they came sniffing around. Now the fox hopped up on the bench beside me and gave me an unreadable look.

"*Fine*," I muttered, and scratched him behind the ears. He began to purr—which was probably the most charming thing about him. "Today's the day, you know. Anwen's getting the crown. She'll be Queen Anwen Sunder."

The fox gave a lazy yawn.

A voice interrupted my morning solitude. "*Queen* sounds awfully pretentious."

I glanced up toward the pergola on the other side of the

garden as a gangly pale white boy in threadbare trousers that barely came down to his ankles, a wrinkled button-down shirt, and a brown vest came in. He had two fresh croissants in his hands from the bakery next door, and a wide smile on his face that made his cerulean eyes glimmer. A sliver of long golden hair escaped his newsboy hat, giving him away. As if his grace hadn't already.

"Shouldn't you be at the castle?" I asked the princess of Aloriya as she handed me a croissant.

"Shush and eat," Anwen replied, lifting the fox up from his spot and putting him on her lap as she sat down.

I twirled a lock of her golden hair around my finger. "Your disguise is coming undone."

"Again?" Wen made a disgruntled noise and took off her hat. Long golden hair spilled down her shoulders, reaching her lower back in soft curls. "It doesn't matter. You'd recognize me anyway whether I was a boy or, I don't know, a *goat*."

I laughed. "I should hope so; we've been friends since we were six—"

"Five," she corrected.

"Are you sure?"

"It was right after your father caught you cutting your own hair and you had bangs like—" And she angled her fingers slantwise across her forehead. "Do you think I'd forget something like that? My brother wouldn't stop making fun of you for weeks."

I shivered, remembering, and handed her the cup of coffee. "Well, *I* certainly forgot until this very moment. Your brother hated me."

"I don't think he did at all," she replied, and took a sip of coffee to wash down a bite of croissant. "I miss him."

"Me too."

We sat and ate our breakfast quietly.

There was still so much to do before the coronation. I had to finish up the rose decorations and tend to the arrangements already in the store, all before I loaded up the wagon and made my way to the castle to help Papa set up for the rest of the afternoon. I felt exhausted just thinking about it. And I kinda didn't want the coronation to come—ever. Because once Anwen was crowned, everything would change.

Anwen rubbed the fox behind his ears. "Cerys, do you think I'll be a good ruler? As good as my brother would've been?"

I gave a start. "Why wouldn't you be?"

She let the fox nibble on the rest of her croissant and gave a half-hearted shrug. "What if . . . what if the crown doesn't take to me? Father died so suddenly, and he never gave me the chance to wear it. It keeps the curse and the creatures of the forest at bay, but how?" She outstretched her hand, and as she brushed her thumb and forefinger together, a flame bloomed in the air. It took my breath away every time she called her magic, the same magic that ran in her ancient bloodline. The same magic that razed the cursewood three hundred years ago. The flame flickered on the tips of her fingers. "Do *I* do something? I don't know."

"You'll figure it out—you're a Sunder, after all. It's in your blood, in your magic," I replied, and put my hand over hers to smother the flame. "And whenever you need me, I'm here. I'll always be here for you."

"Promise?"

I was the royal gardener's daughter. There was nowhere else I was supposed to be. "I promise, Anwen Sunder."

A small smile graced her lips. "Thank you."

We shared the rest of the coffee as the cool morning mists that surrounded the Village-in-the-Valley slowly lifted. The sun was bright and golden, and the sky was blue, and spring grew warm and light in the air. Papa was right. It was going to be a beautiful day.

The fox shook his head, having gotten bored with us, and hopped off Wen's lap. He began to slink around the gardens.

"If you go for those strawberries . . . ," I warned him.

Wen snorted. "He's just a fox. He's not going to listen. Honestly, I don't see why you put up with him."

I cocked my head. "He'll make a great hat someday."

She gave a laugh, and then, unexpectedly, she turned to me. "Cerys, will you be part of my coronation tonight?"

It took me a moment to react. ". . . *What?*"

"You and your papa both—I want you with me up on the terrace, not hiding in the back by the garden wall. You're both family to me. I can't imagine starting my reign as queen without you. You . . . you're the only one who really understands." Her gaze turned hesitantly to the edge of the Wilds, the line of soft green trees that looked innocent, a mask for the curse within. "If I didn't have you in my life . . . I'd be alone."

But if I weren't in your life, your brother might still be alive, I thought before I could catch myself.

Wen smiled hesitantly. "Will you? Please?"

It was an honor, not to mention a breaking of tradition. Only those most important to the royal bloodline were allowed on the coronation steps with the anointed, and my papa and I were simple gardeners. We didn't command countries or save villages from disaster. We tended to flowers. We helped them bloom.

Anwen was asking me to be one of those most important people—and my heart swelled at the thought. I wanted to cry.

But when I looked back into her eyes, I could only see the wood, as it surrounded us all those years ago. On the day she and I survived.

2

THE WILDWOOD KNOCKS

Cerys

ON THE DAY my mother died, there was a shadow at the edge of the wood.

I had pricked my finger on a rose stem that morning. Back then, my blood didn't bloom flowers. It didn't raise forests. It was just a small cut that Mama kissed before she sat me on the counter and braided daisies into my hair. She hummed along as Papa sang in the garden out back. It was a song about a man urging the woman he loved to leave the comfort of her life and sail away with him, and the woman asked the man to stay and put down roots with her instead. My mother had always loved the song.

I missed the way she hummed softly as Papa howled the words. He was a terrible singer, but she loved it when he sang

16

anyway. It was a soft, warm day at the end of the summer, and the shop had been slow.

My mother kissed me on the back of the head and said, "All done, my sweet sprout. I think your friends are waiting."

She motioned to the front of the window, where two children smashed their faces against the glass—siblings with golden hair, barely a year apart. Anwen and her brother. Behind them, a blur through the window, was the shadow of the captain of the guard's squire, tasked with looking after them. I excitedly hopped down off the counter. "Bye, Mom! Be back in a bloom!"

"In a bloom!" she called back as I tugged open the door and sunlight spilled into our quaint shop.

"Papa's got a new gelding in the stables," Prince Lorne said excitedly.

Anwen nodded. "It's black!"

The squire gave a tired sigh. "We're *not* going back up there."

"We are!" the siblings proclaimed. Anwen grabbed my hand and pulled me onto the road that led away from the edge of the village, where my family's shop was. Golden wheat fields surrounded the valley that fall. It was the beginning of autumn; still warm enough to not need a jacket, but the evenings brought a crisp chill. The Wildwood trees had already begun to turn orange and red, and it was between those trees, at that moment dashing toward the center of the village, that I saw it.

The shadow. It lurked at the edge of the Wildwood, and

then it seemed to turn and stalked back into its depths.

"It's nothing," the squire had said, squinting where I'd pointed. He put his hands on his hips and shook his head. "Just your imagination, Cerys. The crown protects us from the wood, you know."

"But what if it's not my imagination?" I asked.

Wen brandished a wooden sword that she pulled from her belt. "Then we'll fight it!"

We were nine, and therefore invincible. The squire turned his gray eyes toward the sky and gave a long sigh. He was tall and fit, with tanned skin and calluses across his hands from years of sword fighting. His name was Seren—seventeen, the age I am now—and while he was tasked with the daily watch of the young prince and princess, he often seemed more like our peer than a caretaker. He certainly was a terrible babysitter, now that I think back on it. He liked to think he was tougher than everyone else, and smarter, even though I once saw him cry over a raven that had collided with the castle wall and broken its neck.

Anwen's brother, who had just turned ten, was different, though. He was anxious and quiet. "I think we should tell Father."

Seren grinned at him. "You scared or something, princeling?"

"No, I just think—"

"That there's something scary in the wood?"

"I'm *not* afraid!" Lorne snapped, and as if to prove it, he puffed out his chest and reached out his hand. He brushed his thumb against his forefinger, and a small flame burst to life. It let off a soft orange glow that made the trees tremble at the sight. He steeled himself and marched toward the wood. "I'll show you. Come on."

Wen prickled. "Wait! But what if there really *is* something in the wood? What if there's . . . an ancient?"

Her brother replied, "I'll burn it."

"Right, like you could kill anything—you can't even beat me in a duel," replied Seren, following him up the King's Road toward the beginning of an old trade road. "You wouldn't last a minute against an ancient."

"How do you know?" Lorne shot back, the flame in his hand flickering brightly. "When was the last time anyone even saw one?"

Someone should have stopped them—*I* should have, but I simply followed behind them, bound toward the edge of the Wilds.

The leaves on the trees we approached were a molten gold, like an artist had taken a sunset and poured it over the forest, and the crisp smell of the coming winter floated on the autumn breeze. It was early afternoon, and the birds sang bright and loud in the treetops.

Of course, the wood itself was prohibited, and the single trade road that cut through the dark forest was now barely a sliver of white rock in the wood—overgrown over centuries of disuse. Some said that the road led to the magical city of Voryn, deep in the heart of the forest, but that was just a story. I didn't know if Voryn still existed, indeed if it had ever existed. The Wildwood met Nor, a neighboring kingdom, on the other side, and beyond that a vast desert. The few people over the years who had defied the royal decree and ventured even a quarter mile into the wood and come out alive told of bone-eaters with razor teeth, and trees that screamed, and shadows that shifted on their own.

My mother was one of those people.

Papa met her on the road outside of the Village-in-the-Valley, having emerged from the Wildwood, badly bleeding but alive. He nursed her to health, and they fell in love, and I was born. My mother's memories of the time before she came out of the wood were few, but Papa didn't need to know anything more about her than that he loved her, and that she loved him. While they lived in this small cottage at the edge of the Village-in-the-Valley, she would sing enchanted songs about the Lady of the Wilds—one of the old gods from before trains and carriages and muskets, the one who, legend said, had gifted the first king of Aloriya with his crown—and the flowers in our small shop would listen.

"We're not supposed to wander into the wood," Anwen said as she walked beside me, wringing her hands together. Her hair was cropped close to her head—not a week before,

20

we had been running through the kitchens to show the king the flame she'd finally summoned in her hand, when she'd tripped and her hair had caught fire. Seren had tossed a bucket of water at her to put it out, but there was no other thing to be done than to cut her burned hair off. Seren was constantly getting us out of trouble.

Then again, now that I thought back on it, he was often the one getting them *into* trouble, too.

"Hello?" Seren shouted into the wood where I had last seen the shadow. "Is anyone there?"

Only the wood answered back, soft and buzzing with life.

Anwen shifted anxiously. "What if Cerys saw an ancient? They take you and turn you into a *bone-eater*."

I shivered at the word. A bone-eater was a person who had been woodcursed but hadn't died, and who wandered the wood in a sort of half-life, empty and hungry. They were the most terrifying denizens in the wood aside from the ancients—monsters that prowled the deepest, darkest parts of the forest. I'd never seen a bone-eater or an ancient before that day. I'd seen wolves and foxes and deer and snakes and all sorts of woodland creatures, but never a bone-eater. I had never wanted to.

Lorne cocked his head, moving the flame from one finger to another thoughtfully. "They wouldn't dare come this close to the edge. The crown protects us. Besides, what if it's someone who needs our help?"

"Wouldn't they already be turned?" I asked.

"Your mom wasn't," he replied, to which I didn't have an answer.

"And there's nothing to worry about while I'm here," Seren added.

I felt my chest constrict. "But . . ."

I should have pressed harder. I should have told them it was a trick of my eyes—that we should just go and see the black gelding. Not dawdle here, on the edge of the Wildwood, where the crown's protection waned. But I didn't—and so what followed was all my fault.

"Do you hear that?" Lorne asked, turning toward the wood again. He raised his hand higher, and the flame shone orange and yellow against the tree bark and autumn leaves.

Anwen strained to listen. "I don't hear anything."

"It sounded like . . . someone crying."

"You're hearing things," Seren replied, but either Lorne ignored him or he wasn't paying attention, because he took a step into the wood, heading for a sunlit clearing about fifty feet away. "Hey, *wait*!" Seren shouted.

Lorne walked into the wood, calling, "Hello? Are you hurt?" to someone none of us could hear. Wen fussed with her short hair, pulling at it nervously, glancing back toward town, but there was no one on the road at the moment, and the golden fields behind us were empty, wind bending the soft yellow stems in waves.

"Don't go too far!" Wen shouted.

Lorne waved her off. "I'm *fine*! I'm just going to that tree, and if I don't find them, I'll turn around."

"He'll be fine," Seren agreed. "It's just, what, fifty feet?"

"You're a terrible babysitter," Wen said.

Seren muttered something under his breath and fingered the hilt of the sword on his belt. When the princess gave him another imploring look, he rolled his eyes and marched into the wood after Lorne. "Slow down, princeling. Don't want you to burn the whole forest down if you get scared."

Lorne was twenty feet into the wood now—twenty-five.

Back then, I knew him. I knew his favorite color, his favorite food, his favorite book. I knew that he could hit a pigeon out of the air with one shot of his arrow. That he could light an entire room of candles with a single wave of his hand, the Sunder bloodline's magic so strong in him that things caught fire when he grew too angry. I knew him better than I knew myself, having spent long nights in the tallest spire of the castle, mapping out just how far we'd go. To the seas. To the horizon. To the world beyond. But that was before that day. Before the wood.

Before . . .

"Hey, princeling, why don't you come back and—" Seren's words caught in his throat. He paled.

Because in the wood there were only trees and sunlight spilling across the green grove, and silence.

The prince and his firelight were gone.

Seren, only a foot into the wood, took off running into the trees, abandoning the sunflower seeds, calling his name. Wen shouted at him to stop, but I just watched him go. I couldn't stop him. I couldn't move. Because in the spilling sunlight I saw the shadow from earlier.

I saw the ancient raise its antlered head. I saw it look at me with its deep yellow eyes, bare its bone-white teeth—

There in the clearing one moment, and suddenly—

Wen took off into the wood after Seren, and this time I followed. He couldn't have gotten far, we thought. Seren shouted Lorne's name, but there was not a response. The farther in we went, calling his name, the more we began to panic. Soon we could barely see the light of the edge of the wood through the trees behind us. Wen slipped on loose rocks and fell into a ravine. She twisted her ankle and couldn't move it, so Seren descended into the ravine, picked her up, and put her on his back.

I didn't even know which way the village was anymore. The trees all looked the same.

Seren called the prince's name, again and again, his voice bouncing off the oaks and pines, and as the sun lowered, a seeping fog began to crawl across the ground toward us. I recognize the fog now, but back then I didn't know what it was. I was scared—but I should've been frightened out of my wits.

As Seren climbed out of the ravine with Wen on his back, the fog thickened.

"I think there's something here," I told them.

A limb snapped to our left and we whirled around. A figure surfaced out of the fog, and Seren reached for his knife—

"Mama!" I cried as a honey-haired woman rushed to me and hugged me tightly.

Seren was perplexed. "How did you find us?"

"You were shouting," she replied simply, though it seemed impossible now that she could have heard us all the way down in the village. We were well into the forest by then. But somehow, she had come anyway.

She inspected Wen's foot. "It's not broken, only twisted."

"My brother's lost," Wen told her, sobbing. "He's lost and we can't find him!"

"Shh, it's okay," replied my mother, cupping Anwen's face in her hands. I remember her voice so well, its soft and sweet cadence. She wore her hair in a long, simple braid, and there were always flowers in it. That day they were daisies, the ones she had braided into mine. "It'll be fine. I'll find him and keep him safe."

And we believed her.

She pointed us in the direction out of the wood and told us to run as fast as we could. She told us not to look back. And we didn't—until we heard a shriek, so loud the wood seemed filled by it. Seren stopped and turned back toward her in the fog. He looked torn.

"We have to keep going," I pressed. "Mom told us—"

"I know," he replied. Then he knelt down and slowly eased Anwen off his back, draping her arm over my shoulder so I could help hold her up. He kissed her forehead and told us to keep running out of the wood. "I'll catch up. I promise."

"But—"

"The prince is my responsibility. I have to find him," he replied, and then he ran back into the fog, toward the shriek and the growls and my mother and Lorne. And Wen and I stood there for a moment longer as he fled into the mists—there one moment, and then gone.

"W-We have to keep going," Anwen hiccupped, sobbing, tearing me out of my thoughts.

But Mom was still in the wood.

I turned to Wen and told her, "Stay here—okay? I'll be right back."

She grabbed me by the arm, her nails digging into my flesh to root me there. "You're not going back in there! You'll never come back."

"I can't leave my mom."

She hiccupped a sob and held on tighter. "But—but what about me?"

"The wood won't come for you if you make it out," I replied, because of the pact the ancient king made with the cursewood. Anwen would be safe, but I couldn't just sit here while my mother—while she . . .

My best friend's fingers slowly released me. She slumped against a tree, defeated. "Please don't leave me."

"I'll come back," I promised, and went into the wood again, deeper than I ever had before. The thorns and briars that curled up from the underbrush picked at the edges of my dress, grabbing at them, as if pleading me to stop. But I couldn't. Around me, the bone-eaters swarmed like bees, but I couldn't see them in the thick fog. When I was sure I was back to where I had last left my mother, all I found were trees. They had just disappeared. When I looked back, I couldn't see Wen anymore, either.

"Seren!" I cried, stumbling deeper into the wood. "Where . . ." I heard something crunch under my feet. I shifted my foot away, and there was a pair of broken glasses. Seren's. I quickly grabbed them up. "Seren! Where are—"

Through the trees, I saw two figures in front of a hollowed-out log. One was Seren—and the other was impossibly tall, powerful, and skeletal. The ancient held Seren off the ground by his throat. Seren kicked and struggled, blood darkening the front of his jerkin from the ancient's claws.

The monster was killing him.

I grabbed a stick from the ground and threw it at the beast. It hit the creature's bone-white skull. The ancient dropped Seren and turned toward me.

Seren slumped onto the ground and didn't move. Why wasn't he moving?

The ancient studied me with gleaming yellow eyes. In the mist, black motes floated in the air like snow. But I'd never seen black snow before. It looked like . . . seeds. Black dandelion seeds.

Something stung the side of my neck, and I quickly brought my hand up to swipe away whatever it was—and I felt what could only be the woodcurse. Something like roots began to burrow into my skin, and I gave a cry, pulling at them, but they were already so deep.

The next thing I knew, the creature was towering over me, flashing its sharp white teeth. I stumbled back, over a root, and fell onto my back. The pain in my neck blossomed into agony, and I could barely move.

The ancient lunged for me. I screamed and flung my arms up over my face—

Then there was silence.

I felt a wetness drip onto my arm. It was bright red like a paint splotch. I turned my eyes upward.

In front of me was my mother. She knelt over me, her back toward the ancient, shielding me from harm. The ancient had its claws in her, so deep they came through the other side. In her honey hair, there were the daisies she had twined into them this morning. I remembered them so vividly. Not her face. Not her voice. The daisies. And I remembered that when she smiled at me that final time, her mouth was filled with blood.

She pressed a red kiss on my forehead.

A shiver ran through me. The pain in my neck dulled.

But that was no longer my concern. The creature pulled its claws out of my mother's side. It snarled, and she stood with great difficulty, turning to face the creature.

"Run, my darling," she said over her shoulder to me. "I'm sorry."

"But—no—"

That was when a loud, commanding voice boomed through the trees—the king's voice. Roots swirled around me; they wrapped around my middle and pulled me away from the danger, through the wood faster than I could stop them. I clawed at the dirt because I couldn't leave my mother. I couldn't leave Seren. Not to face the creature alone—

My mother faded into the fog, facing that monster, and the roots pulled me out of the dark wood, finally letting go. I clawed at the ground to stand, and in front of me was King Merrick on his white horse, his crown glowing, its leaves twining and swaying. Wen was by his side. I would find out later that my mother had sent word to him before she entered the wood. He looked down at me with eyes still alight with the magic of the crown.

"Where's my son?" he asked, his voice detached and cold.

"I—I don't—I didn't—"

"Where's my son?" he said louder, more forceful.

I didn't know how to answer him. He was in the wood—they were all still there, I knew it. They had to be. We had to go in and save my mother. I couldn't leave her. I couldn't leave the prince. I couldn't leave Seren.

I couldn't—

But then the magic in his eyes faded, and he pressed his hands against his face, and he cried.

And none of them—neither the king nor his guard, soon there by his side—went in to save Lorne, or Seren, or my mother, because they already knew what I was too stubborn to believe. That it was too late. That they were dead. They were all dead the moment they met the ancient, the moment the seeds of the woodcurse had descended on us.

And yet, somehow, I had survived.

3

THE CASTLE OF ALORIYA

Cerys

ANWEN SAID SHE would help me close down the shop
before returning to the castle. I told her that she didn't have
to, but she pointed out that the sooner I got done, the sooner
I could help Papa at the castle. It wasn't a lie, but in truth I
knew she didn't want to return to being the *heir to the throne*
quite yet. Or that was her intention. She came into town, in
disguise, to get away from her name and her duties, but even
while she helped me set the rest of the roses in their vases, I
could tell that she hadn't really escaped today. Her mind was
lost somewhere else—maybe in her own doubts at being a
good ruler, maybe in the crown's ineffable power, or maybe
in the wood itself—at least until we noticed that the fox

had gotten into the spool of red yarn I had in a basket at the bottom of the stairs.

He rolled it around the shop, and when he realized that it was *unspooling*, well, you could just imagine his excitement. I didn't have the heart to take it away from him, even though I'd bought the yarn fresh from our neighbor, intending to make a winter scarf for Papa, and Wen couldn't stop laughing. After the fox unspooled the entire thing, he lay in a corner, kicking and nibbling at the thread.

"You're so much trouble," I mumbled, finding the end of the yarn, and began to reroll it.

The fox turned over and watched, flattening his ears to his head. He stuck up his rump, tail swishing, and pounced at the other end of the yarn, but I jerked it out of his claws. Wen watched with a secret sort of smile.

"I think I know why you keep him around," she said as I rerolled the yarn.

"Because I want a winter hat?"

"Because you like the company, and it *seems* he likes yours."

I snorted. "He likes the food."

But really, Wen was right, like she always was about me. I liked his company. He stank most of the time, and he always dug up our garden, but he didn't care that my blood grew flowers. He didn't think I was cursed—not that foxes cared. Or understood.

"You should name him," Papa had said the third time the creature came around, "if you're not going to run him off."

"I don't *own* him, so why should I name him?"

"Fox, then," Papa had suggested, and I'd rolled my eyes.

"Sure, *Fox*."

So the name—or lack thereof—stuck.

The fox looked sad when I rolled up the rest of the yarn and placed it too high for him to reach. "Don't give me that look," I chastised him. "You made a mess, so I revoke your access to the yarn."

"Oh, you're mean," Wen chided, and told the fox, "If you were at the castle, you could play with the yarn all you wanted to."

"You'd spoil him."

"Absolutely."

By the time we finished all the rose bouquets, it was almost noon, and the Village-in-the-Valley pulsed with many more people than usual, all fresh up from Eldervale and Somersal-by-the-Sea for the coronation. They took the newly built railroad into town. You could see the train curving through the gentle mountains from miles away, a plume of black smoke against the otherwise cloudless sky. When the railroad first came to the Village-in-the-Valley, it mostly brought with it produce from the other kingdoms. Aloriya was a small country made smaller by the fact that the Wildwood was forbidden, and our towns were all less than a half day's ride from one another.

The Village-in-the-Valley, despite its name, was the largest city in the kingdom, home to the castle of Aloriya, so our town became the hub of trade—both inside Aloriya and between the kingdoms that surrounded us. We were affluent, and our kingdom's coffers overflowed most years, and everyone knew why. Our fields were always golden. Our harvests were always healthy. Our people were always disease-free. It was all thanks to the crown. It could grow crops and darken the skies and move *mountains* if the wearer was strong enough. We existed in a life of simple splendors while the countries around us were plagued time and again with war and famine and pestilence. But those countries were also filled with new music and new stories and new universities I'd hear tell about in the tavern from merchants from far away . . .

Papa had been the castle's royal gardener long before I was born—his thumb was the greenest in the kingdom, and he knew every flower, every herb, every seed in the castle's intricate maze of shrubbery, because he had almost certainly planted them. And if not him, then his father had, or his father before him. The Levinas had been Aloriya's gardeners for generations, and I'd be the next one, destined to prune Their Majesty's hydrangeas until I died. And sometimes, sure, that thought itched at me in a place I couldn't scratch. Trapped inside the walls of the royal garden felt safe, while the horizon, where the sun met rolling golden wheat fields, was like a yawning mouth ready to eat me whole.

I didn't know what was beyond the valley, or past the Greenhills, or what lay beyond the Saferine Sea. I didn't know if I could belong there. If I could even set foot.

At least here, I knew. My roots were planted, and I was happy.

The Village-in-the-Valley was home.

"Are you sure you want me and Papa at your coronation? Remember the last time Papa was privy to an open bar with elderberry wine," I reminded, putting the last touch on the last bouquet, and felt rather proud of myself. A dozen purple roses sat in rusted tins across the counter. The tins didn't matter—they'd be set in crystalline vases at the castle and given to all the dignitaries as a welcome presents. Wen's late mother loved purple roses; it was a soft dedication to her.

My best friend grinned. "You mean when he lamented the Great Pig Race of the Summerside Year?"

"That one exactly."

"I love your papa's stories."

"That makes one of us."

She elbowed me in the side. "You like them, too."

"I like to forget about them, sure."

Wen finished her last knot in the flower crown and placed it on her head. She looked at herself in the reflection of one of the rose tins and sighed. "I wish the crown were actually made of flowers. It'd be a lot less gaudy."

"But flowers don't have magic."

"I have enough," she said, and with a wave of her hand, flames burst to life on the tips of her fingers. "And magic isn't what makes a good ruler, anyway." She snuffed out the flame, leaving the air smelling slightly of smoke and burning pine.

"No, but I'm pretty sure a lot of people wish they could do what you do."

"It's in my blood; I can't help it. Like you. Well, sort of, I guess."

I waved my hand. "It's not the same. You can control yours, for starters. I accidentally slit a vein and, whoops, there's a forest."

She laughed and picked up a tin of roses to carry them out to the wagon. Out in the square, colorful ribbons were being hung, held up by large maypoles, and lanterns strung up across rooftops. The sweet aromas of sticky cinnamon buns and vegetable skewers from the food stalls mixed with the heavy smell of apple mead from the tavern had even reached the insides of the flower shop. Tonight, there would be song and dance, great ballads of the late King Merrick and his and Wen's ancestor, King Sunder, who razed a path through the wood and returned with the crown.

Wen pushed the tin of roses into the back of the wagon and wiped her hands on her trousers as I struggled over with two more tins and heaved them in beside hers. She didn't move for a long moment, surveying the line of trees where the Wildwood began.

"The wood is too quiet," she said softly. "It must know my father's dead. I should've been crowned the moment he died."

I put a hand on her shoulder. "You need to mourn, Wen."

"I don't have the *luxury* to mourn," she replied. There was a steely look in her eyes—a glimmer of the soon-to-be-crowned Queen Anwen, strategic and perceptive, the hardened shell of the girl who'd come out of the wood eight years ago. "The curse would never give me that. He's dead, and someone needs to bear the crown. And soon. The wood is coming for us; I just know it. Aren't you frightened? After what happened . . . ?"

"All the time," I said, and squeezed her shoulder tightly. "But everything'll be fine. The wood hasn't stirred since then. Maybe it's taken enough for a while."

"Maybe." But it was clear she didn't believe me, and I didn't believe myself, either. But then she let out a breath and pushed the wagon bed's door up, locking it in place so the tins wouldn't come out. "I'll see you later today?"

"I can't wait."

We hugged, and then she scratched the fox behind the ears, lingering at the edge of the gardens as if she would never see them again, and started up the King's Road to the Sundermount.

"She's just nervous," I told the fox as we returned into the flower shop.

It had been years since anyone had seen an ancient at the

edge of the wood. Everything was fine. There was no sign of trouble. But there was a seed of doubt burrowed in my middle that I couldn't uproot, and I didn't know why. The black spots on the orchid, the quiet of the wood, the strange way my blood felt on edge—like it heard a call I couldn't.

It's nothing, I told myself as I busied myself making final preparations to head up the King's Road to the castle.

It was just another day at the edge of the Wildwood.

As I loaded the last of the coronation arrangements into the wagon out back, Lady Ganara came to pick up her orchid bouquet. She was an older woman who lived in one of the beautiful mansions in the center of town. Her family owned the railway that came to the village, so she spent half of her seasons here and half in Somersal-by-the-Sea. She always smelled of salty waves and brisk ocean, and she wore dark blue velvet dresses that matched the sea. She crooned over how beautiful the bouquet was when I presented it to her.

"You have a green thumb just like your mother," she said, and I flinched, even though she meant it as a compliment. "Your father, too, of course, but oh, your *mother* could grow some beautiful flowers."

I gave the gray-haired woman a tight smile. "I remember." Though each day I feel as if I forget a little more.

I saw her to the door, ready to close up the shop after she

left, when she snapped her fingers and turned back to me in the doorway. "That reminds me! Miss Crestshire asked me to ask you if you've found anyone to dance with yet at the coronation. The baker's son is still looking for a partner. Time is ticking, you know."

Yes, I've reached the age to get married and have children, and settle into my place here. And yes, she was right. But there was something about the way she said it—*time is ticking, you know*—that ground against my patience. The baker's son, Mikale, was the kind of boorish boy who I hated on principle. "If Mikale wants to dance with me, he'll ask."

Though it doesn't mean I'll accept.

"Oh, kingsteeth!" Lady Ganara laughed. "You know that's not how boys work. I'll tell you what," she added, coming back to the doorway, "I'll tell Miss Crestshire that you are interested, and she'll tell Mrs. Margerie, who will then tell her son. I do think you would be a sweet couple. I thought, personally, you would have been so happy with the mayor's son, Donnelly, but, well, now he's married! You need to choose them before they're all gone."

"And what if I don't want to choose anyone?" I asked, quite unable to stop myself.

Her eyes widened. She looked aghast. "Well, I believe that isn't . . . *unheard*-of . . ." Though, by her tone, it wasn't something she would have chosen, apparently.

I quickly reeled myself back in and gave a short bow. "I'm

sorry, please forgive me. It's been a stressful morning. I would love to dance with Mikale. Have a wonderful coronation day."

"You as well," she replied hesitantly, and left in her carriage bound for the other side of town.

I watched her down the road a moment longer before I closed the door, pressed my back against it, and slid to the ground. I wanted to kick myself for how unprofessional I'd been—Lady Ganara was one of our best customers. I didn't need to offend her, and she was only trying to help.

The fox poked his head out from around the counter and blinked at me.

"Don't give me that," I told him. "I know she meant well. But can you imagine? Me, dancing with that boorish, *brainless* . . ." I bit my lip so I wouldn't say something I'd regret and pushed myself up to my feet again.

I didn't have time to sit down and take a breath. So I locked the front door, turned the sign to CLOSED, and hitched Gilda, our old mare, up to the loaded wagon out back. She neighed softly, but I fed her a sugar cube for good behavior and led her around to the front of the shop.

"You'd dance with me, wouldn't you?" I asked her soothingly, stroking her long blond mane. "You'd be a terrible dancer, but so am I."

She snorted in agreement.

Making sure I had everything—including a change of clothes for the coronation, tucked into the back of the wagon—I climbed up to the front seat, situating my dress neatly so it didn't wrinkle on the ride up to the castle, when there was a high-pitched whine behind me, and I looked down from my seat on the wagon.

The fox stared up at me.

"Oh, so you're coming along?"

His tail flicked.

"It's going to be boring."

He stared up at me.

"You aren't going to like it."

He gave another loud, high-pitched whine.

I sighed. The fox didn't even know what I was saying, or what he was getting into, but I climbed down off the wagon, scooped him up under my arm, and placed him up beside me on the seat. There was a bit of fur around his front right paw that didn't seem to want grow in properly anymore, a scar underneath from where the trap had snagged—and broken—his leg.

I clicked my tongue to the roof of my mouth and snapped the reins. Gilda neighed, shook her head, and started off onto the road out of the village. The wagon creaked from an old wheel, and on the dirt road the arrangements rattled in their tins.

"You really need to stop stealing food," I chastised the fox. "One of these days you're going to get caught—*again*. And I'm not going to find you in time."

The fox didn't seem to be paying much attention.

As Gilda trotted her way up the side of the mountain, I basked in the quiet. The Sundermount overlooked the valley where we lived, and from the highest spire of the castle you could see all the way across the valley to the countryside beyond. When we were younger, Anwen, her brother, and I—with Seren always yawning and grumbling behind—would sneak up to the spire to watch the sunrises, the smell of elderberry wine and wisteria stuck in our hair from one of the royal parties the night before.

But even from the tallest spire, I could never see far enough, neither past the mountains nor the scope of the Wildwood. Papa said the wood never ended, that the trees went on and on forever—like the tip of the horizon, where sky met land. But I knew the wood ended as all woods did, and met the sea on the other side and the world beyond. I just couldn't see any of it, not with my naked eye.

And the prince, with every inch of his soul, wanted to.

"Why? The Sundermount is your home," I had argued. "The wood isn't safe."

"Because I'd hate to die without seeing something other than the castle and the wood," he had replied. "Anything else."

Anwen had laughed. "Like father'll ever give you the chance to do *that*."

It had been years since I had last climbed that spire—since before the day in the wood, when the prince and Seren and my mother had vanished. I wondered if I would still see as far as I used to, and if I would think of the prince and his yearning for the horizon, or if the Wildwood had taken that, too. I couldn't even remember his face anymore. After his death, the late King Merrick took down all portraits of him, all reminders. Because they hurt too much, Anwen had said. Her father couldn't live with them.

The wagon bumped and jostled up the curving road, skirting the edge of the wood toward the Sundermount. The sun, hot on my neck, was already beginning to ease down toward the horizon again, and in the distance, black clouds dotted the sky. There was a storm coming, bringing with it a chilling bite to the air.

I shivered, hoping it would hold off until after the coronation.

4

THE CASTLE ASUNDER

Cerys

WHEN WE REACHED the gates to the castle, it was already midafternoon and chaos filled the grounds. Servants and guards ran about, making sure that everything—and everyone—was in the proper places for tonight. There would be dignitaries from all across the land coming to watch the princess crowned—it was to be a momentous occasion, and she wanted me to be a part of it.

It was an honor. I just hoped I didn't make a fool of myself.

The castle towered over the grounds, as beautiful as it was old. It was built in a time when the Wildwood clawed and hissed at the castle gates. A thick wall surrounded the outer perimeter of the grounds, with another wall, a little shorter, built of alabaster, encircling the castle itself. Beyond the second wall were the stables and the servant's quarters, as well as most of the larger trees on the grounds—wisterias dating back generations of Sunders, ancient and enduring. There was a smattering of wagons and carriages parked underneath the wisterias by the stable—quite a few dignitaries had already arrived ahead of the coronation. Most stayed in one of the twenty-seven rooms in the castle's keep, but I'd seen a few less-important dignitaries hanging about the bed-and-breakfast in the Village-in-the-Valley.

Of course, there was one city that was not represented. Most people in Aloriya considered Voryn, the city in the wood, to be a myth, a part of the story of King Sunder and nothing more. Perhaps a city existed once, but the idea that any group of people could survive in the wood to this day felt more like legend than fact. And yet, with each coronation, Aloriya sent a raven to Voryn with an invitation, as a matter of tradition. The ravens never returned, and Voryn, if it even still existed, never answered.

I pulled up to the gate in the inner wall and stopped the wagon. Servants rushed in and out of the kitchen door, carrying with them platters of food and large swathes of gossamer tablecloths for the feast. Some ran flowers into the garden, others shouted about the esteemed guests needing towels or a hot bath drawn or food. The castle hadn't been this busy since Anwen's last birthday a few months ago when the King was still healthy.

I poked the fox on the rump. "Okay, up and go—don't want the seneschal to catch you here. She'll skin you and *actually* make you into a nice hat."

The fox didn't move.

"C'mon, stop sleeping. Shoo. Go."

When I poked him again, he finally took the hint, untucked himself, stretched, and leaped down off the wagon a moment before the seneschal burst from the side door. She looked positively exhausted, her peppery gray hair pulled up into a high bun, the wrinkles across her face deeper and darker than I remembered, like a piece of leather too long weathered. She wore the green-and-purple robes of the Aloriya seneschal, speckled with tiny emeralds, embroidery of stags and ravens and foxes on the hems.

"Cerys! There you are! We've been expecting this wagon for hours." She motioned for a handful of servants to come and unload the wagon. "Go and put them in the royal hall where I marked them! Why are you so late?"

"Papa said noon—"

"Noon! Of course he did." Miss Weiss simply gave me one of her disappointed, long-suffering looks, and sighed. I hated the way she sighed. It was like every piece of her soul exhaled through her mouth with the dampness of ever-suffering regret. "I thank the old gods every day that you, at least, are prompt, Miss Cerys. You'll make a wonderful royal gardener when your father retires."

46

I turned down my eyes to my mud-caked shoes. "Thank you."

"And as we are on the subject, Her Majesty informed me that she invited you to join the family for the coronation," she added. "It is with a heavy heart that I must forbid it."

I gave a start. "What—why?"

"You are not of royal blood. It falls to me to ensure that the rules we've followed for three hundred years are honored. I'm afraid that this is not the young princess's decision to make."

"But then she'll be alone up there, and we're her family."

To that the woman replied, "She will need to learn to rule alone." Then she motioned to the sturdy stone wall that surrounded the royal garden, where Anwen would be crowned. "I believe it'd be best for you to stay out of sight tonight. There are too many dignitaries who remember the tragedy years ago, and seeing you might . . . spark some memories of that day. We want this to be a happy occasion."

"I can't go to the coronation at all?" I asked, incredulous. "But—"

"Thank you for understanding," the seneschal added, a little softer.

There was only room for one survivor of the Wildwood tonight. Two of us would dredge up rumors, and there were already enough of those.

"Yes, of course," I replied softly.

"There's a good girl." The seneschal then turned toward

47

the kitchens again without another word, and left. I bit the inside of my cheek so hard I tasted blood, trying to build a stone wall around my injured feelings, because it wasn't going to do any good. Once all the bouquets were unloaded, I led Gilda toward the stables, where the stable hand took her from me and unhitched the wagon. The fox crept out from the bushes finally, and followed me as I set off up the hill to the royal garden again.

"I suppose she's right," I told the fox, but really I was just talking to myself. "Royal gardeners' daughters live their whole lives inside garden walls, so it's rather ironic that I'm not allowed in now. It would almost be poetic if it weren't so depressing."

If the fox understood me, he certainly didn't show it as he went sprinting off toward the bushes after a field mouse and was gone.

~ 5 ~

THE GARDENER'S DAUGHTER

Cerys

PRINCESS ANWEN SUNDER'S coronation was an affair of dazzling dresses and bright, tailored suits. Men and women danced in radiant circles around one another, hands clasped in the official Aloriya dance, passed down for centuries. It was a dance to signify unity and strength. It was mesmerizing to watch. The guests grew happy on elderberry wine and the heady sound of a thirty-piece orchestra. Lords and ladies from across the continent were here—from the farthest reaches of Eldervale to the Salt Strait to the ruby-colored city state of Eriksenburg in the snowy north. The beautiful day had turned into a dazzling and star-filled night worthy of Anwen's coronation.

I had watched dignitaries and nobles dance in the royal

garden for sixteen years. I knew every turn of the music, every step, every guest who would pass out on the grass (I had a feeling a prince from Eriksenburg would be the first one on the ground tonight). Wen wore a gorgeous dress the color of sunflowers and morning stars. Her dress bared her sturdy shoulders elegantly, cinched at the waist, and trailed behind her like a comet tail. I'd seen her earlier, since I had to deliver the sunflowers that her lady-in-waiting braided into her hair, and she looked like the sun we all orbited around. She didn't wear much jewelry, and while other guests had sewn jewels and precious gold into their dresses and waistcoats, hers was simple.

That was what I loved about her.

"She'll make a great queen," I had told Fox. "She's gracious and funny and good."

I sorely wanted to see her coronation. I wanted to see how the crown would react when it was placed on her head, see what feeling would come from the wood. It was the reason each coronation was in the garden, why Papa spent months planning this very occasion, mapping out where every bulb and bloom would be. When King Merrick had been crowned, the flowers had all bloomed at once, the color of cerulean skies. For his father before him, the wisteria trees had sprouted from the ground, before him, the honeysuckles that still climbed across the castle's spires.

And it was my father's job, and my job, to preserve them

and prune them, and help them flourish. We were not just royal gardeners—we were historians of sorts, preserving Aloriyan history in flowers and roots.

And what kind of historian would I be if I didn't see my own best friend crowned?

There was a secret archway on the far side of the castle that led into the garden where the coronation was to be held. I could watch the ceremony from the curtain of vines hanging in the archway, and the seneschal wouldn't know.

I stepped onto the side walkway to the castle, making my way up the stone path toward the royal garden. Lanterns lit the way, dandelions poking up between the smooth stones. The tall wisteria trees bent in toward me, their long lavender-flowering vines hanging like curtains to hide the side entrance to the royal garden. A breeze leafed through the vines like night spirits, bringing in the last bite of winter frost.

I was almost suffocating in my dress. I hadn't worn a corset in nearly a year, and lacing it up had proven a challenge. The beige petticoat was a little too long for me, and I knew I'd eventually muddy the hem by the time the evening was done. The gown I wore had once been my mother's. It was the last bit of her I had left, and while I really didn't want to wear it out where it could be dirtied or damaged, Papa and I could barely afford seeds for the spring as it was—a new gown was out of the question. The dress was the color of sage, pale and soft, with the barest hint of embroidered leaves around the stitching at my waist, curling down the endless expanse of silk like vines. It was cinched at my waist with a deep green sash. The dress was hard to walk in, and harder to stand still in, because my stays would creak and the lace tucker around my neck would scratch at my skin. I almost wanted to tear it all off and go traipsing around in my shift. It wasn't like anyone was going to see me tonight anyway.

I'd forgotten my hair ornaments, so I found a pleasant-looking twig from the wisteria trees with a few blooms still on it, and I picked the scab off the tip of my finger. The twig turned green and sprouted pale blue flowers. I twisted half of my unruly hair up with it. The rest I braided as I stood outside in the pleasant evening air.

In the distance, lightning crackled across the horizon, followed by the deep, low rumble of thunder. A storm was brewing, purple and bruised against the sunset. I hoped it'd hold off until after the coronation, which was to be held on the garden terrace.

Rounding the garden wall, I followed the golden glow of lanterns through the trees—and found that a shadow stood by the wall, staring at the stones before them. I felt the back of my neck prickle. No one was allowed back here, and all the servants were busy tending to the guests.

"Who's there?" I called.

The shadow glanced back at me, though darkness

obscured its face. Then the torches lining the pathway flickered—and the figure was gone.

I hesitantly made my way up to the archway where the person had been, looking to see where they might have run off to. It didn't make sense that they would just vanish into thin air. . . . Maybe it was just a trick of my imagination; the stress of the day getting to me.

But then I inspected the stone the stranger had been looking at, and there were names carved into it. Time had worn them away, but I knew what they said. My thumbs traced the letters, spelling out the names of a prince and his guard, long dead.

"Cerys!"

I jumped at Papa's voice and spun around. He came up behind me, down the dimly lit stone path, looking dapper in a brown suit and a matching bowler hat tipped back on his head, a lily stuck in the ribbon. He grinned at me. "You look as beautiful as a sweet pea in bloom! Put your old man on your dancing card, would you?" He did a quick jig, and I couldn't help but to laugh.

"You're so odd."

"I'm not the one hiding behind the garden wall."

"I'm not *hiding*," I tried to argue, but he waved me off because of course he knew I was lying.

"The fairest lady seneschal talked to you, too, eh?" he

said, and my cheeks burned with embarrassment. The seneschal had even confronted my *father* about Anwen wanting us to be a part of her coronation? When I didn't respond, he had his answer and sighed. "I figured as much. So you've decided to seclude yourself back here, then."

"I like it back here—and the fox doesn't seem to mind the company," I added, waving over to the creature, who slunk into a nearby bush with a bone one of the kitchen staff must've given him.

Papa didn't look quite so convinced. He tucked a piece of hair behind my ear, his rough hand lingering on my cheek. In the soft lantern light, he looked old and wise, with a dirt smudge on his cheek and his wild gray hair sticking out from underneath his hat. He said tenderly, "Never let anyone make you feel unworthy. You deserve the moon just as much as anyone else."

"Yes, well, only if the moon is made of cheese. It doesn't do me any good otherwise." I licked my thumb and rubbed the dirt off his cheek. "Now go out there and find yourself someone to dance with. I saw Gregor over near the endover lilies."

"G-Gregor!" he sputtered. "That son of a— He owes me thirteen shills and three glades after our last gambling night!"

"Mm-hmm," I replied, slinging my arm around his shoulder, and led him toward the entrance to the garden. "I think he also might owe you a dance." I playfully nudged him through the honeysuckle vines that disguised the archway, and into the party.

He spun around and called, "Sprout?"

"Yes, Papa?"

He stood taller, his chin held high, and said, "You're a daughter to be proud of."

My bottom lip wobbled, and I shooed him away. He melted into the crowd of lace and satin, and when he was gone, I let the vines fall back over the archway and turned away. The music was softer on the outside of the garden, but I could still hear the kingdom's most beautiful waltzes. I'd heard them my entire life, watching dresses of licorice and sunflower and marigold blend together in picturesque bouquets.

I sat on the grass beside the fox, who was now curled up, his nose buried in his tail. I leaned back against the ancient wall, humming the song. "I know it's silly," I told him, "but I always wanted to dance at a party like that, in a beautiful gown, with the right partner."

The fox cracked one eye open. His nose twitched.

"Oh, don't give me that. I know I can't waltz. . . ."

The fox closed his eyes again.

"But perhaps with a talented partner . . ." I got to my feet and picked him up before he could squawk a disagreement, holding him against me tightly. I began to hum the song gently, my feet shuffling along because, unlike Wen, no one had taught me how to waltz. I pretended I was in the middle of all those supple silk skirts and rustling bows, the song bright and achingly familiar in my throat.

I understood why I could never leave Aloriya. My father could make the late king's beloved endover lilies bloom year-round, but I could grow a forest in the name of Anwen. When Papa passed, he would hand the mantle to me, and I would prune the lilies and plant the new seeds in spring and trim the wisteria trees in the fall.

And it was safe. I was safe.

The wood couldn't get to me here.

And while it would be nice to dance with someone, to make a home with someone, my home was this garden, my house its walls. I'd known it all my life—what else could I want? And besides, how many people out there could love a girl with dirt underneath her fingernails?

There were no stories of gardeners' daughters. Or bakers' daughters. Or blacksmiths'. We did not bloom where our roots did not grow. So I accepted that I would disappear into history just like every other gardener's, baker's, blacksmith's, or merchant's daughter.

And I would never be asked to dance.

I spun across the soft grass, humming the melody, which I knew by heart. One turn, then another, and another—and suddenly I felt my fingers folded into the hand of another, my hand on his shoulder, his on my waist. Golden hair and a sunset smile and eyes like ocher. My breath caught. Because for half a second—for a blink, a moment—it felt like—

But then I snapped my eyes open and accidentally dropped the fox. He gave a yip as he hit the ground.

I blinked quickly and glanced around, but there was no one on this side of the garden wall. I was alone—

The garden was quiet. The waltz had stopped.

It was time for Anwen to take her crown.

∽ 6 ∾

THE SPLENDORS YOU STOLE

Cerys

"SPROUT! THERE YOU are," Papa called excitedly, poking his head through the vines of the archway. "Hurry! We can't miss the coronation!"

"Miss it? But I can't . . ."

He took me by the hand and said, "We're not missing this."

"But the seneschal . . ."

"What can she do? Fire me?" He scoffed and pulled me through the garden. I glanced around for the fox, but he was gone, and the ivy vines closed behind me as Papa pulled me into the royal garden of Aloriya.

To most other countries and kingdoms in the greater continent of Vaiyl, this probably looked like a rather quaint affair—*charming*, I think I heard the princess from the cold climes of Malvok say. But the royal garden was so much more than charming. It was beautiful in the only way Aloriya could be, beauty that could only exist under the auspices of the Sunder crown. Paper lanterns hung from strings, tied from one tree to another, lacing across the sky above us, their warm, golden glow soft on the myriad of flowers and shaped hedges and bushes with flowering blooms. There was a fountain in the middle of the garden that ran crystalline spring water from a stag's mouth as it stood on the precipice of a mountain, and lily pads grew in the pool beneath it, orange and yellow fish munching on flies that landed on the water. And surrounding us, like ancient sentries, were those old and bent wisteria trees, a spring breeze riffling through their vines, blowing flower petals across the garden.

Papa and I stood at the edge of the crowd so as to not arouse suspicion, but it was still painstakingly obvious how out of place he and I were here. My honey-colored hair was unruly and curly, even after I'd taken a brush to it, and my skin was still fair and freckled even though I spent most days outside tending to the gardens. My hands were callused, scarred from years of pruning bushes and being pricked by thorns. I was not beautiful by any noble standard, but no one expected me to be.

I was the royal gardener's daughter, and my best friend was about to be queen of Aloriya.

I wondered, briefly, as I looked across the crowd, who

Anwen's late brother would have chosen as his partner if he hadn't been lost. Who would *Anwen* choose? A prince, a princess—no one at all?

The seneschal led Aloriya's finest onto the terrace, their silver armor shining in the lantern light, chests emblazoned with the head of a lion. The first king of Aloriya, King Sunder, had broken ground on the Sundermount with a sword that had a hilt carved like a lion's head. King Sunder's portrait looks out over the great hall like an eerie sort of specter, watching over the kingdom and its goings-on. If the seneschal had her way, she would've taken the portrait out and propped it up on the terrace, too, but thank the old gods it was bolted to the wall.

The orchestra trilled a soft note, and our princess stepped onto the terrace, as graceful and beautiful as a swan. A soft white mist began to settle into the edges of the garden and made the lights glow.

"Sprout," Papa said softly, and I glanced over to him. He took my hand gently in both of his. They were tanned and gnarled from forty years of tilling the earth and pruning bushes, never once thanked for his artistry, for a single moment of his labor and love, blown away like petals on the wind. "Is this what you want?"

I gave him a strange look. "What do you mean?"

To that, he chuckled. "This. This garden, this job, this legacy."

"I . . . I don't know what else I would want," I replied, a

little at a loss of words. "I don't know what else I could do. This is my home—of course I want this."

He pressed a kiss to the side of my head, but I got the feeling that I had said the wrong thing, somehow.

On the terrace, the seneschal took the crown out of a gilded golden box and held it up toward the sky. It was made of gold shaped like leaves, twined together like the daisy crowns my mother used to make me. It was the crown that had sat on the late King Merrick's brow for thirty-seven years, and the king before that, and before that, all the way back to the beginning of Aloriya. The crown had been a gift from the Lady of the Wilds herself.

In good faith, to protect our kingdom.

In return, we were never to visit Voryn, never to speak of it, never to bother her fair, magical city.

It had been so for hundreds of years.

This would be no different.

The apprehension in the garden was palpable, and the mist rolled low through the green grass, covering our feet like a tide. A chill passed through me; I shivered and rubbed my arms.

"As her father before her and their forefathers before them," the seneschal announced, holding the golden crown up for the crowd to see, and then went to place it upon Princess Anwen's brow. "I bless you with the gifts of Aloriya and the splendors of the Wilds—"

"*The splendors you stole,*" someone said from the crowd.

A hissing, rumbling voice that seemed to quake the air itself.

I whirled around to try to find the owner of the voice, as did everyone else.

But we found no one.

Papa squeezed my hand tighter. Wen's wide eyes flicked around the garden, trying to find the source of the voice, the guards reaching for their swords, but all we heard was the rumble of thunder in the distance.

On the wind, spirals of black seeds spirited into the garden. One landed in my hand—and shriveled instantly.

The seneschal spoke. "Who said that?"

On the other side of the garden, a pale woman let out a shriek, and a few feet away a bearded man dropped his champagne glass, a third clawing at the flushed sandy skin on his face. The woman in front of me let out a gasp, and I watched as black spots—like the rot on the orchid this morning—bloomed across the brown skin of her hands from where a seed had landed, and burrowed roots down into her skin.

"Sunshine, what's happening?" asked her partner. "Sunshine?"

The woman twitched, turned, another seed curling roots down into the side of her neck—and lunged for her partner.

Papa took my shoulder and pulled me back out of the way. Around us, dignitaries were beginning to tear at one another's dresses and robes. One of them looked at me, and the whites of her eyes bled black—as if ink had been set into them.

The woodcurse—the *seeds*.

"Sprout, you need to . . . to lea—" His hands began to shake as he tried to pry a seed out of his arm, but the roots were too deep, and it pulled at his skin, too. He gave me a fearful look.

"Run, Sprout," he whispered, his breath ragged.

The banquet table flipped as a large man fell back across it, two other diving after him. The woman in front of me began to tear at her dress as she began to change. Her bones popped and the back of her dress split, ridges rising out of her spine like poison barbs.

Roots began to weave up under the skin on Papa's face, his left eye fully black.

"Run," he begged. "Cerys, r—"

Fright clutched at my throat. Papa stumbled forward, reaching out toward me, his teeth lengthening, the wrinkled skin across his face beginning to fracture, a bone-white skull underneath.

"Your Majesty!" I heard the seneschal screech, and I looked up as a dignitary attacked Wen. She barely had room to dodge. In her right hand was the barest flicker of a flame.

"*Wen!*" I cried. I hiked up my dress and ran for the stairs, taking them two at a time, dodging past the guards as they pulled at their helmets. They screamed in pain as the seeds burrowed into their muscles and bones, twisting them.

I knew what it looked like. I had seen it in my nightmares since the day Mother came back to us, not quite herself anymore.

The seneschal howled in pain as an Eriksenburg noble bit into her arm. The crown dropped from her grip and went rolling across the terrace. I shouted at Wen to grab it, but a guard attacked her. She took the sword from the guard's belt and slammed the hilt into their stomach, knocking them off the terrace and into the rosebushes below. She backed toward the crown, fire sparking in her hand, her teeth gritted.

A shadow climbed the steps. The same one I'd seen earlier, outside the garden wall. Now, in the flickering torchlight, I could see his features. Dark hair hung in greasy strands, obscuring his face, and he moved in a jerky motion. He outstretched his hand.

"*Give me the crown,*" the man ordered in that same hissing voice as he prowled toward Wen.

She went to throw her fire at him when another guard lost control and lunged, but instead she slammed the flat of her blade into his face, and he tumbled to the ground.

The stranger stepped over the man, close and closer still. Mist swirled around him like a cape.

"*It does not belong to you,*" he went on, and from the tips of his shoulders, thorns grew like spikes, trailing down the sides of his arms to his hands. His tanned skin was sallow—deathly

64

so—and the twisting, snarling briars that wrapped around his body seemed to make him move like a puppet. *"Give me the crown."*

"What do you want with it?" Wen asked the stranger. She tightened her grip on the sword. "Where are you from— Voryn?"

The stranger chuckled. *"As if Voryn could help you now. I have come for what is ours. What has always been ours."*

The flame in Wen's hand flickered softer—softer— strangely soft. And then it went out.

"Wen . . . ," I whispered fearfully, staring at a black mark on the side of her neck, slowly growing, spreading. "You . . . you're . . ."

Wen stepped back toward the crown on the far side of the terrace. "This thing is a puppet, Cerys. It's from the wood."

"But—but what about you? What do I do?"

She glanced down to the crown at her heel and kicked it toward me. It skidded along the cobblestones and rested at my feet. "Take the crown. Don't let him get it." She grimaced as the veins spread up the side of her neck, toward her face. "Don't let me get it, either," she added. The blade glinted orange in the lantern light as she leveled it against the wood-cursed stranger. "Go, Cerys."

She was giving me time. I didn't want to leave her—I *couldn't* leave her—but I couldn't stay here with the crown, either.

"Take it and *run!*" she cried.

I grabbed the crown—

And I ran.

I ran into the castle and through the great hall, with King Sunder's cerulean eyes boring down into me as I ran away with his crown. There was no one in sight, and the mist covered the entire castle, and in it I saw shapes moving, vaguely human shadows that looked up from whatever they were feasting on and set off after me.

I fled toward the front of the castle, to the impossibly large and heavy wooden doors, and slammed my shoulder against them, pushing with all my might to open them.

The sound of a sword point sliding against the flagstones made me shudder. I glanced over my shoulder, and there was the woodcursed stranger with the sword Wen had used. He looked like a nightmare stalking down the great hall, grinning to show those unnaturally sharp and white teeth.

"*Don't run, Cerys,*" he whispered. How did he know my name? He stretched out his hand. "*Just give me the crown, and I'll save your princess.*"

"She's a *queen,*" I snapped, clutching the crown tightly against my chest, its twig-like prongs poking sharply into my hands, and I pushed harder against the door. It gave a groan and opened just enough for me to escape.

I slipped out into the front courtyard, the gates open in front of me, and past them the King's Road down to the

Village-in-the-Valley. The night was brisk and unnaturally dark, and lightning crackled overhead and illuminated the sea of fog between me and the village. In it, creatures who'd once been Aloriyans prowled with glowing red eyes and dagger-sharp claws, digging their heels onto the soft dirt of the road, blocking me from escape.

The woodcursed stranger opened the heavy wooden doors with one hand, monstrously strong. They swung closed with a thundering boom behind him. *"They won't let you leave, Cerys,"* he said. *"They won't let me leave, either. Give me the crown. Then this will be over."*

"Who are you? Why do you know my name?" I snapped, tightening my grip on the crown. The prongs pressed into my palms so sharply I was afraid they'd cut.

He had me trapped, and there was nowhere to go.

No. I refused to believe that.

He came closer, cocking his head to the side in that same strange jerky motion. But this time he tilted his head back a little, just enough so his black hair parted out of his face. Another streak of lightning lit the skies.

I drew back when I saw his face.

He smiled, cold and cruel. *"I know you because you left me in that forest, Cerys Levina. You left me to die."*

It couldn't be—and yet I knew it was. Unlike the prince, his portrait still hung in his father's tavern in the center of town. He had been dead for years, and yet he didn't appear to have aged a day. Mud stuck to his deathly grayish skin, leaves and brambles knotted into his dark hair. When he smiled, his teeth were white and speckled with dirt, and his eyes were sunken and bled through with black. The woodcurse, it seemed, hadn't gotten to him after all, but it was only because of the gaping wound in his chest, torn open, blood dried to the dark leathers of his armor. He was dead.

Eight years dead.

And yet here he stood, by the wicked graces of the Wildwood.

"Seren," I whispered, his name like a curse falling from my mouth. "But you . . . you are . . ."

He outstretched his hand to me. His nails were dark, dried blood crusted beneath them. *"Give us the crown."*

I glanced behind me, and through the fog, bone-eaters came. Great, hulking beasts with horns and sharp teeth and claws like knives. Some of them still had shreds of their former lives on them—dresses from the coronation, pins in their dull hair. I didn't want to see Papa in the crowd. I didn't want to see Anwen.

I was alone.

There was nothing else I could do. Except . . .

My grip on the crown tightened, and I turned my gaze up to Seren. What was left of him. "I'm sorry."

Then I placed the crown on my head.

"NO!" he cried, but a deep melodic sound filled my ears.

The smell of magic—sweet and heavy—flooded my senses. The moment the crown touched my brow, the fear that had burrowed its way into my bones vanished. There was nothing to be afraid of with the crown on. There was nothing left to feel at all.

Seren reeled back. *"You stupid g—"*

I reached out my hands, and the world obeyed me. Vines burst out of the ground around us, climbing up the stones of the castle, as thick as tree trunks. They reached toward the parapets, curling around them, covering the walls, the doors, the windows, swirling up to claim the castle and everyone inside.

I was lost in the power. Drunk with it. Filled to the brim and overflowing. It was mine. It would always be mine. Wen might've been a queen, but I would be a god—

An orange blur leaped out of the bushes at me and snagged the crown off my head. I fell to my knees, gasping as the magic was wrenched from my blood and bones, scraped away like a scab not yet healed, and left me raw underneath. And I realized what I had done. I had commanded the ground and all that grew from it.

It was terrifying.

Dizzy and disoriented, I scrambled after the fox.

Seren jerked himself upright and jabbed a finger toward the animal. *"Get that fox!"* he snarled. The bone-eaters gave chase.

Even though I didn't have the crown anymore, the vines that I brought forth still twisted and grew, twining themselves across the castle grounds, braiding into a vast thicket of briars no one could get through, until the entire Sundermount was wrapped in this prison of thorns.

I ran toward the edge of the grounds where the wall met the wood. The sound of the forest was so loud it rattled my bones. My heart thundered in my ears as I tripped over a root, catching myself on the ground, fingers digging into the loosening earth, as the man pursued, shouting at me to stop.

The fox leaped through a damaged portion of the wall, and I dived after him, down into the trees and into the deep darkness of the Wildwood.

I slipped on the embankment, tumbling down the steep side of the Sundermount, tangling through the underbrush. I tried to grapple for something—anything—to slow my fall—

I slammed against a tree, and darkness swallowed me whole.

⟡ 7 ⟡

A BLOOD-BROKEN CURSE

Cerys

SOMETHING COLD NUDGED against my cheek.

I groaned and curled my knees up to my chest. I was shivering, and my head pounded. The cold, wet thing bumped against my cheek again, followed by a high-pitched whine.

Five more minutes. I could sleep just a bit more, and then Papa would—

Papa.

I remembered: the coronation in the royal garden, the strange cursed seeds, Seren, the *crown*—

I woke up with a gasp, rolling out of a thicket of roots, clawing myself out of the mud. My lungs burned; my head spun. I coughed, my mouth tasting like soil and rocks. I wiped the sludge out of my eyes and stumbled to stand, my feet sinking into the soft upturned earth. Thick, tall trees towered around me like a wall, thunder clouds rumbling overhead. The trees groaned in a quiet wind, creaking like ancient bones. I was in the Wildwood, and with that realization my hands began to tremble. I pressed them against my mouth, backing up against a thick tree trunk, darting my eyes around the darkness, waiting for the bone-eaters to spring out and eat me.

The Sundermount towered high behind me, the castle like a shard of broken bone on its peak. From here, it didn't look like something horrific had happened, but I knew Aloriya was in danger—

And I had put on the crown.

The *crown*! With a gasp, I began to search the ground. That was when a flash of orange caught my eye. The fox was sitting, his tail wrapped around his paws, looking at me expectantly, as if waiting for me to hurry up.

Beside him was the golden crown, the moonlight catching in its yellow leaves.

I remembered the way its power pulsed through me, the sickening lull of it. I had lost myself in it. I had felt . . . invincible.

It was wrong.

With shaking figures, I picked it up, half expecting it to ensnare me again, but it didn't. The metal was cold and heavy in my hands. A thin line of blood eased down my arm from a cut.

Why hadn't the woodcurse taken me, too? I didn't understand it. The seeds that had latched onto and burrowed into everyone at the coronation, that had turned them into bone-eaters . . . one had shriveled in my hand. Was it a part of my magic?

Was . . . was I the only one left?

Suddenly, the fox's ears whirled around and he jerked his head in the direction of the darkness, as if he heard something. I pushed myself off from the tree, straining my ears to hear it, too.

It was the sound of footsteps crunching in the underbrush. Slow and heavy.

The fur on the fox's back stood on end, and he bared his teeth. With the noise came soft white tendrils of fog, slowly inching over the gnarled roots of ancient trees. And through the fog, in the distance, came a hulking figure, sliding between the flashes of lightning overhead. The blue-white light gleamed off a bone-white skull, reminding me of the carcass of a deer, or the head of the dragon mounted in the trophy hall of the castle.

My heart stopped. The bone-eater was looking right at me—thirty feet away, and creeping closer. Its paws treaded across the leaves in soft and heavy crunches, languid, as if it was prowling, taking its time.

Enjoying the hunt.

Its hair, what was left of it, was a brilliant yellow, like woven gold.

The color of Anwen's hair.

Suddenly, the fox gave an awful, ear-piercing shriek. The sound startled me out of my stupor, and I wiped the line of blood off my arm and dug my hand into the dirt, fingers sprawling across the woodland seeds beneath. Roots began to churn and squirm, and saplings sprouted from the ground, swirling up between the bone-eater and me, hiding me from view.

I scrambled to my feet, hoping that gave me some time, and took off running after the fox. I vaulted over roots and overturned trees, forest limbs tearing at my dress and picking at the knots in my hair.

The fog swirled thicker, clouds of white against dark tree trunks, as the creature barreled after us, tossing young saplings and thick logs out of the way like they were toothpicks. I took another swipe of my blood from my arm and ran my hand along leaves I could reach and hanging moss and vines, and they spread and grew like a greenhouse in motion. I glanced back when I shouldn't have, to see how much distance the monster had gained, and my foot snagged on an upturned root. I pitched forward.

I didn't hit the ground immediately. With a yell, I fell through a thicket of leaves, tumbled down a small ravine, and slammed into the ground at the bottom with enough force to knock the wind out of me. I bit my tongue to mute a gasp, my head spinning.

The crown went rolling out of my grip and into the underbrush, and there it lay quietly.

The sound of the bone-eater lingered at the edge of the ravine as it sniffed in the bushes. It stood there for what seemed like an age, and I felt my head beginning to spin with a lack of air, but just as I was about to give up and gasp for breath, the creature turned and prowled away. With that, the fog slowly began to dissipate.

My heart beat in my ears two—three, four—more times before I made myself take a controlled, quiet breath. My lungs burned as I sucked in air between my teeth and pressed my face against the damp ground. I wanted to cry. To go *home*.

But there was no home to go back to. Anwen and Papa and everyone I loved was . . . they were . . .

They were monsters.

They were the ones chasing me now.

The wood couldn't take the crown. That corpse—Seren, but not, never would be again—couldn't have it. I was just a gardener; I didn't have royal blood or the magic of the Sunders, but I had to keep it from them somehow.

I had no choice.

Slowly, testing myself, I sat up. My arm was still bleeding from the scrape, and where it had touched a tiny weed, the plant flowered into beautiful yellow blooms. But I was otherwise uninjured, if I didn't pay attention to my pounding headache. Gingerly, I got to my feet and fetched the crown. I untied my sash in the middle, looped the crown into it, and retied the sash tighter so it wouldn't come loose. Then

I inspected where I had fallen. A cloud moved away from the moon, and light poured down into the clearing. There was a little abandoned cottage on the other side, about fifty yards away, all the windows dark and the chimney cold. How old could it be? Perhaps fifty, a hundred years old? But no one had lived in the wood for three hundred years.

Or so I'd always been told.

The fog had not come down here, eerily enough. Another shudder of thunder rumbled the trees.

I heard a whimper and glanced down to the fox. He tried to stand but fell back into the leaves again, licking his front paw.

Cursing under my breath, I gently scooped him up into my arms.

I had to hide somewhere in case that monster returned—if I stood out here in the clearing, I would be a sitting duck. Maybe there was something in the abandoned cottage to wrap my bleeding arm. Hesitantly, I started toward it.

The fox whined again, and I hugged him tighter to my chest. The closer I got, I noticed that one of the windows was broken, and the roof was caved in, in places; the fence surrounding the garden was rotted, and the garden soil was as dry as dust. So no one lived here after all.

As I peered into the window, something moved in the reflection of the glass. Broad and hulking. I whirled around on my heels.

A bear, as big as a horse, stood on the other side of the

clearing. She was the color of gray skies, her eyes reflecting the moonlight like silvery disks. She stared at me for a moment longer, breathing loudly through her mouth. Then her lips pulled back to show rows of fierce teeth, and she charged at me.

I screamed and clung tightly to the fox, curling my fingers into his fur as he shifted and wiggled, bracing for the bear attack. I must've squeezed too tightly because he bit me, his teeth sinking deep into my hand. I gave a cry of pain and dropped him.

There was a sound, like a harsh wind through the trees and the pop of bones and the snarl of a beast.

I threw my hands up to shield my face, waiting for the bear to tear me to ribbons—but nothing happened. Fearfully, I lowered my arms to see why I wasn't dead, and in front of me was a person. He held the bear back, paws to hands. The young man's skin twisted and rippled, and I watched every muscle in his back heave as he threw the bear away.

The creature snarled as it stumbled backward, baring its rows and rows of deadly teeth.

"Oh, calm down, you beast. . . . We've had a rough night," the young man said to the bear, massaging his shoulder. He seemed to grow taller and broader by the moment, until he was half a head above me, lean and sculpted like the guards Wen and I watched training out in the yards some summers.

And then I realized—quite suddenly—that he was naked.

I squeaked.

He must've heard me, because he turned around, his back to the bear. A knot formed in my throat. Oh, he was handsome. Sharp cheekbones and a strong jaw and eyes a golden amber that reminded me of autumn. His hair was long and wild, the color of orange sunrises. I'd never seen hair that color before.

I pressed my back against the abandoned cottage, anxiety tightening like a knot in my throat.

His eyebrows furrowed as he noticed how frightened I was. Then he looked down at his hands, his fingers thin, tapering off to black-tipped claws.

The color drained from his face. "Oh."

✎ 8 ✎

MONSTER OF A DIFFERENT KIND

Fox

I WAS . . .

I was a . . .

My hand opened and closed. It was fleshy and long fingered and *wrong*. This wasn't happening to me. This *couldn't be* happening to me. I turned my hands the other way, and the hands in front of me turned.

The girl stared at me like I was wrong. I *was* wrong. This was a dream—a nightmare—some sort of terror I'd wake up from in a few minutes and . . .

I touched my mouth, the remnants of her blood sweet on my lips. I had words. I thought them. Sounds braided together like ivy inching up a wall, forming stories and meanings.

Meaning I was—that I'd become . . .

Black spots danced in my vision—the world was so bright, too bright, and too colorful, and too quiet, and—

And—

9

THE SILENT HOUSE

Cerys

THE YOUNG MAN'S eyes rolled into the back of his head, and he fell on the ground between the bear and me. He wasn't dead—he was still breathing, at least, but he was very much out. And he was the only thing between me and the bear, who inclined her head and sniffed the air.

There was a howl in the wood, and an unkindness of ravens took flight into the night. *The bone-eater.* I couldn't let it find me again.

But where was the fox?

I spun around to the bear in alarm. "Spit him out!" I hissed, ready to cut the bear open and wrench the fox out of her. "He's my friend! He didn't do anything to you. He—"

The bone-eater howled. It was even closer than before.

So close the sound made me tremble. In the wood beyond, something large moved through the underbrush. Big and hulking.

Stalking toward the clearing.

The bear moved around me. She took the strange boy's foot gently in her jaw and dragged him into the cottage, making sure to hit every root and doorjamb on the way. I didn't have time to find the fox, assuming that the bear hadn't actually eaten him. I hoped he had gotten away and was okay somewhere.

The trees shifted, the bone-eater prowling close.

I closed the cottage door softly and locked it as the creature came into the clearing. Golden hair, the shredded pieces of Anwen's beautiful coronation dress hanging in tatters on its bony, spiked spine.

I crawled quietly away from the door and hid underneath the window as I heard it come closer. On the other side of the abandoned cottage, away from the view of windows, were the bear and the stranger, mostly hidden in shadows. I couldn't get over there without giving myself away. I was trapped. The creature outside sniffed at the bottom of the door—and pushed on it. The latch rattled but kept.

It circled the cottage, scraping at the walls, looking in through the windows. Somewhere in the distance, thunder rumbled across the sky.

I don't know how long I sat there, shivering in the cold,

waiting for the bone-eater to leave, but it finally did. Whether it was ten minutes after it had come or an hour, I couldn't say. All I knew was that the skies were still dark, the air smelled like rain, and I was cold and shivering, by the time the bear meandered out from her shadowy corner.

She grunted at me.

I dared not to move.

The bear snorted and made her way over to the other side of the cottage, where she nosed through an old chest, bringing out a moth-eaten blanket in her teeth. She dragged it over toward me. I winced away.

She dropped the blanket and went to curl up beside the hearth.

She . . . didn't want to eat me? Then why had she made to attack me earlier? If this boy hadn't arrived . . .

I couldn't think about any of that now. I had to figure out what to do. I couldn't stay here. The bone-eater might come back, and I had no protection here. But I didn't know where to go, either. The castle was a terrible idea, but if I went back to town—I risked taking the wood with me. How far could the monsters go now, without the crown to keep them in the Wildwood? I didn't want to put anyone in town at risk, but I couldn't stay here.

Maybe another kingdom? Eldervale? Nor? No. They wouldn't know what to do, either, and most of their dignitaries and rulers had been at the castle for Anwen's coronation. If

I showed up in another kingdom without their king or queen or regent—that wouldn't bode well.

I shivered from the cold, from fear, and wrapped the blanket around me. It was warm, and at least I knew now that I was shivering because I was afraid. The blanket smelled like moths and dust, and the edge had a strange embroidery on it. A raven with a laurel in its mouth. It was an insignia I'd seen before in the Sundermount's library. It was a crest—

Voryn's crest.

Voryn. The magical city in the wood. Maybe . . .

No, it wasn't real, was it? It was just a fairy tale. But I remembered the feeling of the crown on my head, and the frightening magic from it that made me so sick I didn't want to touch it again. That was no fairy tale, and neither were the bone-eaters or the ancients.

So neither was Voryn. They'd had the crown before; they lived in the wood. But I didn't know how to get there. No one had been there in centuries. I didn't even know if it still existed. There was only a road, a thin string through the wood, almost completely overgrown with the forest.

But I had to do something. If I didn't, Aloriya was as good as gone. My best friend, my father, everything that I knew—my *home*. It was all gone.

In the corner of the room, the unconscious stranger groaned and shivered on the floor. His hair was matted with leaves, and there were scars across his body, just slightly darker than the rest of his pale skin, one in particular around his left wrist.

I didn't recognize him, but he looked familiar all the same. Though I couldn't remember from where.

Quietly, I took the moth-eaten blanket and walked over to the stranger. Whether I knew him or not, he had saved me from the bear . . . who didn't seem to be very ferocious anymore. But still, he'd saved me.

Calm down. . . . We've had a rough night, he had said.

What did he mean, we? Did he somehow escape the castle, too, and find his way here? I didn't remember seeing him at the coronation. . . . I covered him up with the blanket and finally inspected the wound on my hand; the fox had bitten me much deeper than I'd imagined. I needed stitches.

My hand shook as I looked at it. What if my blood had affected the fox in some way? Turned him into a monster, too? Or . . .

A thought occurred to me, and I glanced back at the unconscious man.

"No, that's silly," I muttered to myself. "My blood helps grow flowers—that's all."

My power didn't approach that of the crown, weighing heavily on the sash tied to my dress. The crown was so much more powerful than I'd thought. Was *that* what Anwen would inherit? That horrible swell of magic, pulling at you from somewhere so deep, it seemed to root you to the earth itself?

It was terrifying.

And I was the only one left who could do anything. Anwen and my father—they were woodcursed now, but if the wood was cursed, then couldn't curses be broken? Couldn't I save them?

It felt laughable, really. Wouldn't the king have tried to break the curse three hundred years ago, when he razed his way to Voryn? If he couldn't break it, then how could I be expected to? This curse stole my mother, killed the prince and his guard, and now was hungry for me.

I had no answers. I only had a destination.

Voryn.

But I wasn't made for this quest—I was a gardener's daughter. I did not thrive where my roots did not grow.

And what if I failed?

↶ 10 ↷

DAISY CHAINS

Fox

I GASPED AWAKE.

I was . . . in an abandoned cottage. That smelled like damp wood and mold. It woke me up faster than a cold splash of water. I almost gagged on the smell. At first, my more recent memories felt like a dream. Until I remembered the damn *bear*, and then I scrambled to sit up. And the horror came flooding back to me.

My body felt too long, taking up too much space. I was too tall, too broad, too—too *everything*. This was wrong.

I was a *human*.

Just the thought made me want to sink my claws into my skin and tear it off, all the way down to the bone, to find myself again, but as soon as I went to scratch at my arm, I heard someone behind me, and a sweet smell, of midnight rain and daisies, cut through the awful dampness of the cottage. I scrunched my nose, glancing over. . . .

And froze.

It was her. The girl. She stood in the doorway of an adjacent room in clothes different from those she'd been wearing before. They were much too big for her, the shirt tucked into trousers she had to roll up at the ankles, her wild honey-colored hair braided down her shoulder. She held her hand—the one I'd bitten—close to her chest, and I still remembered the sweetness of her blood, and how fast her heart raced as she hugged me against her, how she'd been trying to protect *me*, that stupid girl, when I should have—when I wanted to—when—

She was so much . . . *smaller* than I'd thought she was. No, I was larger. Much larger.

She gave me a hesitant look with those strange eyes that were somewhere between green and brown—hazel? Was that the color? I never understood it before. The world had more colors now. The shadows had more depth. The wood more shades of brown and green. Her hair was this twining mixture of red and gold, spilling over shoulders that now stiffened. She was frightened—but of what? Was it the old bear?

She took a step back.

I realized—*She's scared of me*. I quickly looked away. I fisted my hands and sucked in a breath when my nails sank into the flesh of my palms. I still had claws? My fingers tapered to pointed black ends.

The only normal part of me that remained.

The rest of me was . . . human.

Ugh.

"Are—are you okay?" she asked.

I thought of the words to respond, rolled them around on my tongue silently. I'd spoken before, to the bear, but it wasn't like I remembered *how* to. Words were just sounds jumbled together. Finally, I decided to try. "I don't know."

Even my voice was strange. In that I *had* a voice.

She seemed relieved at my answer, at least, and her shoulders sagged a little. "Same."

"Is your hand okay?"

Her eyes widened. "What?"

"Your hand. I bit it—but it was an accident. I didn't mean to—I mean, I won't do it again. Seriously. You tasted terrible."

Her cheeks reddened, like those strawberries in her father's garden. "Did you expect me to taste *nice*?"

"I expected you to run. I fell halfway down the Sundermount after you—I wasn't going to let you die at the hands of *her*." I jabbed a finger at the bear snug in the corner of the cottage, her nose stuffed under her paws, gently snoring away.

The girl glanced at the bear and then slowly drew her eyes back to me. Her skin lost its color. ". . . *Fox?*"

Fox.

She had always called me Fox before, so it felt almost comforting that she did now. I cleared my throat. "Now that you're safe, I would greatly appreciate you turning me back. Please." The sooner I got out of this body, the sooner I could go back to not—not *thinking*. I didn't like all these words in my head, bouncing around, scratching at the inside of my skull.

Her shoulders straightened, and she looked at the old bear as if she could give her an answer, and then she said with so much fake bravado it would've been charming, if not for the words, "I don't know that I can do that."

I blinked. "Come again?"

"I *can't* turn you back," she mumbled to the floor and began to flush with embarrassment. "At least, I don't think I can."

Slowly, I sat forward. "Forgive me, I must be hearing things—I thought you just said you couldn't turn me back. C'mon, stop pulling my leg and let's get back to . . . to whatever we had before—"

"I'm not lying, Fox. I don't know how. I don't even know how I made you human in the first place."

Oh. Well.

Fuck.

That was a new word I had never used before, but it certainly fit how I was feeling right now. I pushed my hands through my hair, my fingers tangling into its knots—why was my hair so *long*?—trying to make myself calm down and think.

But the more I thought, the more I didn't want to think. I didn't want to be here. I didn't want to be in this body. I didn't want these thoughts, or the words in my mouth, or—or the look the girl was giving me.

I didn't want any of it.

And especially not the lingering sweetness of her blood in my mouth.

"But, look, I've been thinking, and I believe we have to get to Voryn. They are a people of ancient forest magic; they're the ones who made the crown. If there's any chance at breaking the curse, it's with them—and maybe we could find a way there to turn you back?" she said hopefully, pacing back and forth across the cottage. "Or maybe when we cure Anwen, she can put on the crown and use her magic?" And then, quietly, she added, "I don't know. I'm sorry."

I massaged the bridge of my nose, because there was a tiny bead of an ache beginning to bloom behind my eyes. "It's not your fault. I did it to myself. I shouldn't have bitten you."

But I didn't want to think that this—this *development*— was permanent, either. I already wanted to scrape my skin off; I couldn't imagine living in this body until I died.

I didn't have a tail. It was a *tragedy*.

Everything was too small, and too loud, and too dull all at once, like the world had suddenly lost a shade of magic.

"I found some clothes in a chest over there. You should see if there are any that fit you." She pointed to a heap of clothes beside me, and I realized that she'd covered most of me with a blanket.

I picked up the shirt and wrinkled my nose. "I'm not putting this on."

"*Fox*," she whined.

"*Daisy*," I whined back, "it smells like someone died in it."

"I'm sure no one did—and you know that's not my name, right?"

"Fox isn't mine, either," I pointed out, though I didn't exactly know *what* my name was. I had never really thought about it before. "And how do you know no one died in them?"

"I don't."

"Have you even *smelled* them?" I asked, and she rolled her eyes and squatted down next to me to smell the collar.

She frowned. "It smells like—"

The sound of a tree branch snapping startled us from our argument. Outside the window, there was nothing but white, impenetrable fog. The bear stood from her pallet and turned toward the door, teeth bared.

Monsters, a voice chimed in my head.

A voice that wasn't mine.

I stared at the bear in horror. I could still *understand* her?

"Do you hear—?" I began to ask Daisy, perplexed, when the bear interrupted again—

Monsters at the door. Corrupted. Bad. The bear's lips

pulled back from her yellow-white teeth, her ears flattening against her skull.

Daisy blinked. "Hear wha—?"

I quickly put a hand over her mouth. "Shh," I hushed, and turned my gaze to the front door. "It's back."

Her eyes widened with fear.

Taking my hand from her mouth, I quickly pulled the shirt over my head and found my way into some trousers. I'd seen Daisy lace them up the front enough times that, even with my aggravatingly long fingers, I managed after a try. Why were my hands so *big*?

While I pulled on my clothes and managed to put on some scuffed old boots, the girl crawled over to her discarded green dress in the corner of the house, tied the sash with the crown to her waist, and started packing her dress with straw.

What are you doing? I mouthed as I shrugged on a coat, pulling my long hair out from beneath the collar, as something outside slammed its hand against the door, making the entire frame rattle.

"*Briars, brambles, bones, and blossom, I smell a girl who can't be forgotten,*" said the monster at the door. The hoarse voice made the hair on my arms stand on end.

Daisy stilled. "It's not the bone-eater," she whispered. "It's him."

Him. The guy from the castle—the one after the crown. The one who smelled like rotten earth and ancient magic. I didn't want to stick around if it *was* him at the door. What had Daisy called him—*Seren*?

We need to find safety. It was that voice again. The bear.

Daisy was still packing the dress, more fervently than ever. "What are you *doing*?" I hissed.

She gave me a meaningful look and then shoved the dress under the blanket and made it up to look like there was someone sleeping there.

"*We can sense you in there, daughter of the Wilds*," the man said, rattling the door again.

Without another word, she grabbed me by the hand and hurried to the back window. Her hands were cold and still— and mine were shaking. I was scared? Is this what true fear feels like?

The bear followed us.

The door rattled again. The hinges wouldn't hold much longer.

My heart was racing, and my skin felt electrified, and there was this metallic taste in my mouth—

Yes, I was scared.

Keep her safe. I will be there soon, said the voice that I knew now was the bear's, as she turned around and headed for the door.

❦ 11 ❧

THE HUNT BEGINS

Cerys

FOX AND I hurried through the cottage to the back, where he
pried open the window in the bedroom. His movements were
jerky and odd, as if he was still getting used to his new body,
and he needed to put a hand on the wall to steady himself. He
flopped out of the window and into the bushes on the other
side, where he scrambled to his feet.

I began to climb out behind him, just as graceful, when I
glanced back to the bear. "We should help her."

Fox shot me an incredulous look. "*Help?* How?"

"We can—"

He put his hands on my shoulders. "Daisy, she's a bear.
We're a human and a—well, I guess we're both humans now.

95

She'll be fine. *We*, on the other hand, will be *eaten*."

He had a point. I nodded and shimmied out of the window the rest of the way, when the corner of my shirt caught on a piece of splintered wood. I cursed, trying to pull myself free, but I couldn't. Suddenly, the door blew open, sent it off its hinges.

At the same moment, Fox grabbed me by the middle and hauled me through the window, tearing my shirt. I fell on top of him with a yelp before he covered my mouth with his hand again, and we lay there, frozen, waiting to move.

I heard the bear grunt.

"*We have no quarrel with you, beast*," the man said, as if he understood the animal, and I heard him walk into the cottage. His footsteps paused and then made their way toward the hay bed.

I pushed Fox's hand away from my mouth and rolled off him. We slipped into a crouch, and I followed him around the edge of the house. The white fog was dangerously thick. I could barely see the wood in front of me.

At the edge of the house, I peeked in through the farthest window.

Seren looked a little worse for wear, his black cloak and armor scuffed and torn by the thorns and briars I had hoped would trap him. His face looked gaunt now, with hollow dark circles under his pitch-black eyes.

He also looked very, very angry.

He snapped his sharp teeth together, so loudly I heard it from where we crouched, and whirled back to the bear. *"Where is she?"*

"We have to go," whispered Fox beside me.

"He'll see us. . . ."

"Then we'll run. We can't stay here. Voryn, you said, right? We have to make it to Voryn."

I shook my head. "But I don't know the way."

"I think I do," he replied, and grabbed my hand in his, and waited a moment longer as Seren disappeared into one of the other dilapidated rooms, looking for me. *"Now—"*

But before we could so much as move, there was a sudden piercing howl, and three bone-eaters lurched out into the clearing. The mist curled around them. Seren spun out of the back room and stalked out of the cottage. The bone-eater with golden hair slunk forward, snapping her teeth together, and flanking her were two others, deep rumbles in their throats.

"Anwen," I gasped. It was finally sinking in that she truly was a bone-eater. That the Wildwood had come into our garden and had changed everything. I had to save her. I had to help her—

Seren jerked his head toward me, but Fox had already pulled me down below the window.

Shit. Of all the times for me to lose my head, it had to be *now.*

He saw me. I know he did, because we locked eyes. He

97

knew I was here. My heart hammered in my chest a hundred miles a minute; I tried to think of how we could run away and not have them follow. The fog was so thick, we'd get lost in it the second we tried to run, but I didn't know if those bone-eaters had any trouble in the mist. It came with them, so I would guess not.

We were at a severe disadvantage.

I was just a royal gardener's daughter. I wasn't supposed to go on quests like this. I was supposed to stay home, and prune the wisterias, and live my life through the stories I heard. I wasn't prepared. I wasn't the right person. I wasn't destined for *this*—

Fox gently took my injured hand, and began to unwrap the makeshift bandage. I pulled my hand away. "What're you doing?"

"Making a distraction," he replied, and held his hand out.

I didn't know what he was thinking, but I unwrapped my hand and handed him my bloodied, wet bandage. He ripped it in two with his teeth and wrapped one half around a sharp stick he found on the ground. Almost instantly, the stick began to lengthen and sprout twigs, leaves flowering into little white dogwood buds.

Then he stood, turned the corner of the cottage, and threw the stick behind him. It spiraled through the air and embedded deep into Seren's shoulder. The limb burst to life, growing into a thick and snarling branch. Seren gave a cry, clawing to pull it out, as roots burrowed into his shoulder.

The bone-eater that was once Anwen shrieked and whirled to us.

"BEAR!" Fox shouted, pulling me to my feet.

Suddenly, the bear charged out of the cottage, knocking Seren off his feet as she went straight for us. Fox grabbed me by the middle and tossed me onto the bear's back, then climbed up after me.

I glanced back at Anwen, at the cottage, but my gaze found Seren's lifeless black eyes as the bear carried us into the fog—and suddenly I felt myself being pulled, as if by a fishhook in my stomach, down into the darkness of his gaze.

There was no light there. It was suffocating, and it was terrifying—

The bone-eaters gave chase.

As we rode by a rather small hybrid poplar—one of the fastest-growing trees in the wood—Fox caught a limb with the other side of my bloodied gauze. Almost instantly, the tree burst from the ground, rushing up in a wave of bark and limbs and triangular leaves.

The bear turned and broke into a gallop deeper into the dark wood. In the clearing behind us, there were even more trees than just a moment before, so dense I couldn't see the cottage anymore. The night was loud, and the wood was angry.

I could barely hold on, my hands beginning to grow numb from how hard I gripped her fur. Fox reached his wiry arms around me to get a better grip of the bear, and also so I wouldn't fall off. I closed my eyes and pressed my face into the bear's fur. I couldn't get the images of Seren, dead but walking, and Anwen, a golden-haired bone monster, out of my head. They replayed, over and over, behind my eyelids like a moving portrait.

Lightning streaked across the skies like white cracks in the heavens, turning the clouds overhead purple for a moment, and then dark again. And then, as a rumble of thunder shook the trees, it began to rain. At first slow, one drop at a time, and then a curtain of water fell across the wood and drenched us in moments.

Still, the bear kept running.

We found a river in the rain, black water rushing downstream with a vicious current. I thought we would stop there, but the bear didn't even pause. And she didn't slow for an hour at least, when the fog began to lift and the rain began to clear. Before I knew it, gray morning light leaked into the sky and slowly turned it pink, and then blue. The storm clouds had disappeared, but so had everything that I thought I knew. Gone were the broad green trees I had studied my entire life, slowly replaced by large and dark pines, their needles little more than slivers of gray, woven around one another in intricate knots.

Fox patted the creature on the back of her head. "Hey, bear, let us off."

She grunted and slowed to a stop. In the sunlight, her fur glittered like spun silver. I wondered what kind of bear she was—she didn't look like any of the ones the late King Merrick had killed and stuffed and put into his great hall. Those were all brown or black bears, and none of them were as large as she, and certainly couldn't run all night with two grown people on their back.

We stopped for a little while by a river. I wrung out my hair and tried to wash the mud and dirt from my skin. My hands were still shaking, and the bite on my hand smarted whenever I flexed my fingers.

"I can go see if I can find some yarrow," Fox said, noticing how gingerly I moved my hand.

I quickly hid it behind my back. "It's fine."

Even so, he tore off a part of the bottom of his shirt with his strangely sharp teeth and took my hand from behind my back. "I know you better than that," he replied as he wrapped my wounded hand. "When we finally stop, I'll see if I can find some."

"Thanks—and, um, that was quick thinking back there. With my old bandage."

He gave a one-shouldered shrug as he tucked in the excess strip of cloth. "I just didn't want to die, Daisy. Simple as that. You could've done it, too."

"I'm just a gardener's daughter—"

"With weird magic in your blood," he interrupted me, as if

he needed to remind me. Which, I guessed, in the moment, he did. "Magic that, it seems, has only gotten stronger since we entered the wood."

I looked away, properly embarrassed. I hadn't noticed, but now that he mentioned it—it *was* stronger here. ". . . Right."

"The bear told us to follow her up the river." He nodded to the bear, who was bending for a drink. "She knows how to get to Voryn."

"I thought you said *you* knew."

"Well, I will. Once I ask her."

"So you can understand her?"

To that, he flashed a smile, all white canines and charm. "I *am* an animal."

Well, I wasn't about to point out that he wasn't quite an animal anymore, but that would've rubbed salt in an already salty wound. So instead I asked, "What's her name, then?"

He cocked his head, as if listening. "Vala," he finally said, and so we followed Vala up the twisting river, deep into the wood that had already taken so much from me.

12

AN ANCIENT BURDEN

Fox

I STUCK OUT my tongue, but it did nothing to cool me down.

The sun beat down from directly overhead like an oven. The few animals we did see were deer and rabbits—out to drink by the river. Which was a good sign. When they disappear, it means something worse is about. Though I couldn't think any self-respecting monster would be out in this sort of heat. It was hot and muggy, and I kept tugging at the collar of my shirt to try to get cooler. The shirt stuck to me, and my trousers were uncomfortable, and I had abandoned my boots miles back. Human bodies were weird. I was sweating— that I did *not* like one bit. It was wet and gross, and I hardly ever allowed myself to get wet. Or gross. I couldn't remember the last time I actually bathed, and I felt every particle of dirt on me, and I hated it.

I hated all of it.

Daisy had pinned her hair up behind her head, wisps of curly hair falling against the back of her neck, and there was a small, dark patch of skin I had never noticed before—almost like a birthmark or a scar.

"When did you get that?" I asked.

She glanced back at me, the water rushing around her feet. She had taken off her shoes, too, but she kept hers in her hands as she waded in the shallows of the river. She touched the spot on the back of her neck with her free hand, knowing what I was talking about without having to ask. "It was where my woodcurse started," she said after a moment.

"You . . . were woodcursed?"

"Yes, but for some reason it didn't take. I don't know why." She looked down uncomfortably, then nudged her head up the river. "Are you sure we're still heading the right way? Voryn is north, but this river keeps inching east, I think?"

I glanced up in the direction the river came from. One of the few things that hadn't changed was my eyesight—at least, the important bits. There was a shadow, soft and subtle, at the edge of my line of sight, and the shadow darkened as I looked toward where the river came. "Yeah, it's the right way."

She gave me a peculiar look. "How do you know?"

"Magic," I replied, wiggling my fingers.

Her curiosity turned to misery. "Ha. Ha."

"I thought it was funny." I shrugged and pointed the way we were going. "I can see the magnetic pull of the world pointing north, which is this way."

The bear meandered into the shallows beside Daisy, pawing at the minnows intently swimming upstream. The river was swift and cold, and the pebbles, from what I could see, unnaturally smooth. Daisy stooped down and took one, and skipped it along the slow-moving surface of the river. The sun glinted in the golden leaves of the crown she'd tied to her sash.

They enraptured me, the colors. All the colors did. The way the sun spiked off the lapping waves of the river, the deep blue of the water, the yellow-green of the trees. It was strange the way the light danced through them, and when I looked straight up, there was only clear blue sky between the twisting trees, never meeting in their crown shyness, veins of blue between emerald leaves.

I found myself pausing more often than I liked, my eyes catching a flower that I knew before, but never that color. It was around midday, while I was watching—somewhat hungrily—a group of trout swim upstream, the sun catching on their silver scales, that I noticed that when they passed Cerys on the river, they circled back and kept time with her. The bear was having a lovely time catching them.

We had picked up a few bees, too, and they hummed in the air as we walked.

That was . . . a rather terrible sign.

They could sense the crown. Like I could, before. It was this singsongy pull, a rapture I had never heard before but somehow knew innately. It was how I found Daisy at the castle, because after she put it on, the song became so loud, it screeched.

If the fish and bees could sense the crown, there were much bigger things in this wood that most *certainly* could, too. Were they also following? I darted my gaze around, but these stupid human eyes could find colors in everything but the shade, and that was where the monsters liked to hide.

I thought it best not say anything—at least not yet. Best to not jinx anything. I'd gotten a good look at those ghoulies back at the castle and the cottage, and I had no interest in seeing them a third time.

I tugged at my collar again, muttering about the heat.

"The water's cool," she said, bending down and taking another rock. She skipped it along the river's surface.

"I'm not very keen on water."

"Well, then you'll start smelling really lovely soon."

I sighed. "I'll work up to it, if I must." I didn't want to think about all the injustices I'd have to endure in this stupid, ugly body. "We should start traveling at night, I think, and sleep during the day. There are fewer predators then."

She waved me off. "We should travel as long as we can and put as much distance between us and Seren as possible.

Reaching Voryn is the only chance you've got of getting back to being a fox and my only chance to break the curse on Anwen and return to the castle."

"But I'm so *tired*," I complained, and could hear the whine in my voice. I kicked a pebble, and it skittered into the shallows. "We've traveled all night, and this body is so heavy. My feet hurt, my back hurts, and I think I'm getting what you call a sunburn."

"I know," she replied, sounding equally as whiny. "But I'm scared that if we stop, then they'll catch up. And I don't know how much my magic can actually hold them off without me putting on the crown again—"

"Which you will *not* do."

She pursed her lips. "If I have to—"

"No. You won't."

"Fox—"

"No." The word was sharper than I'd meant it, but I didn't take it back. "It's a bad idea."

"And how do you know?"

"Because you're good at two things, Daisy." I held up two fingers. "Gardening and getting in trouble."

Her face began to turn red. "I do *not* get into trouble!"

"Mmh, how about last week with the blacksmith's son?"

"I honestly thought it was *you* stealing bites of my meat pies from the windowsill, not him," she replied pointedly. "If I'd known it was him, I'd have put something in them that would have given him something much worse than a good bowel movement."

I folded my arms over my chest. "And the week before—at the tavern?"

"Lord O'Hare was cheating! If Papa wasn't going to call him out, then I had to do something."

"Last I saw, he still had the ace of hearts glued to his fingers."

She couldn't stifle a laugh even though she most earnestly tried to. "Like you're one to talk. You do nothing but laze about and steal strawberries out of the garden and chicken bones out of the compost!"

I gave a morose sigh. "Ah, those were the days! And if you put on that crown and attract attention, you'll be the one being eaten."

"Hi, you're human, too, now."

"I doubt I'd taste as sweet as you."

"The sarcasm in your voice is astounding," she commented dryly, and I grinned at her. She rolled her eyes and pulled me toward the river. I narrowly missed tripping into it and hopped onto one of the rocks instead.

The bear grunted, *Stop flirting, children.*

I gave a start. "We are *not*."

Daisy blinked, confused. "Not what?"

"Flirting. The bear said we were flirting."

"With you?" This time, she actually did laugh. "Not a chance. Besides, I have standards."

"And I'm a fox," I pointed out.

"And you're a fox," she agreed.

The bear gave a grunt—probably in denial—and caught another fish in her mouth. I found a long, sturdy limb in the underbrush along the riverbank and took the fish from her, spearing it on the limb. We didn't have any food, clean water—nothing to survive in the wood. Might as well start collecting food. We would need something to eat tonight.

The deeper we went into the Wildwood, the darker the pines grew, until they were almost black, their needles thin and sharp. That meant more shadows for predators to hide in, and more places for *me* to hide, too. We stopped to rest at an outcropping of rocks, and I stuck the limb deep into the ground. We had five fish by then. Enough for a decent meal.

Spires of sunlight fell through the leaves like spools of yellow string, and absently I tried to paw at one, but my hand slipped through the light—and I remembered.

Right—human.

"Do you remember anything?" Daisy asked, startling me from my thoughts. She was sitting on a rock on the sun, the light catching her honey-colored hair, turning it bronze and red and gold. It was a color I'd never seen before, iridescent and soft all at once. I stared—I couldn't help it.

When she finished lacing up her boots, she must've felt me staring, because she glanced up—and for a moment she wasn't sitting there, but a child was, with honey-bronze hair and wide hazel eyes and dirt on her cheek—

I cleared my throat. "Remember what?"

"From when you were a fox," she said.

"Everything," I replied. All the times she cried in the gardens, wishing she'd never gone into the wood on the day her mother and her friends were lost, and all the times she'd felt guilty at how much she loved her magic, and the mornings she would bloom wildflowers in the gardens just to make a chain of flowers, and sometimes wrap them around me, and the first time we met, when I'd caught my foot in that bear trap.

It was a question that was so simple and so complex all at once. Yes, but I was a fox. Yes, but it was different. Yes, but I couldn't ever stop you, tell you that you were not broken, that you were not alone, that it was never your fault.

But . . . they were words I had now.

And there was just so *much* to her now that I noticed, it was ridiculously hard to ignore, but more than her hair, or the slight pout of her lips, or the crown that hummed at her waist, there was—

"But I especially remember your scent."

I froze. Had I just said that out *loud*?

She stared at me, quickly growing mortified. "My . . . *scent*?"

Not as mortified as me, however. *Shit.* I clamored for some explanation, but everything sounded even *more* mortifying. Why had I opened my mouth? I hated words. I hated them about as much as I hated—

"You—you stink," I lied.

Her cheeks flushed red. She hopped to her feet, ready to fight me or, I don't know, something equally embarrassing. "Says the guy who refuses to bathe!"

"I shall be a fox again soon," I replied. *Or I shall die of embarrassment.*

"Oh, you'll make a fine hat," she threatened. "I'll wear it every day—even in the summer."

"You're kidding," I scoffed, crossing my arms over my chest. "I'd make a better muffler, and you know it."

She glared at me, her hazel eyes dark and stormy, but then she sighed and said, "Let's not fight. I know I'm grumpy, and you are, too. Let's keep going?"

Then she started up the river again, the bear ambling on behind her, giving me a knowing look as she went.

I wanted to die.

For a while, Daisy led the trek up the riverside, and ambling behind her was Vala, the bear, grunting to herself like a tired old nanny. Grunting about *me*, but I was the only one who understood her, and for a satisfying moment I envisioned her as a nice throw rug, before I relinquished the idea that she was right.

Telling a girl she stinks . . . what charm, the bear grumbled sarcastically.

Which . . . okay, yeah. Fair.

We walked quietly for a mile or so, trekking up the river as the smooth riverbed stones turned jagged and toothlike, and the trees darkened and grew bare. The shadows, as always, lengthened again, like night beginning to bare its fangs. The temperature had dropped considerably as the day wore on and as we neared the Lavender Mountains, with snow on their peaks. I hated snow, and I shivered just thinking about it.

Daisy was unusually quiet the rest of the afternoon.

The bear ambled between Daisy and me, but after a while she slowed down to lumber on beside me. I knitted another flower into the crown I'd begun to weave a while back, full of different wildflowers I'd picked up along the riverbed. "What is it, bear?"

She is worried.

"I know," I replied quietly, glancing to her to make sure it was soft enough for Daisy not to hear, but she didn't seem to be paying attention at all. "Aren't you, too? There are bone-eaters after us, and we're tired and hungry. She's going to pass out soon if we don't stop."

The bear wagged her head back and forth. *Then tell her.*

"She won't listen to me. She never did."

You never had words before.

I opened my mouth to argue, but then I closed it again and frowned. The bear gave me a knowing look. I sighed and tossed the flower crown onto her head. It sat prettily over one ear. "Fine. Daisy," I called a little louder, "I hate to be the *bear*er of bad news, but I think we should stop for the night."

The bear's nostril's flared. *That is your idea?*

"Trust me," I hissed out of the side of my mouth.

Except Daisy decided to ignore me. Though I knew she couldn't do so forever. I knew her one weakness. I went on, "What can I do to *honey* you up? *Sweeten* the pot? This is as *fur* as I can go."

Her shoulders stiffened. *Aha!*

My lips twitched up. "I can *bearly* take another step!"

She turned about-face to me. "You are the *worst*."

I grinned and leaned against the bear, flicking her flower crown so it righted on her head.

"I'll *beary* the jokes if you let us stop for the night—hey, hey now—I was just—" I ducked as she came to strangle me. I laughed, and finally she managed to crack a smile, just as she grabbed me by the shoulders. "Oh, come on, now! Those were quality puns."

She shook me one good time. "No! They were terrible, and you should feel terrible!"

For a moment, I thought she was actually mad at me, but then she cracked a smile. A giggle bubbled up from her throat.

She pressed her face into my shoulder, laughing. Howling, in fact.

I—I didn't know what to do.

Had I broken her?

But then her laughs . . . changed. The way her shoulders shook, the way her breath caught in her throat—and suddenly she was sobbing into my chest, and I *definitely* didn't know what to do now. If she cried louder, she might attract unwanted attention, and I wasn't in a position to defend myself. But I couldn't *leave* her like this, either. I didn't know where to put my hands or what to say—humans didn't lick each other, did they? No—think, think—

Hug her, you stupid fox, the bear growled.

Oh. Right.

But how did that work? Did I do one arm first and then the other? Where did I hug her? What should I do with my fingers?

Before I could figure out my plan of action, she began to steadily slide to the ground, and I— mostly because she had a fistful of my shirt—followed her. *Kingsteeth, just do it*, I told myself, and pulled my arms around her tightly. It . . . only made her cry harder. No, I wanted the opposite. I wanted her to *stop* crying. Because my eyes were beginning to burn, too, and it made my chest ache.

"I'm so scared," she whispered between sobs. "I've been scared all day, and it's just getting worse. I don't know if I can do this. Wh-what if Voryn doesn't exist? Wh-what if there's n-no way to break this curse? I'm j-just a gardener's d-daughter. I'm not built for th-this."

Oh, Daisy. I held her tightly. "Doesn't that seem silly? Just because you are born a gardener's daughter doesn't make you any less worthy than someone born into royalty."

"You're a fox; you don't understand."

"Maybe, but I'm not a fox anymore, and you have the crown." I finally unraveled from her and sat back. She wiped her eyes with the palm of her uninjured hand. "There's no one else who can do this, Daisy. Whether or not you can, you *have* to. And I'm here."

"Promise?"

"Yeah," I replied without thinking. I just wanted her to stop crying. "Let's camp here, okay? We're all tired, and we need to sleep. We'll take turns keeping watch, and at the first sign of trouble we'll run."

She nodded. "Okay."

Though the idea of setting up camp *outside* sounded dreadful. I was still terrified by the idea of those bone-eaters and whatever other creatures lurked out here. And after so many years of having a warm place to sleep in the flower shop, the idea of sleeping on the cold hard ground had me wishing for Voryn. I never in my life wanted a hot bath more than I did just then—and I *hated* baths. Ugh, I was turning into someone I didn't even recognize.

We settled down near a set of rapids, where a short cliff, and a waterfall, shielded us from most of the weather. Daisy found a small alcove by the rocks to make a bed of dry grass. I just wanted to curl up on it and sleep, but I didn't have a tail anymore, and I didn't want to think about how I was going to sleep in this body. How would I keep my nose warm?

Daisy and I gathered some dried branches and twigs and built a small fire on a dry spot on the river's edge. As she prepped the fire, I shimmied the fish off the spear.

"Oh, use this," she said, digging something out of her pocket. An iron knife. She handed it to me.

"Where did you get it?"

"I found it in the cottage with these clothes. They were all in an old chest." She shrugged and went back to stoking the fire.

I looked at the knife, then at the fish on the stick. "Um. What do I . . . ?"

"Run the knife against the scales. Then we have to cook them."

"Can't we just eat them raw?"

She gave a grin. "The prince once did—on a dare from Seren. He had parasites in his intestines for *weeks*. Just about shit himself to death."

I blinked at her. "Well, then."

"Yeah. That was before . . . you know. Before."

I did know. It was hard not to, really. I did as she instructed, and the scales began to pop off the trout like heated corn. "You addressed that woodcursed man—the dead one—as Seren."

She nodded. "Seren Penderghast. He was the prince's personal guard, and one of the best squires on the Sundermount. I think the wood did something to him. The curse . . . it didn't turn him into a bone-eater, but it's inside him. I think it's taken over his body. It's using him as some sort of puppet or something."

The wood is cunning like that. The ancients want the crown very badly, the bear said, nibbling on one of the raw fish.

The word *ancients* made me shiver. I'd seen them in the wood before, prowling in the shadows, long antlers and bony fingers and moss curling through their skeletal rib cages. "Well, I don't have any reservations about putting a sword through Seren's skull," I assured Daisy, and finished scaling the fish.

We cooked them until they were crispy. Daisy tried to take a bite, but burned her tongue.

I stared forlornly down at my fish. How did humans eat?

I watched her nibble at the belly of the fish again, and gently I drew the fish to my mouth. It smelled so good; my mouth was already watering. The taste took me by surprise. It was something I couldn't describe, like a color I had never seen before, and I'd begun to take another bite when I realized—I shouldn't.

If I liked it, then I liked it as a *human*, and I didn't need to like anything about this body. And it would only be something

I missed when I turned back, and food was the one thing I did not want to miss.

I didn't want to miss anything about being human.

I quickly offered the fish to the bear. She sniffed at it before she ate it.

"Is it not good?" Daisy asked.

"I'm just not hungry" was my reply—until my treacherous stomach grumbled and gave me away. I folded my arms over my chest, feeling the tips of my ears heat up with embarrassment. "And I don't think I like fish."

"You've eaten out of the *garbage*, Fox."

Only because there weren't any rabbits nearby, and the pigeons were too fast to catch, and my paw never quite— I grabbed ahold of my wrist, feeling the scar over it, annoyed. "I'm just too tired to eat—"

A scream tore through the wood, so shrill it sent shivers up my spine.

Daisy spun toward the sound, beginning to rise to her feet, but I grabbed her by the arm before she could. My claws sank into her skin so tightly, she winced. "Ignore it," I advised, scanning the shadows of the trees.

"But what if someone's in trouble?" Daisy asked.

"Then we definitely need to ignore it."

"You can't be serious, Fox."

I glanced over to the bear, who was looking off into the direction of the shriek but wasn't moving to go investigate, so that was answer enough for me. "Look, the wood is scary, and it's almost dark. You're a human in the Wildwood. You'd taste very good to a lot of creatures here, and I'm sure that crown is attracting a whole host of terrible things."

She glared at me. "That's no excuse. I'm going."

"*No*," I said a little more forcefully, and then to my own regret I added, "I'll go. Just . . . just stay here."

Where it was safe.

Then I forced myself to stand, against everything my instincts told me, and went into the trees, toward the sound. Even though I was positive that it wasn't anyone in need of help, I could find whatever was hunting us and maybe we could get a head start before they found us.

I didn't like how quiet the wood was. Where there had been all sorts of noise before—birds or insects or the rustling of rabbits in the underbrush—there was . . . absolutely nothing anymore. It was silent.

I liked silence about as much as I liked being human.

At least as a fox, I had enough sense of smell to figure out exactly *what* lurked in the underbrush that made the wood so still, but with my nose dulled and my ears muted, I felt trapped. My eyesight at night, which I somewhat retained, couldn't make up the difference. No wonder humans invented weapons. They certainly didn't have the capacity to fend for themselves without any.

And now neither did I.

119

There was no sign of the creature that had screamed, or any sort of struggle, but I could feel it—like eyes on the back of my neck. There was something prowling in the distance, as sure as the chill that crept up my spine.

I knew very well what it felt like to be hunted. That feeling, whether fox or human, hadn't changed.

I had to get back to Daisy. We had to leave—now.

I tore through the underbrush as quickly and quietly as I could. The shadows on the ground grew longer as the sun began to touch the horizon, filling the trees with a pinkish orange that began to bleed red, like blood. I didn't like this at all.

"Daisy, put out that fire and . . ." I froze on the outskirts of camp. It was empty. "Daisy?"

She and the bear were gone.

13

LIKE A RIVER RUNS WILD

Cerys

I DID MY business by a poplar tree, and I was lacing my trousers back up when I heard it again—another scream.

Closer this time, and coming from downriver.

I didn't care *what* Fox thought it was—someone was in trouble, and Papa taught me never to turn the other way. Gathering my courage, I crept toward the sound of the voice. Because the sun had almost set, the shadows were long and soft, painting the wood in an orange-and-purple shroud. I pushed my way out of the thicket and stumbled onto the shoreline again. There was no one there, only the rush of the water down the smooth stones, washing all the way down into the valley to the Village-in-the-Valley.

"Hello?" I called, but no one answered.

I could've sworn the scream came from this direction, but maybe I was mistaken. I kicked a branch into the river, and it was quickly swept away in the swift current.

When I was little, I used to make boats out of fallen flower petals and clipped-off twigs from Papa's garden, wondering if the current would carry them all the way to Somersal-by-the-Sea. And Voryn waited at the beginning of this river. If it still existed.

It *had* to.

The river even smelled different this far into the wood. Cleaner, like a crisp spring morning. A little upstream, I watched Vala, nosing down into the river to grab a fish. Every time she came back up empty-mouthed, she dived back down with more vigor.

"Daisy?" I heard Fox call, parting a pair of thick tree limbs, and he looked annoyed when he found me. "Really, if you're going to go wandering off like that . . ." He visibly paled, his tanned skin draining to an awful, deathly white. He swallowed thickly and said, "Daisy. Don't move."

I rolled my eyes. "I didn't go *that* far—"

"I mean it," he snapped, and the sharpness in his voice made me pause. He stared intently at something . . . just behind me. At first I thought it was Vala, but when I turned my head, I saw it out of the corner of my eye.

The thing behind me exhaled, and its hot, rancid breath heated the back of my neck.

Slowly, I turned all the way around—and wished I hadn't.

Large yellow eyes returned my stare. It was a creature at least twelve feet tall, bent down as if to smell me. Moss grew over parts of its soft brown fur like armor, its face thin and deerlike, with large antlers arcing out of its skull. It had long, thin arms and long, thin legs.

I knew this creature—I had seen them before at the edge of the Wildwood. I had seen one the day Prince Lorne and Seren and my mother died.

It was an ancient.

Across its shoulders were small pods burrowed into its skin like tiny, misshapen holes—where the seeds of the woodcurse dispersed. They were the carriers of the woodcurse.

I had trapped most of the bone-eaters in the castle, but I dared not put on the crown again, and the crown was the only thing that could stop these monsters.

The creature lowered its yellow eyes to the crown tied to the sash on my hip. It whispered something in a language I didn't understand. I quickly looked ahead of me again, trying to suck in breath—but I couldn't. My lungs had stopped working. I was frozen in fear.

And what was worse, Fox—who had been standing on the river's edge just a few moments before—was gone.

The ancient raised its gnarled hand and curled its twig-like fingers around my neck, whispering that strange language, its bone teeth clicking together.

Click. Click.

I slowly slipped my hand into my pocket for my iron knife—and quickly realized it was back at the campsite. I didn't have it. I was defenseless.

Out of the corner of my eye, I saw Vala come closer, her ferocious teeth bared, the fur on her spine bristling up.

The creature's hands slowly trailed down my back, reaching for the crown. Its fingers began to pry at the knot in my sash, the whispering growing louder and louder—

Vala took a step toward us and gave a thundering roar. It was so loud it left my ears ringing. The ancient's grip loosened, and that gave me the moment I needed.

I acted before I thought, bending down into the river and scooping up one of the sharp shale rocks at the bottom. I didn't have time to unwind my bandage; I simply raked the rock across my palm as hard as I could where I had previously cut myself.

Pain seared up my arm, but I ignored it and shoved my hand against the ancient's strange face. The thing gave an anguished cry as green bloomed where my blood touched it. It screeched, an ungodly sound, as it tried to reel away, but as it did, its skin sloughed off like bark into the water, and the green moss ate up its face and burrowed into its yellow eyes, daisies blooming as it did.

As it tried to flee, dark roots burst out of its chest, swirling around its thin arms and legs, digging deep into the riverbed, until it stood frozen in the river, arms now limbs, legs now trunks, a nightmarish tree covered in moss and flowers.

A rivet of blood swirled down my arm and dropped into the river. I quickly pressed my hand against my shirt to stanch the bleeding.

My knees felt like pudding, and I sank down into the shallows of the river. My heart thundered in my ears, black spots dancing in my eyes.

Vala ambled up to me and pressed her shoulder against my face. I curled my good hand into her fur and let myself cry into it. Hot tears burned in my eyes. I was scared. I hated the wood. And I didn't want to be here at all.

I almost died. I almost died and—and—

"Is it gone?"

The voice of Fox came from behind me, and I turned.

He stepped out of the trees, picking leaves out of his hair. I wondered how far he'd fled, where he'd hidden. I wondered if he watched the whole thing, waiting to see if the ancient was going to rip me asunder. A hot anger bubbled in my stomach.

"You left me!" I cried, pulling myself to my feet. "You went and hid!"

"Of course I did!" he snapped, untangling a particularly gnarled limb from his long orange hair. "What else was I supposed to do? That was an ancient! You think that I

would've been a match for *that*? I could've been woodcursed!"
I was frozen in anger, and when he caught the look on my
face, he rolled his eyes. "I'm flattered that you think so highly
of me, Daisy, but trust me when I say I would've only made
things worse. Besides, you handled yourself pretty well. I told
you that you weren't a useless gardener's daughter."

I rubbed the tears out of my eyes. "It isn't about being useless, or about my magical blood. I thought we were in this
together, Fox. I thought we were friends. But I guess I was
mistaken."

"No, Daisy, that's not what—"

"Forget it," I said, and headed back to camp, not caring if
he followed.

ᔕ 14 ᔓ

FORSAKEN FORESTS

Fox

IT WASN'T WHAT she thought.

I *wanted* to help her—but the moment I saw that monster, something deep down beneath my rib cage, hidden and forgotten beneath my heart . . . broke open. Something I didn't understand. I had never seen an ancient before, and the sight of it filled me with the sort of fear I couldn't fight against. It was the kind of fear that came from looking at a nightmare you had seen in your dreams your entire life, finally made flesh and bone. That fear flooded me, and a voice as clear as day said, somewhere in the back of my head—

Run and hide.

Besides, it wasn't like I could have helped. That thing was twelve feet tall! Even as a human I was still small compared to it.

Though Daisy was smaller. I remember when I barely came up to her knees, and now she barely came up to my shoulders.

. . . And *she* had faced the ancient. While I cowered.

What was wrong with me? Running and hiding always worked when I was a fox. It was how I survived. I didn't fight. She couldn't fault me for that.

Daisy sat quietly by the fire, knees curled up to her chest. She held the crown in her hands, and the firelight caught the leaves, spinning pinions of light across our camp. The crown was humming very softly, but I wasn't sure if she could hear it or not. She just ran her fingers along the thorns and gold-foil leaves.

Vala slumped down on the other side of the fire, tossing a fish up and swallowing it in one gulp.

"How did it find us?" Daisy asked, startling me from my thoughts. Her voice was soft, and it sounded brittle around the edges. "The ancient, I mean. What *are* they?"

I glanced at Vala, who snorted a *Humans do not know.*

"They're old gods," I started, "back from when the world was not as dark, and magic lived everywhere. They used to be the sentries for the Lady of the Wilds, but when the crown was given to the first King Sunder, they grew corrupted, and now they spread the woodcurse. As for how that one found us, my guess is that it was attracted to the crown."

Surprised, she looked down to the golden circlet. "Really?"

"You don't think that sort of magic is silent, do you?" I folded my arms behind my head and reclined back onto the bear, who just grunted. She made a rather comfortable chair. "You put it on, so I think you understand the temptation."

She hesitated as she stared down at the crown. "I wouldn't have ever taken it off if you hadn't knocked it off me."

I looked up into the night. I guessed this was as good a time to tell her as any. "You were screaming. You were screaming because it hurt."

Her eyes widened. "I . . . don't remember that."

"Well, I can't forget it." Sighing, I massaged the bridge of my nose. There was a needling sort of pain behind my eyes, but I wasn't sure if it was from a lack of sleep or the stress of this situation. I closed my eyes and rolled away from her. "Go to sleep, Daisy. Maybe you'll unpack some of those bags under your eyes."

"You're the worst, Fox."

I felt the same.

She curled up on her mat of grass, and soon her breath evened out as she fell into a deep, soft sleep. I sat up and rubbed my face. Someone had to keep watch tonight, and it was going to be me.

The bear flicked her ears toward me. *She wore the crown?*

"For a moment," I muttered, remembering the way her honey braid began to ignite at the ends, the smell of burned hair flooding my nostrils. Her eyes had rolled up behind her eyelids, roots crawling up her legs, a scream tearing from her mouth, bloodcurdling and horrible. I remembered it so viscerally, it made me shiver, though I told myself it was from the cold. "I took it off her before anything could happen."

How did you know what it would do?

I pulled my long orange hair over my right shoulder, began to meticulously pick out the knots, and frowned. "I don't know. I just know not everyone can wear it."

How? How do you know?

I opened my mouth to tell her, but I realized I had no idea how I knew. "Aren't all animals from the wood? Don't we all know, in our bones, how the crown works?"

I only know it calls to us.

I picked another knot out of my hair. "Why does it matter? She's not going to put the crown on again."

The bear gave me a look, her eyes dark and unreadable. *And if she does? Will you be here again to take it off, or will you slip off and hide, like you did today?*

"I can't protect anyone, bear," I told her. "I just make things worse. I mean, look at me now. I saved her from the crown, and she turned me human."

You don't know if you don't try.

"And if I don't try, I won't fail."

In reply, the bear only snorted, laid her head on her paws, and dozed off. I got the sense that she wasn't any normal bear—I mean, just *look* at her—but I didn't know what she had to do with this quest, or Daisy, or the crown. Or why she was helping us.

Or why, even though I didn't know any of these things, I still trusted her. Being near the bear made the rest of the forest lose its sharp edges, as if the trees knew a secret, and with that secret they behaved. I felt safer near her.

I stayed up for the first half of the night, listening to the fire crackle and the wind bend the trees. Daisy mumbled in her sleep and rolled over, the dim orange light of the campfire catching in her soft hair. Small white flowers began to bloom through her braids, and I couldn't remember if they had been there before. She turned her face into her arm, tensing in her nightmare, mumbling words I almost caught. The crown sat tied to the sash on her waist, knotted so many times it would've been impossible to take off.

I watched her for a while, until I could barely keep my eyes open, and then I woke up the bear and told her that it was her turn to watch the wood.

I'd had enough of creepy old gods and mumbling stubborn girls for one night.

✌ 15 ✌

A MEMORY OF TEETH

Cerys

MY MOTHER CAME home three days after she died.

On the first day, we had mourned the prince's death. The kingdom hung black cloth over their doors, they prayed to the old gods, and they wept for a boy who we lost in the wood. The king was never quite the same after that. Sometimes, I imagined he wished he had pulled his son out of the wood with the power of the crown, and not me. Sometimes, I could understand why.

On the second day, the chapel at the edge of town held a small service for Seren. I didn't go. I know I should have, but I was too afraid. I was the one who came out of the wood alive, after all. Even though the villagers were never anything but kind to me after that, I knew they felt that it should have been someone else who had survived that day. Why had the royal gardener's daughter been spared, and not the heir to the crown of Aloriya? Or at least a bold young squire?

On the third day, we burned a casket for my mother and spread the ashes across the doorstep of our home, as was Aloriyan tradition. *Traveled on, but never gone.* That morning, the king had told Papa that he could have the day off to mourn, but Papa had insisted on opening the shop. I thought, back then, it was because he knew my mother wouldn't have wanted him to lose any potential customers, but the truth was a lot simpler: If he worked, he didn't have time to cry.

It was also the day my mother returned. And the day I found out the wood gave me a curse all my own.

I was sitting at the counter. The door was open, letting the rays of the afternoon sun fill the shop. The golden light danced with motes of the ash we spread across the doorstep. The entire shop smelled like burned wood. Papa was in the garden out back, picking a bouquet of lilies to place on the doorstep, though I remember my mother loving daisies best.

That was when I saw it—a familiar shadow in the doorway.

"Mama!" I hopped off the stool and raced around the counter. Papa heard me from the garden and came in as quickly as he could. But it wasn't quick enough.

The sunlight backlit my mother, so I couldn't see her face until I came up to her and hugged her around the middle. She smelled of freshly upturned earth and an irony scent I couldn't quite place. Not at first, anyway. Not until Papa called my name, and I drew away from her enough to see the blood on her shirt, the holes torn into her gardening trousers. Just enough to see the maggots worming through the gash in her side. I took a step back.

"*Cerys*," she breathed, and her voice was all wrong. She looked down at me from beneath matted honey-red hair. Her eyes were dark and sunken. She reached toward me. "*Cerys.*"

"CERYS!" Papa shouted, pulling me back behind him. I stumbled, trying to catch myself, but ended up knocking a vase of flowers off the table. It shattered on the ground, and I cut my arm, but I didn't notice. Papa held a pitchfork at the ready, one he had brought in from the garden out back.

My mother, who was not my mother, stared at him for a moment. Her mouth was too wide, set with too many teeth; antlers curved from her forehead like devilish horns. She jerked a hand toward him, reaching, pleading.

"*Arthur*," she gasped. "*Arthur.*"

Then—and I remember as clear as day, she said—

"*Kill me.*"

I looked away. I don't remember what happened next, or I chose to forget. What I do remember, however, was watching a line of blood travel down my arm and drip onto the floorboards. And from it sprouted a single daisy.

I hadn't dreamed about that day in such a long time, I had almost forgotten how beautiful it had been until then.

I had almost forgotten the smell of the ash on the doorway. I had almost forgotten that the wood had come knocking at all. But I found myself standing there now, in the late-afternoon light, the shop empty and silent. In my dreams, in the wood, I had returned.

From one of the shadows a blurred figure appeared. He was tall and thin, and he put his hands in his pockets as he came toward me. His image grew sharper, dark leathers and long black hair. But he looked different from when I saw him at the castle just as the curse arrived, and then at the abandoned cottage. He looked as alive as he had years ago, with olive skin and a catty smile.

"Isn't it quaint," Seren said, "what we thought we could destroy?"

I stared at him, perplexed. "You're dead."

"And yet I remain."

He took a step toward me, and as he did, he morphed into a familiar face—incisors as sharp as a fox's, eyes burning like stoked coals. A river of orange hair flowed down to his shoulders. The scar on his lip deepened into a scowl. He ran a claw down my cheek, pressed his lips against my ear, and whispered, "*You will never leave this wood, Cerys Levina.*"

16

THE POISONED TONGUE

Fox

I NUDGED DAISY in the side with my boot. She was having a nightmare. She jerked up instantly, gasping for breath. Then she looked up at me and screamed. I winced as she scrambled out of her pile of dry grass and onto a rock by the river, her chest rising and falling rapidly. Her eyes were bloodshot, her cheeks glistening with tracks of tears. I held up my hands to show that I didn't mean any harm. At least that's what most humans did to me when they wanted me to calm down.

"It's okay," I soothed, moving a dandelion stem into the corner of my mouth. The yellow flower bobbed at the end. "You were having a bad dream."

She finally seemed to come to her senses and moved back off the rock onto her makeshift bedding. The crown clanked against the rock as she did, and she wiped her tears away with the back of her hand. "It's nothing."

"It didn't seem like—"

"It's *nothing*," she insisted.

The sky between the trees was gray with dawn, and the campfire was little more than smoldering embers. I'd woken up some time ago to take the last watch, because Daisy seemed to need the sleep, and so I'd taken a brisk wash in the river. The water wasn't as cold as I remembered, and without fur it didn't hang on me. It was the first time I had a chance to really inspect this body, long limbed and strange. I managed to get most of the knots out of my hair, and I scrubbed the dirt from my skin. I'd spent a little too long in the water than I'd readily admit to anyone. I didn't like it. It was just . . . more *convenient* for washing as a human.

Daisy rubbed the sleep out of her eyes. "Give me a few minutes."

"Oh, sure, I'll just ask the ancients if they can wait until we've had our morning coffee before they try to kill us again."

She clenched her jaw and glared at me. "Why do you care? You'll probably just run away again, anyway."

I winced. "It wasn't like that."

"Sure," she said, and forced herself to her feet. She went over to the river to wash her face, and I followed to toss the bones of the fish Daisy had eaten into the current, so it would be harder to notice that we'd camped here.

The bear gave a lazy yawn. *Can't we sleep a little longer?*

"Daisy had a nightmare," I told her.

Daisy spun around, bristling. "It was a good dream!"

The edges of her voice sounded thin. I cocked my head. "Oh? Then what was it about?"

"I was—I was dreaming that you were a nice fur hat," she said weakly, drying off her face with the end of her shirt. Ah, the fur hat again. Honestly, I'd make better mittens, but I digress. "And I was the talk of the town in Voryn."

"Assuming the city hasn't been overrun by ancients for centuries."

"Of course not. They're magical—they know how to live in the wood. That's why they gave King Sunder the crown. And when we get there, all of this mess will be fixed. They'll know what to do—right, Vala?"

The bear gave a grunt of affirmation—which was all Daisy could hear—but what she said was *It will be there.*

I kicked dirt into the fire to snuff out the remaining embers. "Fine."

Daisy began to brush her hair out, and with the brushing came those small white flowers that had bloomed in it overnight. She seemed not to have noticed. "Haven't any of the animals talked about it? A hidden city in the wood? I mean, surely you must've heard *something*."

"Daisy, I eat rabbits, I don't converse with them," I replied. *Be truthful. You probably talk them to death,* the bear

138

said, and I shot her a glowering look.

Daisy wilted a little. "Oh."

"And to be fair," I added, because I didn't like seeing her wilt, and she wasn't like a flower I could water to make better again, "I've spent more time in your garden than I have here in the wood, but yes—I've heard rumors. About the city. But what if they can't help us?"

"They will," she replied softly.

I rubbed the back of my neck doubtfully and decided to change the subject. "C'mon, if we stay here much longer, we'll both be food for the carrion birds, and you won't get your nice hat."

"You're right," she agreed softly, following the bear and me up the river again. She tugged another flower out of her curls and frowned. "Why did you put flowers in my hair?"

I glanced back at her, surprised. "What?"

She rolled her eyes. "I get the irony, you calling me Daisy, but isn't this a bit much? Even for you?"

I opened my mouth, closed it again. *They* grew *in your hair*, I wanted to say, but it sounded as farfetched as a secretive city in the forest. "I thought it was funny."

Tugging the last flower out of her curls, she sectioned off her hair and began braiding, a morning ritual of hers. I remembered from when I was a fox—she would often come out to the gardens in the morning to do it, her thin, graceful fingers weaving the strands together delicately, as entrancing as a soft wind through the sunlight-sprinkled trees. I could have watched her for hours.

"Well, next time you decide to be *funny*, why don't you gather a bouquet of different ones? We could use them. Goldenrod's good for teas if you're feeling anxious," she said, and again my chest began to feel weird, like there were bees knocking against my rib cage, buzzing. "Dandelion roots for upset stomachs."

"Aren't daisies good, too?"

"For a variety of things, sure. Coughs, inflammations, disorders of the liver and kidneys, purifying the blood . . . They're weeds, but they're still good. Still important." She glanced over to me then. "Why're you looking at me like that?"

I quickly trained my eyes at the ground again. I didn't want to tell her that my reason for calling her Daisy had nothing to do with the fact that it was a weed. Instead, I said, "You talk too much."

She didn't take offense, though; she simply smiled. "Prince Lorne used to say that, too."

A pang of something unfamiliar shot through me, and a word—*jealousy*? The bees inside my chest buzzed louder. I pushed the feeling away before Daisy could see, but she wasn't paying attention to me anymore. She had a soft look on her face. The rush of freckles across her cheeks reminded me of nighttime constellations, and her eyes were the shade of gray just before a spring rainstorm. My gaze settled on her mouth.

What was *happening* to me?

Once she finished braiding her hair, she flipped her braid behind her shoulder. "Anyway, we should hurry and find Voryn. It can't be that much farther."

"After you," I replied.

As we traveled, the trees stretched taller and became harsh and jagged. Their needles coated the ground, which grew uneven, with craggy rocks and ridges. The Lavender Mountains towered over us, the snow at their peaks visible between the branches and looking like dollops of frosting. It wasn't until midday that a thin white fog began to settle between the trees once again. I ground my teeth. What little I *could* smell didn't help anymore, and my hearing didn't make up for it. The bear kept stopping to sniff the air, growing wearier the deeper we traveled. She smelled something I couldn't, but when I asked, she'd just grunt and amble on.

Soon, as the afternoon wore on and the sky began to turn a dark orange, the fog became so thick, Daisy slowed her pace and took hold of the bear's fur. She was frightened—her eyes were wide and kept flicking to every sound in the wood.

I drew close to her, and she eyed me. "This can't be good if you're sticking so close to us," she remarked dryly.

I inclined my chin indignantly. "I simply don't want to lose you in the fog."

"Oh? And I thought you'd want to be as far away as possible so you could run at the first sign of trouble."

To that, I flashed her a grin. "Ah, but why would I run

when I could just hide behind you?"

She bit the inside of her cheek, and then she turned on her heels to face me. "Is this just a game to you?"

"What? No—"

"My best friend and my papa are both monsters, and the only way for me to save them is to break a three-hundred-year-old curse—and you're just *joking* around."

"Daisy, I didn't mean to—"

"You're a coward."

As if I didn't already know that. Whenever I closed my eyes, I saw those bone-eaters, or the baker's son coming after me with a shotgun, or the hunters' traps in their gardens, or the wolves and coyotes and snakes. As if I weren't afraid of all those things, and helpless against them, and . . .

"I'm a fox," I replied. "What do you suppose foxes do? We run, and we hide, and we steal. That's it. If you wanted someone loyal or brave, maybe you should've befriended a dog."

Then I started ahead of them up the river. I didn't want to have this conversation.

"You're not a fox anymore!" she shouted behind me. "You're a person, and people are . . . they are . . ."

I knew very well what *people* were. I knew it even better than her. She was scraping for words like *loyal* and *brave*, but I knew that humans could also be cruel and petty, and they could hurt you with words and deeds just as quickly as with blades or bows. If that was what being a human was about, I couldn't get back to being a fox fast enough.

"Courage gets you killed, Daisy. I'm in the business of staying alive."

I expected her to yell at me, and I braced myself for it, but all she said was "Of course."

It was the first time I ever heard her sound disheartened—not the disappointment of running out of your favorite food, or waking up to a rainy day, or getting your tail wet, but a different, deeper sort of disenchantment. I didn't understand why, but thinking back on it, I probably should have. Hindsight and all that.

Because she said softly, "Then you shouldn't be with me."

"Wait—no. Daisy, I—"

"It's fine. I didn't even ask you if you wanted to come along, anyway." She wasn't looking at me anymore, and I felt my heart begin to sink, sink, sink, down into my toes. "I just assumed. I'm sorry for that. You don't have to come any farther. I'll go and find Voryn. I'll find a way to break the curse, and to change you back, too. It's my fault you were transformed anyway. None of this is your responsibility."

"That's not what I meant, Daisy. Tell her that's not what I meant," I pleaded to the bear, but Vala didn't come to my rescue at all. She simply stood beside Daisy, leaning toward her, as if to protect her from me.

"Then why did you run when the ancient came?" Daisy asked. "What'll happen next time?"

I ground my teeth and looked away. That was all the answer she needed.

"Go find a hole somewhere and hide. I'll find you when this is all over. I'll be fine, Fox. Trust me."

Then she turned into the mist with the bear. The last expression on her face stuck with me—that look that told me that she would fix everything herself, even if it killed her. I bent into a crouch and put my head in my hands. What was I supposed to do? What *could* I do? If I told her how afraid I was of that ancient, she would think less of me than she already did.

She was right. I should just stay here. Just wait until I could return to myself, until I become a fox again, however that happened. Then, I was certain, I'd forget this whole ordeal. It would feel like a dream. I just needed to wait. I just needed to— -

"What am I *thinking*?" I stood. No, she never asked me to come along, but she never had to. Daisy thought I was always running around by myself, but the truth was, I was never alone.

I had always had her.

"Daisy—wait!" I cried. They were shadows in the fog, but I could still see them. I took off in a run after them until I was upon their shadows. I reached out to touch her shoulder. My hand went through it.

The shadows vanished.

They were gone.

⤳ 17 ⤳

THE SCREAM IN THE SILENCE

Cerys

KINGSTEETH, I HATED him. I hated him so, so much.

As the last of the daylight burned on the horizon, a knot of dread curled tightly in my stomach. The white fog that had become a suffocating constant on my and Vala's trek upstream had darkened into a dull, stormy gray. It grew thicker the farther we traveled, and I found myself clinging to Vala's fur as the last of the light was leaving us. The trees were so tall now, they disappeared up into the night sky. All the cracklings and stirrings in the underbrush were tenfold louder than they'd been just a few hours before, as though the night and the fog amplified them— or it might've just been my fear amplifying the noise. I kept my hand curled tightly into Vala's gray fur.

I didn't need Fox. I was the only person I could count on—I had gone into the wood before and come out. I had survived when my mother, when Lorne and Seren, had not.

And even if it was foolish, I couldn't *not* try to save Wen. I couldn't just return to the Village-in-the-Valley, and I couldn't leave, find another land to call home, knowing for the rest of my life that I could've done something. I hadn't been able to save my mother or my friends before, and I didn't expect the fox to understand what sort of weight that left on me.

I knew we must be drawing closer to Voryn, but how close I couldn't be sure. Perhaps Vala knew, but unlike Fox, I had no idea what her grunts and *haroooms* meant. If Vala and I didn't camp tonight, if we could perhaps fashion some torches and push through once night had completely fallen, maybe we'd reach it soon. . . .

But maybe we wouldn't.

I was a little afraid to stop in this thick fog, but I was more afraid to keep going after dark, when we could stumble into a ravine or any number of hazards beyond just the beasts that walked this wood. So, as the red-orange sky finally faded to an inky black, we set up camp by the thin spools of moonlight that broke through the dark trees. We thought it'd be safest under the shadow of a large rock, and I made a small fire that was hopefully hidden by the overhang. It would've been so much quicker with an extra pair of hands.

"Honestly, he was getting on your nerves, too, wasn't he?"

I asked the bear, who flopped down beside the campfire.

There had been no fish in the river today, and my stomach grumbled. I was hungry, and when I drank the water from the river, it tasted strange. The fire was small and barely gave off any warmth in this fog.

"I mean, I can't fault him." A knot formed in my throat, and I swallowed it down thickly. The memory of that nightmare— of my mother, woodcursed and hungry—hid under my eyelids, waiting for me to fall asleep again. *Don't cry*, I told myself. *Don't cry.* "Truthfully, I'm glad he turned back. Everyone I've ever loved died because of this wood. I was the only one who survived. I didn't want Fox to get woodcursed, too. Like Mama, like Seren. It would be all my fault."

Vala grunted and curled herself near me. I sank into her warm side and blotted my tears with her fur. I didn't want to be in this terrible wood. I had lived my whole life trying to escape it. And yet here I was, lost in the Wildwood that took my mother and my best friends, and it was coming for me, too.

After a while, I finally began to drift off to sleep. But just as I closed my eyes, a scream cut through the trees, and I jerked awake.

Vala's ears pinwheeled about, and she faced the direction of the noise, but there was only fog and trees. I sank deeper into her side, curling my knees up to my chest.

"Fox said not to listen, right?"

The bear made another noise—I hoped in agreement—as

I settled back into her fur. Until I heard the scream again, and this time it sounded like—

"Cerys!"

"Wen?" I jerked to my feet, as did Vala. "That was Wen. I'd know her voice anywhere. Maybe she—maybe she broke the curse?"

The bear shifted on her feet, rocking back and forth indecisively.

"Cerys!" she cried again through the mist. "Cerys—help me!"

If the curse had somehow been lifted, and she found herself in the middle of the wood, she'd be terrified. And calling out like that . . . It wouldn't be long before an ancient found her.

"I'm here!" I called. "It's her—I have to go. I have to find her. I'll be right back, I promise," I told Vala, quickly fashioning a torch from a fallen limb and a length of cloth I ripped from my oversized shirt. I lit it, and the fog around us warmed to a pumpkin orange. It didn't help me see much farther, but at least I had some light. Though I didn't know how I was going to get back to camp—the fog was too thick to see anything beyond the reach of my hand, and I didn't have any string to tie to me so that I could lead myself back, and all there was in the surrounding area were river stones and dead trees with hanging moss—

Moss.

I grabbed a tuft of moss from a nearby tree, returned,

pulling my iron knife out of my pocket, and pricked the tip of my finger. A bead of red blood bloomed, and I pressed it into the moss. Almost instantly—faster than it ever had back in the Village-in-the-Valley—the magic in my blood took root, and the moss in my hand grew, curling down over my fingers, until it was as long as I was, and still it kept growing. When there were about fifty yards of it (and by then it was slowing), I took up one end of it, gave it to Vala, and made her promise not to let the end go no matter what happened. It would be my only way back to the water through the fog, since I certainly didn't trust myself to find my way back on my own.

"Cerys!" Wen called again, closer.

I steeled myself, tied the other end to my sash with the crown, and set out into the mist.

There was no path, and the underbrush was thick, so my going was slow as I picked my way through the wood. The trees bent and swayed in the wind, the thin black leaves rustling, sounding like laughter. When I looked straight up, the branches were so thick and the fog so consuming, I couldn't see even the moon or stars. I couldn't see anything.

The fog was suffocating.

"Wen?" I called, holding tight to the hanging moss, the torch in my other hand. There was no answer. I wandered a little farther. I'd go as far as the string would let me, and then I'd turn back—with or without her.

"Anwen!" I called again.

"Ceeeeeeryssss."

I froze in my footsteps. A cold chill crawled down my spine. I spun around to try to find the owner of the voice, but there were only the shadowy trunks of ancient trees and fog.

So much fog.

My torch flickered. Something was wrong. I should never have left the campsite.

The wind tickled against my ear, and I swatted it away, ducking beneath a low-hanging limb. On the other side was a clearing where nothing grew. Trees lay bent and broken on the ground, old and rotted, while the soil itself crinkled dryly as I crept across it. There was a strange smell here, too, like smoke from Papa's pipe and something I couldn't quite place, so pungent I almost gagged.

"Ceeeeeeryssss," the voice whispered again, this time closer—close enough for me to hear the honeyed edges of it. My heart panged with familiarity.

It *was* Wen.

I spun around toward the voice, but as soon as I turned, all I saw was that unending white fog.

There was no one.

With my free hand, I began to wind the moss tight, until I realized that I was winding too long without it going taut. Frightened, I dropped the torch as I reeled in the plant and found the end. It had been crudely cut.

"Ceeeeeeryssss," the voice of my best friend hummed

again, and the sound of footsteps, light and brisk, followed.

There was no denying that there was something in this glen with me. I felt its eyes on me now, as sure as I smelled the pipe smoke and the rot—like death. I remembered that stench now.

It came with the ancient as it breathed its hot breath on my neck.

I slipped my hand into the pocket of my trousers, my fingers curling around the iron knife there, my other hand on the crown at my side. I should've left it with Vala, but I hadn't thought of it at the moment. Fox was right—I shouldn't have kept it on my person.

"Ceeeeeeeeeerysssss . . ." The whisper came again, as soft as snow through the trees.

The fog was so bright and disorienting, and it clung to me like a damp towel. I searched the ground around me for my footprints, but when I looked down, I found mine—and another's.

Large, taloned, and deep.

A tree branch snapped in front of me, and a hulking figure appeared in the mist. With a bolt of fear, I realized that I was well and truly lost, and the thing that was once Anwen had found me.

18

THE EMPTY PROMISE

Fox

"DAISY!" I CALLED, but she didn't answer.

The damned fog was everywhere. If it hadn't been for the shadows in my eyes that picked up the magnetitic fields, I would've been lost ages ago. They were like dark spots at the top of my vision, always pointing in the way that I now know as *north*. If she and Vala had continued following the river, I couldn't be that far behind them. Or at least, I thought not.

As I traveled, the fog continued to encroach on the path, silent and thick.

Where *was* that impossible girl? My throat began to constrict, even though I tried to stay calm. She was just ahead of me. She wasn't that far—why didn't I keep her in my sights?

The wood grew more dense, the rush of the river was

muted by the fog, but there were small tracks in the earth from wild animals. Nothing too wild or beastly, but I bristled at every crinkle in the underbrush. While I wasn't the one carrying the crown, there were still things in the wood that wouldn't mind crunching on my bones, too.

And one of them decided to pay me a visit.

"Where did your flower girl go, fox-boy?"

I jumped, tripping on a root as I spun toward the voice, and fell backward into a hollowed-out tree.

The monster faded out of the dark wood—a shadow made flesh. He propped his hand up on the side of the tree and leaned in toward me. "Frightened you, did I?"

Shit. It was that guy—what had Daisy said his name was? *Seren?* I hadn't even heard him sneaking up on me.

I pushed myself back into the hollow of the tree even more, but there was nowhere for me to go. I was too big for the tree; my shoulders jammed into the sides, brushing against the dry moss.

He cocked his head. Black rot had crept up the right side of his face, disorienting because his left shoulder was full of blooms: a bouquet of wildflowers blossoming across his chest and down his arm. The branch I had thrown at him was still embedded in his shoulder, though it looked like he'd been trying to dig it out to no avail.

Daisy's power really *was* terrifying.

His black eyes settled on my face. "Look at you, cowering

like some poor little creature. Is that why she left you?" His voice—it wasn't like before. Back at the cottage, he had sounded like a thousand crows in unison, but now he just sounded like a man. "Did she kick you out of her adventuring party?"

I clenched my teeth together. Every piece of me wanted to sink into the shadows of the tree and hide. Get away from this corpse. The wrongness came off him in waves.

He cocked his head to the other side, like a raven assessing something shiny. I fisted my hands so he couldn't see them shake.

I can take him, I thought, though I wasn't very sure.

He was slightly taller than I was, wiry and thin. He carried no weapon, but he wore the remnants of what looked like armor. It was dirt covered, the leather peeling and the metal bits orange with rust, but I noticed Aloriya's sigil on his chest. I recalled Daisy saying he'd been the prince's bodyguard before he'd been lost in the wood.

But then he pushed himself off the tree and gave me space to wrench myself out of the hollowed-out insides. I darted my eyes toward the shadows of the trees, wondering if I could hide, slip away, disappear—

He said in a bored tone, "I would like to call a truce—a deal, you could say. All you have to do is lead me to her."

I turned my attention back to him, eyebrows raised. Was he joking? No, he seemed perfectly serious.

"Listen, *Fox.*" He said my name like it was beneath him

154

and began to circle around me, like carrion birds over a carcass. "Have you thought about what you'll do if she fails? Look at you—you aren't fit to be human. You're cowering in your boots. You're scared. You want to run—"

"Any self-respecting creature would wanna run away from you," I interrupted. My voice shook. "Have you smelled yourself? You smell like decade-old rotted meat."

"Well, that's because I am," he replied simply, and reached toward me. I flinched as he picked a bug out of my hair and flicked it away. "Just think, if she fails, you'll be trapped in this body forever."

"But let me guess, you can turn me back?"

He flashed a toothy, delicate smile. "With the crown, of course—"

An earsplitting shriek startled an unkindness of ravens in the trees above me. *Daisy.*

"Well," said the corpse, "what fortunate timing."

I spun back to the corpse. "Call it off! Call your stupid beasts off!"

"I can't."

"Can't?" I echoed, and my shaking fingers grabbed at the collar of his jerkin. I pulled him close to me, realizing that we were about the same height, really. I was bulkier than he was. Stronger, too.

Not a fox against a human.

I tightened my grip and growled, "Call. It. *Off.*"

"I can't. Can a puppet call off its master? That's why I need the crown, you idiot," he snapped in reply. "And if you don't find her, she's as good as dead and the wood will have the crown and *everything* will be over. I can't find my way in this ridiculous fog, but you can."

"So you were *literally* lost in the wood and just *happened* to find me?" I asked, astonished.

The edges of his lips twitched, as if my realizing that bothered him. "Most fortunate for me, isn't it? This interminable fog is as much a hindrance to me as it is to anyone else roaming the wood. It's a protective barrier for Voryn, you could say. To keep beasts such as me outside their walls."

So Daisy was close—we were so close to that stupid city, and we didn't even know it.

"But *you*," he went on, shifting beneath my grip. I could smell the wildflowers blooming from his shoulder. "*You* are not quite all human yet, are you? I'm sure you can follow her scent even now. Let *me* have the crown, and I'll turn you back. I'll make you what you want to be. What loyalty do you have to her? She made you this way—"

Somewhere in the distance, Cerys screamed again—and then came the sound of a shrill, toneless cry. A bone-eater . . . or an ancient?

Startled, I glanced toward the sound of her.

I didn't know what to do. I couldn't lead this corpse to her, but if I stayed here, she would be wood food.

But the bear is with her, I told myself. *The bear'll protect her.*

But . . . what if they'd gotten separated?

What if—

"She's in danger, fox-boy," the corpse murmured.

Suddenly, thorns struck out through his jerkin, piercing my hand, and I hissed in pain, releasing him.

"Stop thinking and *go!*" he snapped. "I doubt you want to abandon someone else in the wood."

Someone . . . *else?*

The thought scratched at the edge of my mind. Had I abandoned someone else before?

I took a step back, holding my hand. It throbbed from where his thorns had pricked me.

This time, it wasn't Daisy who screamed. It was a creature—familiar, loud, like a death cry.

A bone-eater.

My heart beat in my throat, and all I wanted to do was run in the opposite direction. I wanted to get out of this fog. I wanted to run away. I wanted—

I wanted to save Daisy.

My legs acted before I did. I left the riverside, running headlong into the wood. As I ran away, toward the sound of the screams, I heard him laughing behind me, far back in the distant fog, but never far enough.

ᡒ 19 ᡒ

THE EVIL OF THE HEART

Cerys

SHE WAS WEN, but not.

She still looked something like herself, golden hair now littered with leaves and moss, the flesh on her face cracked and torn to accommodate a too-wide mouth filled with too-sharp teeth, grinning and hissing. Antlers twined with upturned roots and dried flowers had burst from her forehead, and the black emptiness of her eye sockets was inset with pinpoints of red light. When she spoke, a black tongue clicked against the roof of her bloody mouth. Her arms were too long, and her fingernails too sharp, her skin eaten by scales and feathers. The seed that had been planted on her neck throbbed, its roots thick as they curled into her skin and wound themselves down her body. With a scream, I backpedaled to the edge of the small clearing, where tall firs towered over me with spindly branches. She reached out with sprawled, grasping fingers.

"*Ccccccerys*," she hissed again. "*Crown.*"

"Wen—Wen, it's me." My voice was tight and trembling. She advanced, and I fell back against a tree trunk. Her hot breath stank of carcasses and rot. I shuddered.

I curled my fingers tighter around my iron knife.

My hand shook.

I was going to die.

"Wen, please, this isn't you," I begged, and I remembered it too well—my mother's figure in the doorway, the wood-curse spreading across her skin in rotting threads. I couldn't do anything then. I couldn't now.

"*Crown*," she repeated, and one of her claws caught the tip of a golden leaf on the crown and began to pull. All I had was my iron knife, but I couldn't draw it and slice my hand open again. My blood could surely stop her, but what if it killed her, like it had the ancient? I couldn't do that.

Whatever the wood had done to her, Wen was still my friend. She was all I had left.

"*The crown doesn't belong to you, gardener.*"

I felt Wen's fingers tug at the crown on my waist to free it. I tightened my grip on the blade but couldn't move otherwise. I held my breath—

That's when something darted out of the fog and slammed into Wen's side with enough force to send her stumbling away.

"It doesn't belong to you, either," said Fox, standing where Wen had been a moment before, massaging the shoulder he had used to ram into the side of the creature. He turned his attention to me, and his eyes flashed like mirrors in the torchlight. His chest heaved as if he'd run miles to get here. "Now, what's a pretty flower like you doing in a wood like this?" I could tell that his attack on the creature had dislocated something on his shoulder. He grinned through the pain.

I wanted to cry; I was so happy to see him. "What are you doing here?"

"Something very stupid!" he replied, and his voice was tight. He was frightened. His eyes were wide, and he was shaking, but he was here.

He'd come back for me.

Wen growled, righting herself. Fox and I both fell backward in fear. *"Crown! Crown!"* she raged, her eyes flaring a bright red. Once they'd been cerulean, but I was beginning to wonder if my Wen was truly gone.

Was there was no one left inside?

She launched herself at us, but I grabbed Fox by the arm and rolled us both out of the way. Wen shot past us through the fog, and there was a loud crack, like a tree snapping.

"Daisy—run," Fox told me frantically. "You can't fight her."

"What about you?"

"I don't know! I'll try to distract her, buy you some time,

160

and then I'll get away and hide somewhere."

"But—"

"Daisy, there's no time. I can see and hear better in this fog than you can. Besides, you know hiding's pretty much the only thing I'm good at." He tried to flash me a smile, but it just looked like he wanted to vomit.

Wen let out a shriek that quaked the trees.

"*RUN!*" he cried.

The ferocity in his voice made me scramble to my feet, and I took off before Wen could find me again. The fog was thinning, letting a little starlight through, which was lucky, since I'd dropped my torch back in the clearing. Still, I couldn't see much, and I groped blindly at the limbs and bushes, feeling my way to somewhere.

Anywhere.

Behind me, a toppling tree shook the ground. And then there was a yip, like the sound I had heard years ago, when I'd first found Fox in that hunter's trap.

Fox was in danger.

And I was running away.

He'd come back, and I was running *away*.

My feet slowed to a stop. I trembled. I wasn't brave or strong. Just like when the wood attacked the castle, I was helpless to save Wen, Papa, and the kingdom. I couldn't save anyone. I had gotten mad at Fox for running away, for being a coward. But who was the coward now?

I'd be a fool if I turned around, I thought.

But at least I'd be a loyal fool.

I pivoted on my heels, my iron knife tight in my free hand, and rushed as quickly as I dared back toward the sounds of shouts and splintering wood. I dodged between trees until the hulking shadow of the bone-eater came into view in the fog. Anwen towered over Fox, her claws bloodied and her teeth bared, snapping and snarling like the feral wolves that sometimes came to the edge of the garden wall.

Kingsteeth, I was going to die.

I pressed the iron knife against my wounded palm and sliced it open once more. Blood pooled in my hand, and I flung it out toward the ground. My blood seeped into the leaves. Saplings shot out of the ground underneath Anwen, growing thick and large as they swirled up into the sky, taking with them the monster she had become.

Fox struggled to his knees. His shirt was dark with blood. There was a gouge in his shoulder, still bleeding, from where Anwen must have raked her claws across him.

"Get up," I told him, putting his arm around my shoulder and pulling him to his feet. The light of the moon cut through the dissipating fog, giving us just enough light to see. "Come on, please. We can run—can you run?"

He turned his unfocused gaze to me, and my chest tightened. "You . . . run."

"No." I held him tighter, if only to prove I wasn't tempted to leave him behind. Above us, my best friend howled as the trees slowly stopped growing and she had to pick her way down through the thick, thorn-sharp limbs. "Together. We're in this together."

His brow furrowed. "But I—"

"*Together*, Fox."

I grabbed onto him as tightly as I could, and we ran. There were only fog and trees—an endless expanse of them, it seemed—but I knew there must be an end to it. Voryn had to be near. The river began in the Lavender Mountains, and Voryn was at the beginning of the river—

Or, at least, I hoped.

Against me, Fox groaned. The wound must be serious; sweat beaded on his brow, and his eyes were clouded. But it wasn't the bleeding that alarmed me.

It was the thin black veins that crept slowly across his skin from the wound.

"It's the curse," he told me when he noticed that I was looking. "It's—it's in my shoulder. I can feel it."

"Can I dig it out?" I asked, even though I already knew the answer. I remembered my mother's face, streaked with black roots. I remembered her skin breaking apart, the monster inside emerging like a nightmare from a cocoon. Like how Wen's face looked, torn and peeling, something monstrous underneath.

His resigned gaze locked to mine. We both knew there wasn't a cure. He was already as good as dead.

Anwen must have climbed down finally; I could make out her hulking shadow, a few dozen yards behind us, prowling through the thicket. Twigs snapped under her feet, leaves crunching. She was closing the distance between us with ferocious speed, and so I leaned Fox against a nearby tree and did the only thing I could. I threw my hands out, droplets of blood flying off the tips of my fingers, and where they landed, flowers and vines and trees burst to life underneath the decomposing underbrush, rushing up like a wall. She jumped back, eyeing the new growth.

"Daisy!"

I heard Fox's anguished cry, followed by another monstrous howl. Another bone-eater had burst through the trees behind us, wearing the remains of a beautiful set of robes. As it came in to attack, I stooped to grab a fistful of dirt. An acorn I had scooped up burst into a sapling in my hand, and I lobbed it at the creature. It grew in the air, doubling, tripling in size, and slammed into him with enough force to knock him back.

Two more bone-eaters crept out of the fog, snapping their sharp teeth, red eyes flickering. I could have sworn one looked like Papa, but I told myself it wasn't. It would make the next part harder.

I threw out my hand once more and blinked the black spots out of my eyes. Flowers gushed from the ground, but the bone-eaters had begun to anticipate my movements. They hurdled the growth before it could block their path. I flung my hand again, thorny bushes spreading across their path, but they just began to pick their way through them. When they got through the briars, they would tear us to pieces.

Wen came to the head of them, looking at the briars that swirled up between us like a barrier, thorns sharp and flowers bright. She stretched out one of her long, monstrous hands, and her black tongue formed words in her too-wide mouth. *"Crown. It is mine!"*

"It's not yours," I replied.

She snarled. *"MINE!"*

Suddenly, there was another roar in the fog, loud, thundering, and deep, and the sound of a heavy creature moving fast through the wood followed.

An ancient.

The bone-eaters inched toward us. I held on to Fox tighter. His breath was labored against my collarbone, and I felt him jerk in my grip, convulsing. If he turned into a monster now, he would shred me in two before the others even got their claws on me.

The roaring shadow came closer, galloping faster than the bone-eater. Out of the fog, I began to make out a shape—

Round ears and large paws and gray fur.

Vala.

Her eyes caught the silver moonlight as she came out of

the fog and grabbed me by the shirt with her teeth, flinging first me and then Fox onto her back. I gripped her fur with one hand, my other around Fox so he wouldn't slip off.

Anwen reached for me, her long claws catching the edge of my braid, but I slammed my foot against her and knocked her away. She gave a cry of pain as she fell back, writhing, into the wood.

I hoped she was okay.

Vala ran until the fog began to clear, and the moon broke once again through the corkscrew trees, and her fur was slick with sweat. After what must have been fifteen minutes, she slowed to a walk. Fox struggled to sit up, and I helped him get one leg over her back. It took all of his energy. His eyes were dull, their topaz darkening like ink dripped onto gold. It shivered me to the bone.

"Let me off here," he gasped. "I can walk. . . ."

In reply, I grabbed his hands and pulled them around my waist. His left hand, the one closest to his wound, was already a strange purple, like a bruise, and his claws were long and gnarled. His muscles twitched and shifted beneath the skin of his arm, as if they were changing, and his fingers played across the leafy gold of the crown at my waist. He could've taken it then, and for a breathless moment I thought he was going to, but then he clenched his fist and curled his arms around my waist.

I held fast, too.

"You stupid, stupid fox," I whispered. "You shouldn't have come back for me."

"You said I was a coward. I had to prove you wrong," he replied with a pitiful laugh.

"I shouldn't have said those things. I was just . . . I was letting my anger out on you when I was angry with myself. I'm the coward."

He sighed and pressed his forehead against my back. "You're stronger than you think."

A knot formed in my throat. "We'll find a way to help you. We'll do something. Once we get to Voryn—"

"Cerys."

It was the first time he'd ever said my name, and it made my breath catch in my throat. The end must be closer than I feared. I bit my bottom lip to keep from crying and held tighter to his hands around my stomach. He gave a long sigh and leaned fully against me, his face pressed into my loosely braided hair.

Vala walked in silence. She must have known the way to Voryn, but I couldn't begin to think how she could've found Fox and me in that fog.

After a while, Fox mumbled something.

I glanced over my shoulder, and he looked at me from under his long dark eyelashes. His eyes were still that milky, filmy white. "What was that?"

"You don't stink," he said softly. "I lied. Before. When I

said that. You smell like . . . daisies."

That took me off guard. "Oh."

"It reminds me of . . ." His voice trailed off, either because of the curse or something else, I didn't know. He closed his eyes and pressed his face into my hair again. "I like daisies."

Oh no, he was being truthful. The curse must've addled his brain. I gave a small laugh. "I'll make you a daisy crown when we get to Voryn."

"I'd like that." Then, quieter, "I don't want to become a monster."

"I don't want you to, either."

The silence that fell was terrible and foreboding. It couldn't have been more than a few minutes later before Fox made a sound I couldn't describe. It wasn't human or animal. He shoved his face hard into my back. I quickly glanced down at his hands. Now his other had been taken by the strange black roots, and they bulged out of his skin, throbbing.

My heart skipped.

"Vala—quickly!" I cried, and the bear took off at a gallop again. I hung on to her silver fur, my other around Fox's arms. His hands grew strange and knobbed in my grip. I could feel the muscles underneath his skin shift, his bones popping, his hands tightening into fists.

How much farther to Voryn? I didn't know—the wood seemed endless. Did the city even exist? Did it still stand, or was it just ruins? And if we made it, would the haughty, mythical people said to live there even let us in?

There wasn't enough time.

Fox growled, a rumble deep in his chest, and in my fright I glanced behind me at him and met his inky-black eyes.

In them I didn't see Fox at all.

Bruise-like roots spiderwebbed across his face. He bared frightfully sharp teeth and grabbed me roughly, his claws sinking into the flesh of my arms, and I prayed he wouldn't break the skin, afraid of what would happen if I were to bleed on him now.

Suddenly, Vala burst through a dense wall of trees. A thick limb slammed against my chest and threw both Fox and me off her back. I tumbled to the ground with great force and felt something inside of my chest pop—and then a sharp pain.

Black spots danced in my vision. I took an excruciating breath, and the black spots bloomed, but the moment before I fell unconscious, I thought I saw a city of shining obsidian built into the wall of the mountains, torchlights gleaming across the rooftops like rubies.

Voryn.

It was real.

20

CORRUPTED

Fox

I DREAMED OF blood. The city colored in it. Guards chained me up, dragged me through the streets, people screaming. I remembered the smell of blood pumping through quick, fearful hearts. And the smell of fear.

That smell was not like Daisy. It was vicious. Hot and sharp and sweet.

"What do we do with him, Grandmaster?" one of them asked. The words tumbled through my head. I almost knew them. I clung to them. He held a sword, and it glinted in the torchlight.

"Wait until the woodcurse takes him," a woman replied. "I doubt the public will want to see a half-human monster die at the pyre."

I shifted in my chains, curling in against myself, trying to hold on to what I was—who I was.

Who was I?

The flower girl had called me a fox—what was her name? Soft and sweet. Sweet like blood, sweet like food. Sweet—I wanted to taste how sweet. I was starving. I was hungry.

I was—

What was—

Who was—

I?

~ 21 ~

THE MONSTROUS

Cerys

I OPENED MY eyes.

Sunshine spilled in through a small window by my bed. My first thought was that it was strange that light would come in through my window—my room faced west, toward the baker's shop, and the only light I really saw was just before sunset.

Until I remembered the forest, and Wen, turned into that hideous bone-eater, and Fox.

Fox, who was turning into a monster, too.

I tried to move, but my side flared with a sharp pain, and I sucked in an agonizing breath. My hands went to a bandage against my side, just underneath my arm. I had to find my clothes and find Fox. I wrenched the blanket off. Purplish-yellow bruises covered my skin—they didn't look fresh. How long had I been unconscious?

The room I found myself in was small, with blue-patterned wallpaper and old wooden paneling. The mattress was lumpy, and a sweet-smelling incense burned on the nightstand. There was little else in the room—a washbasin on the other side, some liquids in various vials, my boots below them. My sash—the one with the crown tied to it—was nowhere to be found. I hoped Vala had it.

But where was Fox?

As I gingerly pushed myself to the edge of the bed, a girl, maybe ten or twelve years old, came into the room. Her dark hair was in a braid down her back, the kind my mother used to wear and weave dandelions into in the spring, and her skin was a warm brown. She wore a simple uniform emblazoned with a raven crest. I'd never seen that sigil before.

My heart began to race.

She gave me a wide-eyed blink and dropped the bowl of soup in her hands. The contents spilled out over the floor. "You're awake!" she cried. "I must tell Petra—and the Grand-master! I'll be right back; stay there!"

"No, wait!" I tried to stop her, wincing as my side flared with pain, but she was already turning out of the doorway.

It was then that I remembered seeing, just before I blacked

out, a city carved into the cliffside of the mountain, sharp and black as obsidian.

Was this—*Voryn*?

I didn't have time to wonder. Voryn or not, I had to find Fox and Vala.

Pushing myself to the edge of the bed again, I tried to stand, but my legs wouldn't cooperate. I hit the floor hard, pain shooting up my kneecaps. I took a quick breath, doubling over. I could barely stand, never mind *walk*, without pain piercing my side.

The girl came back a few minutes later with a woman in pristine white robes, and they helped me back onto the bed. The woman appeared to be a doctor. Her hair was long and brown, pulled into a simple bun, and her face was narrow and solemn. She looked about thirty, but when she spoke, her voice was old and crackling, like a wood fire, a sound that matched the smoky orange-gray of her eyes. She told me that I had two bruised ribs and stitches in my injured hand, and I had been asleep for four days—but she told me that I was safe.

Vala had brought us to Voryn.

The impossible city.

It was real, and we had made it.

I grabbed the doctor by the wrist and asked, "What about Fox? Is he okay?"

She didn't say anything. Instead, she dedicated her

concentration to unwrapping my injured hand and applying a salve that smelled like honey. Then she started to rewrap it meticulously.

"Please answer me."

"I cannot."

"What do you mean you can't? Where is he? Is he okay? He needs help and—"

A cold, sharp voice interrupted me. "Your... *companion*... has been detained in the prison."

A woman stood in the doorway. She wore long emerald-green robes, much like the seneschal's coronation attire, and she looked to be around Seneschal Weiss's age as well, her graying eyebrows thin and her long hair fixed in a high ponytail. Her pale skin was old and leathery, speckled with brown freckles. She held herself with the regal authority of someone of royal blood, and I resisted the urge to bow to her. I was too angry for that.

"What do you mean," I snapped, "by *detained*?"

The woman gave the doctor a glance, and she promptly gathered up her medicines and gauze and slipped out of the room. Then the woman came closer, her arms tucked into her long sleeves. "Your companion has been corrupted by the wood."

"Yes, but surely you can save him," I argued impatiently, and she gave me a strange look. One that found an uneasiness settle in my belly. ". . . *Can't* you save him?"

"There is no saving one who is cursed, child."

"But . . . but this is *Voryn*. You have survived in the wood for centuries. It was you who gave us the crown that protects us from the wood. The Lady of the Wilds must know how to do *something*!"

"Ah. So you *are* an Aloriyan." She gently sat down on the stool the doctor had occupied and gave me a scrutinizing look. "No one else would believe such lies."

"Wh-what?" My vision began to narrow. I'd traveled through the wood. I'd risked my life. To get *here*.

And—and Fox had been right.

The woman went on. "Our Lady has not been seen for centuries. And we are no more capable of surviving the woodcurse than you. I'm surprised you even made it through the fog. It's near impenetrable. It's a miracle that only your companion was taken by the curse and not you both."

Her words were like stones dropping from a terrifying height. *Crack. Crack. Crack.* I sucked in a breath, trying to keep myself calm, but the room was beginning to spin.

No, this couldn't be right. It didn't make sense. In all the legends, the Lady protected the enchanted people of Voryn. She had given King Sunder the crown.

All of this—everything—was *wrong*.

I had so many questions. But one was more important

than the rest, at least at the moment.

"What will happen to Fox?"

She smoothed her robe across her lap. "He will be relieved of his curse."

A seed of hope blossomed in my chest. "So there *is* a cure?"

"No, child. I mean we will execute him."

My eyes widened. The hope burst in my chest.

"We rarely allow the woodcursed through our walls to begin with," she continued. "Your friend had not been fully infected when you had arrived, but that is no longer the case. We cannot risk a cursed person within the city walls any longer. We will set him aflame tonight."

"Aflame?"

"We burn the wicked of the wood," replied the woman coldly, and left me speechless.

Fox was going to die.

"Your companion is gone. Only the husk remains," she added, trying to be tender. She set a hand on my arm, soothing. She reminded me of the villagers who told me that my mother was gone. That the wood took her that day when I survived, along with Prince Lorne and Seren.

They're gone, they repeated, over and over again.

And now, again, I was the only one to have survived the wood.

"Let me see him," I said. I curled my hands into fists and

felt the blood squelch out from between the stitches on my hand, dampening the gauze. "Please. Let me say goodbye."

"And why should we do that?" the woman asked. "You are from the outside. For all we know, you could be another trick of the Wildwood. Another attempt to destroy us. We have not survived this long by trusting anything that comes to us from outside our walls."

"I'm not."

"Then how are you not woodcursed? The scar on your neck says you should be."

Shit. I touched the bloom-shaped mark on the back of my neck. It was something I couldn't deny. From what little I knew of Voryn, I was sure they could spot any sign of the woodcurse, living with the wood as they did. But maybe I could use it to bargain. "I'll tell you," I replied. "But you must let me see him first."

The old woman inclined her head. Her eyes were the color of butterscotch. They should have been warm, but they reminded me of gems instead—cold and old and rare. She wouldn't be taken for a fool, and I had the distinct feeling that she wasn't the kind of person I could lie to and live to tell about it.

"Very well," she said. "I will take you to your companion."

The entirety of Voryn was carved from the mountainside; every building was chiseled from the rock face in crisp detail, and I could hardly believe that such a thing was possible. It must have taken hundreds of years to sculpt a city like this, and as half a dozen Voryn guards led me out of my room and into the mountain itself, I didn't know how far it went. I just swallowed the pain in my side and followed the old woman down into the depths of the stone city, staircase after staircase, until we reached the damp bottom, where the prison was located. There was an open square, and then a line of cells at the other end. A torch sat outside each one, but there was only one occupied.

The woman, who was probably a seneschal herself, or a high-ranking soldier since the guards obeyed her, said, "Your companion is there."

I swallowed the knot in my throat and walked down to the cell to which she was pointing.

There was no mistaking it; it was Fox and yet . . . not.

"May I have some time alone?" I asked the woman.

She inclined her head, debating. She must have realized I couldn't cause any harm and stood no chance of freeing him. I could barely walk without wincing from the pain. The stairs had been brutal. "Very well. Five minutes. Say your goodbyes."

The guards left on her order, and soon I was the only one remaining in this strange underground courtyard prison. I rubbed the gauze on my wounded hand and turned to face the dark cell.

Fox shifted and looked up. He was a shadow in the corner

of his cell, but his eyes caught the firelight, shining like disks of moonlight. I took another step closer. He pushed himself farther into the corner, his arms wrapped around himself.

The woodcurse had taken my mother, leaving nothing of the person I had known. The same could be said for Anwen. I didn't entertain the hope that Fox was still in there.

The shadow shifted again, the chains that bound him rustling. But then, quietly—quivering—I heard my name. *"...Daisy?"* His voice was strange and pained, like the syllables were hard to form.

I curled my fingers around the bars of the cell. "Fox, you're still alive!"

He didn't say anything beyond a low moan. *Think*—I had to do something. He wasn't gone yet. And I couldn't lose him. I didn't know what I would do without Fox, and for the moment there was still a piece of him left.

Maybe a piece was enough.

My fingers shook as I began to unwrap my wounded hand.

When my blood had touched the ancient, life had taken over the monster's body, destroying the creature and leaving nothing but a withered tree behind. But when it touched flowers, it made them bloom. It turned a fox into a man, and it trapped a castle in briars and thorns.

Before the curse came to Aloriya, I had thought I understood my magic. In truth, I knew nothing about it.

180

But I knew, whatever the cost, I wouldn't let Fox burn.

"Fox," I called again, reaching out my hand.

As he stepped slowly out of the shadows of the cell and into the torchlight, every bone in my body wanted to run from there and never look back. Fox looked so much like my mother had, like Anwen had, skin cracking as something terrible began to emerge from beneath. My heart thundered in my ears, because I could see my mother again, standing in the sun-drenched doorway, no longer my mother at all but something that ate and ate and never had its fill. I had been helpless then, like I was helpless now, standing in front of this bone-eater, unable to stop the curse from festering inside. Rotting black roots crossed over his cheeks, curling up around his eyes. He looked like he was drowning in the darkness.

All I could hear was Fox telling me that he didn't want to become a monster. And it was my fault that it was happening now. If my blood could make wilting flowers bloom, and foxes into men, maybe it could . . .

He stepped up to the cell bars, and I placed my wounded hand on his cheek. His skin felt feverish to the touch, but I didn't pull away, even as I knew what he would do.

His yellow eyes widened, his lips pulling into a snarl because, oh, he was hungry. His turned his head toward my hand, his lips brushing across my bleeding stitches.

Oh, kingsteeth, he looked like he could tear me apart.

I steeled myself and said, "Bite me, you stupid fox."

His voice sounded like boots treading upon dead leaves. "Daisy—"

"*Trust* me." Then as I held my hand up to him, hoping that I wasn't wrong, the last bit of white in his eyes blackened to an inky, terrible abyss, and he opened his mouth to show me rows of sharp, terrible teeth.

And then he bit down to the bone.

～ 22 ～

SWEETER THAN SORROW

Fox

I WANTED TO grind my teeth through her. I wanted to tear her flesh off her bone. I wanted to snap her fingers between my teeth. I wanted—

I wanted . . .

I . . .

She ground her teeth in pain, her eyes bright with tears, and the hunger in me wanted to bite harder, to tear her flesh open and—and—

And . . .

I couldn't. I was hurting her. And moment by moment, it began to hurt me, too. I loosened my mouth from her hand and sucked in a shuddering breath, and the hunger unhooked its grip, and I tasted her on my tongue. I knew the flavor, from before. The world came back into focus. Honey-bronze hair and a constellation of freckles across her heart-shaped face and lips, which parted into a smile as if—

As if she was happy to see me.

She smelled so nice, like a field of wildflowers, and—a dream. Of running through the Wilds, daisies underfoot, someone pulling my hand. The sun was bright through the trees, but even so, the wood was dark, and there was a sound behind us. It tore through the underbrush, snarling and snapping, and still the woman didn't let go.

"Hurry," she said as she pulled me through the wood. Her hand was tight around my wrist. "We can't stop—we mustn't stop."

My feet were tired. I wanted to go home. I was crying.

The sound was an ancient, and it caught up to us. I knew it would. Somehow, I had seen this moment before, a hundred times it seemed. It was my fault, what happened next. She spun to me and took me firmly by the shoulders. Her hair was honey and her eyes were hazel, and she looked so familiar. "I need you to hide."

"What about you?"

"I told my daisy I'd keep you safe—now go!" she cried, shoving me toward a fallen log. I crawled into its hollowed center, my hands pressed tightly over my mouth, to stay quiet—stay safe—no matter what happened—"

"Fox—can you hear me? Fox?" I heard Daisy call through

the memory of the forest, and her face faded out of the darkness.

"You . . . you taste sweet," I murmured, and my knees gave as I fainted.

23

TO PLEASE A GRANDMASTER

Cerys

AS HE FAINTED, I tried to catch him through the bars, but my hand was slippery with blood and my side flared with pain and—and I failed *miserably*. He slumped across the cold stone floor, and I quickly knelt down and pressed the back of my hand against his mouth and let out a relieved sigh. He was breathing. The roots that had burrowed around his face shriveled, rotted, and turned to ash.

"We're going to be okay," I whispered to him. "We made it."

To Voryn.

We survived the wood.

I leaned against the bars of the prison, cradling my bleeding hand against my stomach. I knew I should've been relieved, but there was a knot in the back of my throat—because everything was wrong. This city was wrong.

When the woman came back and saw that Fox was no longer woodcursed, she quickly left again and barked an order at the guards—to detain *me*.

"Wait—no, stop!"

Three guards grabbed me and forced me to my feet. I didn't have the energy to fight them off.

"I didn't do anything!" I fought weakly, trying to wrestle out of their grips, but it was to no avail, and my side ached with pain. I told the woman, "You can't do this!"

I was a fool.

Of course she could. I was powerless, and this was not the Voryn I'd imagined.

Earlier, as I'd been led to the prisons, I hadn't wanted to admit it, because I kept tricking myself into thinking that these ornate buildings in this forgotten city of Voryn couldn't have been made without magic, that these people couldn't have lasted this long within these walls without some enchanted help—well, the fog *was* enchanted, I found out later, but very little else was. There were no enchanted weapons. No enchanted lampposts that popped on when night fell, like in Somersal-by-the-Sea, or enchanted armors like the ones in Eriksenburg, or enchanted *people*.

Fearing me, I guess, they locked me in one of the other empty cells as they dragged Fox away. I didn't know where, even though I insisted that he was cured, that he wasn't dangerous. But they didn't listen to me. So, I sank down to the cold floor, and I waited. Powerless. I didn't know how long I sat there—long enough for the blood from Fox's bite to dry—but finally a handful of guards came to get me. As I was led out of the prisons again, toward the fortress at the top of the city, I realized how much of a fool I really was. These denizens were just *people*. They reminded me so much of the people of Aloriya. They looked like people from Eriksenburg, and Eldervale, and Nor. Had they all gotten lost in the Wildwood and found their way here? Or had their ancestors been in the city since the curse?

The city was beautiful, each building ornate and old, but it was gray and quiet and . . . hopeless. I imagined—I don't rightly know what I imagined, but it wasn't this. The Sundermount looked like the sun against the grayness of Voryn. There were stone creatures perched at the edges of the rooftops and carved across the trim work in the old stone buildings. The wallpapers inside the buildings were old, as were the furniture and decorations, as if Voryn itself had been trapped in a bubble of time hundreds of years back, or at least trapped in the stuffy, unused halls of Castle Sunder. And the citizens of Voryn had this look in their eyes when they caught a glimpse of me—I could feel the animosity at the back of my neck, jealousy and bitterness intertwined. Like people trapped.

Nothing about Voryn was what I'd expected.

Where was the magic? Where were the riches? The power

that could hold back the curse, that could create the crown itself?

Where was the Lady of the Wilds?

And, more worryingly, where was the *crown*?

I hoped Vala was okay. I hoped even harder that, wherever she was, she had the crown. I didn't want to think about whether we'd lost it in the wood, or if Seren had gotten it— or something even worse. If Vala was out there in the wood with it, I knew she would keep it safe until we could find her again.

"The Grandmaster wants to see her alone," said one of the guards, a woman with bright blond hair and pale skin. I didn't like the sound of a *Grandmaster*. Was he some sort of leader? A king?

The Lady herself?

"*Alone?*" one of the guards who had me by the shoulder asked. "Are you sure that's wise?"

"It's her wishes."

Inside the fortress at the apex of Voryn, the half dozen guards led me up a large stone stairwell to a large set of ornate doors, carvings of bears and cougars and ravens across them, and pushed one open.

The guards jerked me to a stop just inside the door.

". . . It cannot be that she was able to cure the woodcurse once it takes hold, and yet she *did*," said a soft, sure voice. It belonged to a young woman, her back turned to me as she faced

189

the older woman sitting behind what I could only describe as the fanciest desk I'd ever seen—bronze gilding and animals carved into the wood. Stacks of papers were piled high atop the desk and almost blocked the older woman completely. I recognized her—she was the same one who led me to the prisons. The woman who I'd thought was a seneschal.

Could *she* be the Grandmaster? Behind her was another set of closed doors, framed by maps of what must be the wood and other information about the city.

The young woman went on, "Think of all the people we could save if we could force her to—"

"We have no idea where she came from," the older woman replied. "She could be woodcursed herself. She could be part of the wood's plan to take us unawares. No, this is a nonstarter, Petra. Oh—you're here," she added when she noticed me.

The young woman—Petra—glanced over her shoulder toward me. Now that I was closer, I was surprised to see how tall she was. Her dark hair was short, barely brushing her ears, and her skin was the color of bark wood, her eyes a warm brown, eyelashes long. I couldn't help but blush, because she was very beautiful. She turned to me with the grace of a dancer. Her lower left leg was wooden, gleaming with metal bits that strapped it to her thigh. She wore leather armor emblazoned with the raven's sigil, like the guards.

The crest of Voryn.

"So *you* are the one who cured that young man," said

Petra, narrowing her brown eyes. "How did you do it?"

I gave a start. "Oh, um—"

"Was it a poultice? Magic? Are you a witch? A *god*?"

"No," I quickly replied, shaking my head. "You see, I don't really understand it—"

The woman went on, cutting my babbling short. "Then some sort of talisman? An array? A—"

"Petra," the older woman interrupted. "Leave us."

The young woman looked like she wanted to say something more, but then she bit her tongue and turned to leave. As she passed me, she gave me a glance that sent a chill down my spine. The door swung closed behind her with a deep and sullen thump.

"Forgive my apprentice. She's very curious."

"It's, um, all right." If *that* was curiosity, I didn't want to know what it would be like to be interrogated by her.

"The question she should have been asking," the older woman said, and reached behind one of the stacks of paper, "is why you have the crown of Aloriya."

She set the golden crown on her desk.

Oh.

I stared at the crown. I'd tell her, but . . . "Where's Vala?"

"Who?"

"A bear—about this tall and sort of a sooty gray color . . ."

"*Ah*, that beast," the Grandmaster said. "She was very protective of the crown. We had to subdue her. But she's fine," she added quickly when I made to yell at her. "You see, I'm in quite the predicament. You seem to be able to cure the wood-curse, and on top of that you have the crown of Aloriya. You can just imagine what I might be thinking of you."

I clenched my hands again. "What might that be?"

"That you're from the wood," she said. "That you're a magic user of dark intent who has stolen the crown from Aloriya for a purpose I cannot yet guess."

"That . . . is definitely not true."

"Then how did you cure your companion? I'm no fool—you knew he was cursed, and you walked into that prison with a plan." She stood abruptly. The legs of her chair screeched loudly against the stone floor. "Now tell me why I shouldn't lock you up or put you to death—if not for being woodcursed, then for the safety of my city."

I clenched my teeth. "I didn't *mean* to deceive you. I have some sort of . . . power in my blood. I don't know how it works, but I somehow knew that it would either kill Fox or . . ."

"Or cure him."

"Yes. I hoped it would be latter, obviously."

The Grandmaster narrowed her eyes, but then she swooped up her robes and sat back down. She waved to one of the other chairs in front of the desk. "Sit. Tell me who you are, why you are here, and what you're doing with this crown. And I warn you, do not lie to me."

Behind me, the guard who had been posted on the outside

of the room stepped in, his hand resting on the hilt of his sword. I knew that stance—I had seen enough guards at the Sundermount take it in the village when people at the tavern got too rowdy, or a villager's voice rose too high in the great hall. It wasn't casual; it was threatening.

"I didn't come all this way to lie, milady," I said. "My name is Cerys Levina. I'm the daughter of the royal gardener of Aloriya." My hands were shaking with fear and frustration, but I made myself stay calm and sat down in the chair she had motioned to. I told her about the assault on the castle during Anwen's coronation, and how I didn't know where else to go but to Voryn. I told her of how we were chased through the wood by the bone-eaters—by Anwen herself—and of the wood-animated corpse of Seren Penderghast that haunted our trail, and how Fox fought off the bone-eaters and got cursed.

The Grandmaster listened as I spoke, nodding, and when I was done, she shifted in her chair. The crown shimmered in the low lamplight between us. Finally, the woman said, "You still haven't told me why your blood is magic."

"Because I don't really know," I replied, somewhat truthfully. "Folks in Aloriya thought it was a gift from the crown—a gardener's daughter to make the late king's endover lilies bloom year-round," I added, not as truthfully, because I knew where my magic had come from. I knew it had come from the wood.

"And do you expect me to believe that?"

"Anwen has magic, so why can't I? Didn't you once have magic, too? Or was that a lie in all the stories I was told?"

The Grandmaster gave me a look I could only describe as pitying. "Once upon a time, we did, but no longer." She stood again then, and I had picked up enough from Wen's etiquette training to know to stand with her. "You'll find your companion has been evaluated by our healers and deemed cured, miraculously. He's been taken to a room in the infirmary for the night. You may go to him, and you both may recover and restock your supplies before you leave."

"*Leave?*"

"Yes."

I gave a start. "But I came all the way here—"

"And for what? For help you thought we would give?" She took a step forward, and I shrank back. "We have fought against the Wildwood for three centuries without your help. Powerless. Isolated. *Trapped.* While you and the other thieves in Aloriya prospered. We have no idea what this crown is capable of, or if there's even anyone here who would be able to wield its power. What are two Aloriyans and their cursed crown to us? Nothing but trouble."

"But you *must* be able to do something!" I pleaded, and then I remembered. "How about the Lady?"

"The Lady?"

"The Lady of the Wilds! Can't she do something? Where is she?"

The Grandmaster's face hardened. "*Where? Where* indeed. She isn't here."

"But—but she—"

"She's gone. She's been gone for three hundred years, and we have lived generations in this wood without the help of that crown or the Lady or Aloriya, and I will not let some little girl destroy that. You may stay a week and no more—"

"The wood will come for you eventually," I interrupted. "It'll come for you just like it came for Aloriya!"

"I'm sure you think it will," she said, "but I see no threat. Our city is safe behind the fog and behind our walls, and I won't risk my people for you." She sat down again. "Now, you may stay until your and your companion's wounds are healed, but then I expect you to be gone from my city—"

"And if I can bring you proof?" I challenged. My voice shook.

She inclined her head. "Of this threat of yours?"

"Yes."

"I make no promises about helping Aloriya." When I made to protest, she held up a hand. ". . . But I will listen."

My shoulders unwound a little. It was better than nothing. "Okay. I'll find you your proof." When I went to grab for the crown, she was quick, drawing a dagger from the inside of her robes. She slammed it through the middle of the crown. I jerked my hand back.

"I keep the crown," she said. "I do not know its power—it's

as much an object of legend to us as our city must be to you. And I do not trust you with it in my city walls."

"But it's not yours!"

"It's not yours, either."

I hated that she was right.

She drew her knife away and returned it to her robes. "Oh, and take this *ghastly* beast with you." She flicked her hand, and a door to the left opened. Three guards hauled out a gray bear, bucking against her chains, snarling and snapping her sharp teeth.

"Vala!" I cried as I rushed over. "She's not going to hurt you! Take those shackles off—"

"She about mauled one of my men!" one of the guards snapped at me, and looked to the Grandmaster.

She said, "Do as the girl says."

Begrudgingly, they obliged. I unhooked the heavy iron collar from around her neck and hugged her tightly. Vala gave a content grunt and shoved her snout into my face. She was an ounce of familiarity in this strange place, enough to give me a little more courage.

"Now leave." The Grandmaster flicked her hand in dismissal.

My fingers curled tightly around Vala's fur. "Thank you," I replied, giving her a short bow. My gaze lingered for a moment longer on the crown. I didn't have a choice in the matter, and there wasn't anything I could do with it anyway.

The only thing that mattered was convincing the Grandmaster to help. Hopefully before the curse overtook this place, too.

As I left, Vala followed me out of the chambers. I tried to keep a handle on my anxiety, and the guard returned to his post by the door. Outside the chambers, leaning against the opposite wall, was the young woman from earlier—Petra.

"Your friend will be in the infirmary for observation for a while," she said, and without waiting, she turned down the hallway.

Vala and I followed her to the infirmary in the east wing, where I had woken up, and down the hall to the farthest room on the left. I hesitantly stepped inside. The room was bright and spacious and old. Wood paneling lined the walls, along with wallpaper designed with golden filigree. The scent of jasmine and another herb I couldn't quite place filled the room, and at the other side was a bed where Fox lay. The young girl I'd seen earlier sat on a stool beside him, dabbing a damp cloth across his forehead.

Fox's chest slowly rose and fell. He didn't look monstrous—the purple veins across his skin were gone, the wound on his shoulder bandaged. I breathed out a slow sigh of relief.

And suddenly, my own exhaustion caught up with me. I slid down to my knees and sat. Everything hurt, and my side ached.

The girl glanced back to me and smiled. "Oh, hello again!"

"Hello."

"You just missed him. He woke up a few moments ago, but he was in quite a bit of pain, so I gave him something to sleep. My name is Briath, by the way."

"Cerys," I said. "What did you give him?"

"Some tea, of course." She laughed.

I didn't want to find out what kind of tea that was.

"Ooh—there's a—" She gave a squeak as Vala poked her head into the room.

"That's Vala. She won't bite," I assured her.

Briath's eyes brightened. "I've never seen a bear this close before! You have such beautiful fur!" she said, rushing over to smoosh Vala's face in her hands. The bear let her, looking like a dog who is content with letting a child pull her ears.

Fox appeared to be sleeping soundly, and yet something seemed off about him, though I couldn't quite tell what. Perhaps it was just from all that we had been through, and now I saw him in a different light. "Thank you for taking care of . . ." I realized what was different. "Where . . . where are his claws? He had claws."

"Oh?" She glanced over at his very human-looking hands as she rubbed Vala under the chin. "I don't see any."

"No, but he had them!" I gently turned his face to me, putting my thumb between his lips to find that his teeth were blunted, too. I quickly drew my hands away. ". . . He's *human*?"

"He wasn't before?"

198

"No—no, he was . . . he wasn't as . . ." I didn't know how to describe it. That he'd had claws and slitted eyes and sharp teeth, and now he didn't. "I changed him again," I said, realizing it with dread. "Oh, kingsteeth, he's going to kill me."

"You saved him, so I don't think he's going to kill you," Briath patted the bear one last time, muttering, "Good girl," before she gathered up the herbs and bandages that were scattered around the bed.

"You don't know him like I do. He almost lost it when he realized he didn't have a tail. I don't want to imagine how he'll react now."

She gave me a strange look and then shook her head. "My sister told me not to ask strange questions, so I'm just not going to say anything. I'll be back if you need anything." She left, with one last pat on the bear's head.

Vala sank down in the corner of the infirmary room, put her nose under her paw, and started to snore.

The candle beside Fox's cot burned low. His breath was long, eyes closed in a restful sleep, and it was then that I dared to take his hand. It was much larger than mine. At the ends of his fingertips where his claws had been were smooth nails, and his fingertips held calluses not unlike those of the guards who had been leading us about here in Voryn. I rubbed my thumb over Fox's knuckles gently, up to the paper-white scar that circled his wrist.

"Thank you for coming back to save me," I whispered. "It was a bad idea, but I'm glad you did it. I couldn't have faced Wen alone." My fingers wove between his like a braid. I had held hands with boys in town before, but it had never been a particularly memorable experience.

But this felt . . . it felt—

Groggily, Fox's long eyelashes fluttered, and I was falling into eyes that were no longer slitted like a fox's, but round, the irises golden, like an endless expanse of wheat. I sat back, trying to get control of my suddenly racing pulse—and realized I was still holding his hand. I quickly let go.

Kingsteeth, what was wrong with me?

For a long moment he didn't say anything, and then: "Am I dead?"

"No."

He sighed. "Well, that's a relief."

∽ 24 ∾

THE TONGUE AND THE THORN

Fox

DAISY DIDN'T KNOW what to say after I'd awoken. I didn't think I could stand her crying again. I didn't want to start crying, either; it looked like terrible business—one of the many things I did *not* want to experience as a human, but my chest felt tight thinking about it. She quickly let go of my hand the moment we both realized she had it, but my skin still tingled.

As the haziness slowly faded from my brain, memories of the last few days came back in flashes. I curled my hands around the sheets of the bed, trying to hold myself together, but the more I remembered about the corruption, the hunger, the change—

"I'm glad you're awake," Daisy said, oblivious of my

white-knuckled grip. "I was worried you'd be passed out for a while."

"I'm fine," I replied. Was it too short? Was my voice too thin? I remembered the taste of her blood in my mouth, the smell of her fear on her skin, the warm pulse of her heart, quick like a rabbit's—

It revolted me.

My bottom lip trembled. No. I didn't want to unravel—I couldn't. I had to keep myself together in front of Daisy. I didn't want her to worry about anything being wrong with me.

A young girl parted a curtain of what looked like glass in the door and said, "Lady Cerys? I need to treat his wounds. You can come back later, though. You also should take it easy with your bruised ribs. You don't want them to get worse."

She had bruised ribs? It took her a moment to get to her feet, but when she did, I noticed that her lips were pursed into a thin white line, her face purposefully neutral, trying to hide how much her own wounds hurt.

Here she was with bruised ribs and a torn-up hand and she was more concerned about me?

She curtsied a thank-you to the girl and turned to me. When I didn't say anything else, she left the room.

It wasn't until after I was sure she was gone that I exhaled, pressed the palms of my hands against my eyes, and sucked in a ragged breath. The memories came back like a rainstorm, and my chest tightened. I clenched my teeth against a sob, but

I couldn't keep it down. They were so visceral—the pain, the bits of me that I'd lost, moment by moment, as I descended into hunger.

Nothing but hunger.

I shuddered, and my eyes burned, the telltale sign of the one thing I didn't want to do. *Kingsteeth, no. Don't cry, don't cry,* I told myself, sucking in a breath. It turned into a sob. My vision blurred, eyes hot with tears.

I was crying.

I was right. It felt terrible.

I hurt everywhere, and the pain wasn't like some thorn I could pluck out of my paw. It was sharp and throbbing, and I pressed my hands over my mouth to keep myself quiet. A hand touched my shoulder.

It was the girl. The one who had sent Daisy away. She couldn't have been much more than a child. Ten, maybe.

"It's okay," she said softly. "I won't tell her."

I pushed the tears out of my eyes, but they just kept coming. When Daisy had been at that cell, I had wanted to kill her—more, I had wanted to tear her limb from limb. I had wanted to feel the crunch of her bones under my teeth. I had wanted to taste her and savor her—

I hated this feeling. I needed to get out of this body. I needed to get out of this head. I needed to return to my old heart.

That corpse of a man—Seren—had said he could do it. If I got him the crown, he could change me back. With the memories of that hunger quaking in my bones, I considered it. If I gave Seren the crown, then he could turn me back into a fox, and I could be on my way. I could forget about all of this.

But then the woodcurse would go on. And Aloriya would be lost.

And Daisy would be alone.

You should rest came a grunt from the corner of my room. I wiped my eyes and glanced toward the sound. It was the bear. I hadn't even noticed she was in here.

"I'm fine—don't worry about me," I replied.

The bear pulled her nose out from underneath her paw. *You are crying.*

I rubbed at one of my eyes again. "Am not. I just—I just got something in my eye."

You hurt.

"I'm fine," I insisted. "It was just . . . a lot. I don't like it. You're lucky you don't have these emotions. You don't cry. This this wet stuff on my face? Tears! Actual tears! Because I'm—I'm . . ." My lip wobbled.

Because the stupid bear was right. I wasn't okay.

I sucked in a stilted breath. "I just need . . . to stop being human. I need to go back to my old life. I need to stop feeling *this*, whatever this is."

I was done with being a human. With these *adventures*. If I was a fox, then none of this would've happened. I would never have become woodcursed. I wouldn't have that vision in my head. My heart wouldn't burn every time I saw Daisy. I needed to get out of this form.

The bear gave me an unreadable look. *You aren't alone, fox. Burdens are meant to be shared.*

I gritted my teeth and looked away, clawing at the skin over my heart. Why was it burning so badly? "Foxes don't have burdens," I replied roughly. "Not a one."

And they certainly didn't share them with girls who smelled like wildflowers and had blood like honey.

25

FOX TALES

Cerys

THE NEXT FEW days came and went in both a blink and eternity. Briath and some of the other caretakers tried to keep me in bed, but I couldn't just sit around and do nothing while Anwen prowled the wood as a bone-eater. I refused to believe that there weren't answers to the curse in this city. Someone had to know *something*, or perhaps there was a book on the history of the wood or a tapestry detailing King Sunder's meeting with the Lady of the Wood, or—or . . . I didn't know. There was something the Grandmaster wasn't telling me about the crown and the Lady. I could feel it.

I had reveled in the Somersal parades for seventeen years, enjoying golden fields and peace and safety, without ever knowing—without *caring* about—what was happening in this city. I never questioned the legends. And the more I saw of Voryn, the more of a fool I felt.

The few times I came to see Fox, he was either sleeping or pretending to be asleep; either way, I could tell he didn't want to see me. So I wandered the halls, the pain in my ribs growing lesser by the day. I didn't know what kind of herbal concoction the Voryns made me drink, but whatever it was seemed to heal me a lot faster than any medicines in Aloriya. It was strange how much alike Voryn and Aloriya were—we believed in the same old gods, the same ancients, the same bone-eaters and curses, and yet—how strikingly different. They didn't seem to have a bloodline hierarchy. They bartered instead of exchanging coin. Women were everywhere—brandishing their swords in the barracks and debating policies in the streets. There were bakers' daughters, sure, and gardeners' daughters, and blacksmiths' daughters, but here they weren't defined by that.

What was that like? I wondered.

How did they know what they *could* be if no one told them what they couldn't?

Wandering through the fortress—there was very little else to call it, since it reminded me of the garrisons in some of Anwen's tactical books—gave me some reprieve from the anxiety that kept building and building, and sometimes I felt like I would explode if I stood still. The walls of the city were so high, and the wood beyond it was dark and vast and held everything I'd ever loved in its cursed roots.

The more I thought about it, the more I began to hate myself for surviving. For thinking I could save *anyone*. For—

"Stop it," I muttered to myself, following a stairwell down into another dark level of the fortress. I was exploring again, trying to stay a step ahead of my thoughts. But they kept catching up to me.

I reached the bottom of the stairs and found myself in a smoky and sweet-smelling kitchen. The staff must've been on their break, or serving the Grandmaster and other Voryn lawmakers in her meeting room, so I helped myself to a few plates that were still left out from dinner and placed them on a tray.

He was always a glutton as a fox. Even though he hadn't eaten in the wood, I thought I could at least try to get *something* into his stomach.

I was so focused on trying not to drop anything as I ascended the first flight of stairs to the infirmary that I didn't notice the person standing in my way until I almost ran into him. The man sidestepped and put his foot out. I tripped over it, barely saving myself and the food.

"Thieving trash," he sneered, and disappeared down the steps.

Thieving . . . ?

Was that what I was to the people of Voryn? They saw me as an outsider—an Aloriyan who'd lived in safety her entire life while these people here warred with the wood. But my own people would call me a traitor, too, wouldn't they? I had abandoned my queen. I had run—I couldn't have done anything to save her, or anyone else, but I ran all the same.

I had decided to find Voryn, because I thought that Voryn could fix our problems—but perhaps that was wishful thinking. Perhaps I just tricked myself into running away. Into coming here. Instead of facing the horrors of the coronation and the nightmare that followed.

I didn't want to think that was the case, but it was a thought I had been having since my meeting with the Grandmaster. The curse had been part of the trees for centuries, and I was just a gardener's daughter. Whatever power my blood held, even if I bled myself dry, I wouldn't be able to save the whole forest, all the people of Aloriya who had turned the night of the coronation. I was only one girl.

And now I had well and truly failed.

I tilted my head back and blinked the tears out of my eyes. *Crying won't do any good, Cerys*, I reminded myself. I waited until I had collected myself and moved the rest of the way down the winding stone corridors toward the room Fox had been in since being moved out of the infirmary. The room was connected to the bathroom I had bathed in earlier, but I hadn't gotten a chance to really look at the room itself. It was small, with lit candles flickering in sconces on the walls, giving off a soft orange glow. Through the balcony door, I saw the sun slowly ease beneath the tree-lined horizon like a sinking ship.

Fox was sitting on the bed, his back to me, watching the

sunset with the stillness of stones. He was awake. I was so relieved I wanted to cry. His orange hair caught the color of the sky, shimmering like fire. I tried to creep quietly inside, but the plates on the tray clinked together.

"You're terrible at sneaking," he said dryly, not even turning around.

I winced. "I'm not that bad."

"Who told you that lie?"

Sighing, I set the tray on the edge of his bed. "I brought you some food."

"I'm not hungry," he said dismissively, only a moment before his stomach grumbled.

"Well, I *am* hungry," I replied, and pulled a chair from the desk up to the bedside. I lifted the cover off the nearest plate. The smell made my mouth water. "Let's see, this looks like some sort of meat—"

"Duck."

"*Duck,*" I repeated, "in some sort of sweet sauce, and roasted carrots and potatoes . . . Hey, didn't you steal a roast duck from the baker's windowsill once?"

He glanced rudely at me, the first time he'd looked at me since I'd entered. He was bare chested except for the bandage around his wound. He was trying really hard to make me feel like I was unwanted, I'd give him that, but it wasn't like I hadn't given him the same look a hundred times when he was a fox.

It was strange, but I think I missed him.

"C'mon, here's a fork. You need to eat," I said, offering him the utensil.

Finally, begrudgingly, he took the fork.

I ate a bit of duck and tried the roasted carrots. "It's good to see you awake. Are you feeling better?"

"Yeah. Briath said you came to visit me a few times while I was asleep."

"I didn't want to wake you, so I left." *And when you weren't asleep, I know you pretended to be*, I thought, spearing another carrot. His hands looked strange without claws, and he kept running his tongue over his teeth, as if he expected to find sharp canines, but they weren't there anymore.

"I'm sorry," I found myself saying.

He poked at the duck with the prongs of his fork. "For what?"

"For not being able to protect myself in the wood. If I'd just fought back against Wen, you probably wouldn't have gotten cursed. I just . . . froze." I bowed my head. "I'm sorry, Fox."

I waited for him to agree that it was my fault, that I was weak and stupid, that all the trouble he'd been in was because of me, but . . . those words never came. Instead, he sighed and put his hand on my head, like my father used to when I was younger, a soft touch of affection. He said softly, "I would do it again to save you, Daisy."

I pursed my lips tightly, trying not to cry. Again.

I ate the rest of the plate in silence.

Later that night, I came back Fox's room to find him leaning against the window. He was looking out to something in the city. The sun had already set, bringing with it blue-and-black skies. He didn't notice I was there until I almost tripped over my own feet, and then he turned around and smiled at me.

"Fancy seeing you again," he greeted me. He was dressed in a simple dark shirt and trousers that were a little too big for him. His hair was tied back into a ponytail with a ribbon— one that I'd seen Briath wearing around earlier.

Oh, I'm glad he's made a friend, I thought as I set down a tray full of food from the kitchens again—some sort of vegetable concoction that looked much less appetizing than the duck we'd eaten earlier.

Fox was clearly *not* interested. He made a face as soon as he bit into a leek. "Oh, that's *gross*."

"Not a fan?"

He eyed the food as if it were about to turn on him. "Nothing tastes like I remember it."

I poked at what looked like a carrot, but I couldn't be sure. "Does it taste that bad?"

"Most things, no. This? Yes."

"Huh. I just thought you'd lost your appetite when you turned human."

"Lost my appetite?" He leaned forward. "Daisy, I *love*

food—there's hardly a thing I love more. If I could *marry* a meat pie, I would—why are you laughing?"

"I'm just trying to picture the sort of meat pie who would marry someone like you."

"I'd make a nice meat pie quite happy, thank you," he replied haughtily, taking a knife from the tray, and cut off a slice of eggplant. He held the utensils like Wen did, I noticed, his forefingers along the backs of the fork and knife. The proper way had been drilled into her by her etiquette instructor. The same woman who scolded her every time she muddied the hem of her dress.

He took two bites before he noticed me staring. "Is there something wrong?"

"Oh no. Just . . . I have a lot on my mind."

He moved the food around on the plate, like I did with green peas I didn't want to eat, to try to trick Papa into thinking I did. "I guess you've asked the leader here in Voryn for help already."

"I did—the day you awoke."

"I'm sorry I didn't ask earlier."

"It wouldn't have made a difference," I replied with a sigh, and told him what had happened at the meeting while we pushed this horrible vegetable concoction around on our plates. I ended up pouring myself a cup of tea and calling that my dinner for the night.

"Well," he said, sniffing at what looked like a tree of

broccoli, "it seems like things got a whole lot more complicated, Daisy."

I scoffed. "You *think*? I don't know what to do now. I don't know where to go." I frowned into my tea. "I thought this would be it, but Voryn is no more able to deal with the curse of the wood than we are. I just don't understand it, Fox. In all the stories we have of Voryn, they live free of the curse. The Lady protects them against it. But where's the Lady? The Grandmaster isn't telling us something. I can feel it—about the woodcurse."

"Technically, *you* can cure it," he pointed out.

"Sure, if I had enough blood for every person in Aloriya," I said, and then fell silent.

"There has to be another way."

"And if there's not?"

"There is," he replied, so surely that I almost believed him. "Didn't you say that Grandmaster or whatever told you that she'd act if we got proof that the woodcurse had grown stronger? I don't know what kind of help she'd give us, but it's gotta be better than us going back to the wood alone."

"And how are we going to get that before they kick us out of the city now that we're almost healed? We don't have the crown, we don't have any way out of the city—"

"Well, it's a good thing I have an idea, then," Fox said.

I was a little afraid to ask, but I did anyway. "What . . . sort of idea?"

He grinned, all white teeth and trouble. "How opposed are you to stealing?"

Oh. Oh *no*.

"Fox, I don't know what you have in mind, but I'm sure the guards will be all over us if we go anywhere. We're Aloriyans in Voryn, and as far as I can tell, all the stories I've heard are wrong. Honestly, I wouldn't trust me either if I came here with magical blood and a crown—"

"That's why we need to throw them off our scent," he replied, wiggling his eyebrows, and pushed himself off the bed.

I put the covers back on the plates and set the tray on the floor. "What do you mean?"

"There are lights down in the city. It looks like a market. I'd say we should start by going and finding some *actual* food."

"What, you didn't have your fill of the vegetable surprise?"

"Daisy, it tastes like old shoes."

"I've seen you chew on an old shoe, so I believe you."

He rolled his eyes and outstretched his arm for me to take.

"Well, Daisy? Are you gonna come with me, or do I have to do this all by myself?"

Then he grinned. And oh, what a dangerous look that was, trouble tucked into the corners of his mouth like sin. I hesitated, because I wasn't sure what taking his arm would mean. We were supposed to stay in the building, and stay out of trouble, and leave the city.

I bit the inside of my cheek. *No, Cerys. This is a terrible idea, Cerys.*

I took his arm and said, "No stealing."

And then his grin turned into a smile—and as strange as it was, it felt like, for the first time, I'd been found in my safe little garden, and asked to come outside.

❧ 26 ❧

FOR WHAT TASTES SWEETER

Fox

VORYN WAS . . . HOW to describe it—*immense*. The entire city had been carved out of the side of the mountain. It was old but beautiful, made of ancient stones, smoothed to the touch by centuries of wind and weather, hundreds of secret alleyways and hidden doors scattered across like a game of hide-and-seek. The city was composed of layers built atop one another—like dusty cakes in a bakery fallen into disrepair. Atop the city stood the fortress, where the Grandmaster lived, and as the city cascaded down to the lowest layer, more and more people filled the streets.

About halfway down the city was what I was looking for—the night market. I rubbed my hands together as soon as I heard two passing women talking about some sort of celebration planned for this evening. Where there was celebration, there was food, and where there was food, there was my happy place. And a celebration also meant lots of people, and a crowd to get lost in. Which was exactly what we needed, as two Voryn guards had trailed us since we'd left the fortress. They kept enough of a distance, however, that I was pretty sure Daisy hadn't noticed.

At least, not until she said, "I told you we'd be guarded."

"Just act like you don't know they're there," I murmured in reply. We squeezed through a particularly dense group of people and came out on the other side in some sort of crumbling balcony courtyard, overlooking the fifty-foot wall beneath and the wood beyond.

I turned my face to the clear night sky stretching overhead and basked in the openness of it all. The wind smelled fresh and sharp, brisk in the way the first breath of winter was. Behind us, orange lanterns illuminated most of the city, the shadows on the stone a dark blue.

"It's so beautiful," Daisy said softly.

"It looks to me like a pretty cage."

She glanced at me and then back at the city. "I suppose it does."

"But maybe, if we can find a way to break this curse, we'll free the Voryns, too, along with your friend and your father and everyone else in your village."

Her shoulders stiffened, and she turned away from the

city, and leaned against the banister, gripping it tightly. "I hope so. So what's this plan of yours?"

I took another glance at the guards, who were still standing at the stairwell we'd come out of onto the street. Then I leaned in casually, like we were sharing a secret joke. "Your corpse friend—"

"Seren?" she asked in surprise.

"That's the one. He offered me a deal in the wood when you and I were split up."

"What kind of deal?"

"He said that if I gave him the crown, he'd turn me back into a fox." As I said it, I watched her, waiting to see what her face did, if she thought I was tempted. If she was disappointed in me.

But all she said was "You would probably have better luck with him, in all honesty."

I couldn't help it; I smiled. "Yeah, you're right. Too bad I like being the underdog. Besides, you're cuter than he is."

Finally, there was some emotion on her face: horror. "You turned down giving him the most powerful object in the kingdom because he wasn't *cute* enough?"

I gave a shrug. "His whole . . . *dead* . . . thing really wasn't doing it for me."

She shoved me on the shoulder. "Fox! You're prime evil, you know that?"

"I can't be *that* evil." I laughed. "I chose you, didn't I?"

She gave a heavy sigh and turned away, but before she did I could've sworn I saw a pink tinge flood her cheeks. I grinned. "I guess you did. So, Seren wants the crown. That isn't new information."

"No, but before I came running after you in the wood, he seemed pretty sure I would give it to him—like he knew something about me that I didn't. Like he knew *me*. But I've never seen him before in my life, Daisy."

"*Oh*"—she began to catch on, and her hazel eyes brightened—"so if we bring the crown to him, like we mean to give it to him—"

"We can capture him, bring him back to the old hag, and present our proof that the woodcurse is worse than she knows."

"And capturing him may give us some answers, too, as to what happened in the wood, how the curse grew powerful, why it attacked now," Daisy added, nodding. "This is, of course, a *terrible* idea—"

"It's not *that* bad."

"—but I think it's the best we have."

I spread my arms wide. "Thank you! Finally! Some confidence!"

She rolled her eyes. "You'll never change. What do you want me to do? Say *good job* and scratch you behind the ears?"

"I do love those scratches," I teased, and glanced back to the guards again. "But I think that might have to wait. If we're going to nab that crown from the Grandmaster, we're going to need to shake them first."

"And how do you suppose we do that?"

I offered my hand to her. "We have some fun."

"Fox," she replied exasperatedly. "I feel like I could burst into tears at any moment."

"I'd be worried if you didn't say that. Don't worry, we just have to be convince them that we're planning on being here awhile." I glanced at the guards again. They thought they were so inconspicuous, leaning against the wall in the shadows. They clearly didn't think either of us a threat. That gave us our best chance.

"Okay." She put her hand in mine, and I held on to it tightly as I pulled her away from the balcony and into the night market down the street.

There were vendors hawking modest but lovely items: intricate glass jewelry, roll upon roll of cloth that seemed to shimmer in the torchlight, and flowers that had such unique smells I was sure they were Wildwood grown. None of them, however, were more enticing than the smells coming from the food stalls. Worn lanterns draped from building to building, crisscrossing down the market like lacing on a bodice as music drifted from the square, bright and loud, chorused with the telltale song and dance of . . .

"It's a wedding." Daisy marveled.

I licked my lips. "Oh, I do love the food at weddings."

She gave me a deadpan look. "I don't know that you even need Seren—seems to me like you're turning back into your old self already."

"Well, if there's anything that could bring it out of me, it's this!" I stretched my hands out toward the night market and the celebration beyond, people dressed up like delectable pastries. "All the food I could want, and not a single angry townsperson in sight trying to drive me off. It's practically *begging* me to plunder it."

"Just as long as we don't attract too much attention," she warned.

I waved my hand. "You're talking to a professional," I said, and quickly stepped up to the nearest food stall, taking a skewer of sweet-smelling meat.

Daisy grabbed my arm. "You can't just take that," she hissed.

I blinked at her. "She didn't ask for anything in return."

"It can't be free."

"Of course it is," said the woman, a strange look on her face. "Wait, are you the Aloiryan we've heard rumors of—"

"What's down there?" I interrupted, steering Daisy toward another stall. The last thing we needed was to be recognized; we'd never lose the guards if everyone we passed knew we were outsiders. Besides, here there were fish cakes and meat skewers and crepes and— "Is that *fried*? Excuse me, two of those."

Daisy followed me with a hapless sort of resignation as

I dodged through the crowd, going straight for another food stall, and then another. I was having the time of my life. But at every stall I would glance behind us, and the guards were always there. Finally, after following us to our sixth stall, they must have been content that we were here for a while, as one of them went to get them mugs of beer, and then they went over to the stall with the meat skewers.

Daisy looked wistfully at the celebration. She missed her village, her father, Anwen—I could tell. The long sigh, the drooped shoulders, the way she twined the end of her braid around her fingers. Watching her even made *me* miss Anwen, too, though I shook off the feeling immediately.

It was so strange. I'd lived so much of my life alone, being chased out of gardens and trash cans, and yet here I was . . .

"We've almost got them fooled," I noted, offering Daisy a paper bag full of sweet, round cakes.

She eyed them cautiously. "What's wrong with them?"

"Do you really think I'd eat something that wasn't delicious?" When she hesitated, I added, "Yeah, I know, trash. Look, just try it."

She picked up a small potato cake and cautiously ate it. Her eyes brightened. "Oh, that *is* delicious!" Then she smiled at me—and her smile was bright and genuine, and I felt like I was falling even as I stood still.

She ate another one, and then gasped. "Ooh! You know what would be great with this? Warm wine—let me get some."

She hurried over to another stall, and just as she came back with two cups of mulled wine, the dance quieted. We looked toward the center of the market, where a procession had been set up in front of a bonfire. A woman with gray hair pulled back into a bun, wearing a stark white ceremonial robe, stood between two other women dressed to be wed.

Daisy bristled. "That's the Grandmaster," she whispered to me as the ceremony commenced. "Great, now how're we supposed to disappear?"

"Patience," I replied, taking a cup of wine from her. "If she's here performing the wedding rite, she can't be in the fortress, too, can she?"

She sipped her wine. "No, now that you mention it. But we still have to deal with the guards first."

"Patience," I singsonged, and we stood quietly as the wedding ceremony went on.

". . . Even as we are surrounded by darkness, love surrounds us with light," the Grandmaster said, and tied the ribbon around the couple's clasped hands. "Let the other guide your way, let them be your light, for even apart you will be together, your roots always intertwined."

Then the two women leaned in and kissed each other. The crowd around them cheered, throwing flower petals into the air. The wind swirled them high into the night sky and out into the Wilds beyond the wall. The Grandmaster went to sit in an old wooden chair, and the moment she did, the celebration commenced with cries of delight. A small band of musicians started up the songs again, and the couple took their first dance. The way they looked at each other made me feel like I was watching something intensely personal that I wasn't supposed to see—we hadn't been invited to this ceremony, after all.

"The wine merchant told me this wedding almost didn't happen," Daisy began, as dancing partners grabbed each other and swung into the circular clearing in the middle of the night market.

The wine was already making me hot, and I pulled at the collar of my shirt to loosen it. "Mmh, why's that?"

"Because there was a rumor that a man came into the city woodcursed."

"Ah. So, me."

"So, you," she agreed, and took one of the skewers from my hands. I squawked in protest, but she didn't care.

"Remind me never to bring up the fact that I almost became a bone-eater around anyone tonight," I muttered.

"Oh, you don't think it'd be a great conversation starter?"

"Yeah, in ten years, maybe."

She laughed. "Bold of you to assume you'll be invited to parties in ten years."

"I probably won't be. Foxes aren't really invited to anything."

To that she smiled warmly. "I'd invite you . . . as my hat."

I went to point out that in ten years, hat or not, I would probably be dead, but the words fell from my mouth because

I . . . I *wanted* to be invited by her to a party. I wanted to watch her arrange flowers in her father's flower shop, and I wanted to sunbathe on the windowsill while she hummed and made beautiful bouquets of lilies and goldenrod, and I wanted to sit beside her on the ride up to the castle, and I wanted to look out of the tallest spire with her and imagine following the river all the way down to Somersal-by-the-Sea, and I wanted to eat more food with her, and laugh with her, and—

And—

What was *wrong* with me?

It was the wine. I wasn't thinking straight.

I shoved an entire skewer into my mouth and moved on through the night market, toward the wedding celebration, telling myself that what I wanted was idiotic. What I wanted didn't matter.

And that I really didn't want it at all.

Because there were no stories of foxes and gardeners with happy endings.

❧ 27 ❧

THE LADY OF THE WILDS

Cerys

THE WINE WARMED me, inside and out.

As we wandered around the bonfire and through the wedding celebration, we kept to the edges of the dance floor. One of the vendors called to Fox, "Would your pretty partner like a bite?" He offered some sort of sugar-sprinkled fried pastry. "It's a lover's knot!"

Baffled, a blush ate up the sides of my face, and I tugged at the hem of my shirt in embarrassment.

"Aw, look," teased Fox, "you made her blush!"

I wanted to *kill* him. Which only made him grin wider. "I think we'll pass on the knot," he told the merchant, and we kept moving through the crowd. He lifted his nose and sniffed the air. "Ooh, is that . . . Daisy, it's a *meat pie*!"

"Oh, good, you can try proposing," I said, and he smiled at our earlier joke. "I can't eat another bite. Go on without me."

"Don't mind if I do," he replied, handing me his warm wine and shoving the rest of a sweet pancake into his mouth as he made a beeline for the meat pie food stall. I'd never seen anyone so gluttonous in my entire life. There were boys in the guard who could put down some food, but none of them could best Fox. He was an endless chasm of hunger.

As he went to pester the stall owner, I spied a small temple-like entrance carved into the side of the mountain. Flowers adorned the exterior, and large braziers lit the entrance. Fox would be busy for a while, so I slipped inside the cave.

It must have been a shrine to the Lady of the Wilds. There was a large statue of her inside—I recognized her features from storybooks I'd read as a child. I nodded to one of the citizens leaving as I went in and found myself alone staring up at the beautiful woman. Long chains of flowers stretched throughout the temple—across the walls, over her arms, and down across the floor. Her stone hair was untamed, made of vines and moss and wildflowers, and she stood naked on the pedestal, but where I was usually embarrassed by such things, I was simply awed. The way the statue carried herself, the way she looked out to the entrance, welcoming everyone inside . . .

The smell of flowers was sweet, and my heart ached because it reminded me of the flower shop, and Papa, and how far away I was from home, and how, at the moment, my home really did not exist anymore.

Everyone I loved was a monster.

I don't know how long I stood there, but it must've been long enough for Fox to come and find me. "I wondered where you wandered off to," he said quietly, but still his voice echoed in the cavernous shrine. He came up beside me, and I handed him back his warm wine as he looked up at the stone statue of the Lady of the Wilds.

I wondered where she'd gone, if she wasn't here in Voryn. I wondered why she'd left all these people defenseless. Was the Lady of the Wilds responsible for the curse? Had she lied to her own people?

And that made me think of the things we believed in Aloriya. The things that had since proven false. Did King Sunder know they weren't true when he returned from the wood with the crown all those centuries ago? Was Aloriya built on a lie, too?

The music from the bonfire drifted into the small shrine, and the candles danced to the melody. A gentle breeze swept into the shrine and played through Fox's long hair. Some parts of his skin were still a little red and blotchy from the wood-curse. He looked . . . tired.

I was tired, too.

"What was it like?" I asked.

229

"Oh, the meat pie was *excellent*—"

"No." I laughed a little, and then said more quietly, "The woodcurse."

He stilled. He didn't say anything.

I took a deep breath. "When I was nine, I got lost in the wood, and my mother came to save us. She . . . disappeared. With the prince and his guard. But a few days later, she came back. Or at least a part of her did. The wood had taken her. She tried to kill me. So I guess I just wanted to know . . ."

"If she knew it was you?" he guessed.

I swallowed the lump in my throat and nodded.

He took a deep breath, as if steeling himself, and then said, "I was hungry. Not like I am now."

"Like you pretty much always are."

He nodded. "Not like that. I was *voracious*. It was the kind of hunger that burrowed down to my bones. It was all I could think about. I don't even remember feeling it start. The hunger just *was*. So, to answer your question . . . she might've known it was you, Daisy, but she didn't care anymore."

That was the answer I was afraid of. "And you? Did you care?"

He didn't say anything for a long moment, and then—

"No. I doubt Wen would, either. Seren, though, he was different. He seemed to have control over himself, even if he is controlled by the wood like the rest of the bone-eaters. And that's why . . ."

"What?"

"I think you did something to him, Daisy. Or your blood did. When he found me in the wood, he was . . ." He breathed out through his nose in frustration. "I don't know how to explain it."

"Maybe it was a trick. Seren was good at those when he was alive. He was good then, though. The best squire on the Sundermount, and he knew it, too. Kingsteeth, he was so full of himself, and he always complained about having to babysit us, but . . . we knew he liked hanging out with us brats."

"Because he got reassigned, but he asked to stay where he was."

I cast Fox a surprised look. "Yeah—that was a good guess."

"He seemed like the type," he replied smoothly, and nudged his head toward the exit of the shrine. "C'mon, let's go see if we've lost our guards yet." We started out as another woman came in to honor the Lady. She braided a flower into the chains that looped over the stone woman's arm. The braid was familiar—it wasn't a style anyone in Aloriya knew, but my mother had taught it to me. I touched the braid in my own hair.

As we made our way toward the bonfire, even more people arrived to join the wedding celebration. The two brides swirled in the middle of the dance, their gowns fluttering behind them in trails of blue and gold silks. Most people lingered on the outskirts of the dance, clapping along to music that reminded me of the ballads played in my village's tavern in the evenings, when everyone had had just a little too much beer. It reverberated against the stone buildings, and laughter sang across the expanse like shooting stars.

In the middle of the courtyard stood the gigantic bonfire, decorated with beautiful golden chains and feathers laced into ribbons slowly catching fire as the flames climbed higher. The brides spun each other around the fire, joining with the rest of their wedding party.

And the guards were still there.

Annoyed, I returned my attention to the dance—when an idea struck me. "Fox, dance with me."

He snorted. "Foxes don't dance."

"Fine." I stopped a man with cool, tawny skin and a neatly trimmed beard, in a waistcoat the color of saffron seeds, and asked, "Would you want to dance?"

The man gave a grand smile. "It would be an honor."

I handed Fox my half-empty cup. He squawked in protest, but the man was already leading me onto the dance floor, and all he could do was watch. The steps were familiar—I moved slowly at first, my feet unsure, but I had been the witness to too many garden waltzes to not catch on quickly. The charming man guided me around the dance floor, and I stumbled after him, but I was laughing nonetheless, and he was gracious enough to correct me when I misstepped. I tried to keep up, staring down at our feet.

Three steps to the left, one back, one over, turn—

On the next spin, the man grabbed my hand again. But his hand felt different, softer, not as callused—

I glanced up, and Fox smirked at me. "Your partner had to move on," he said almost apologetically. Over his shoulder, I saw that the man was dancing with another partner now. I suspected that he hadn't changed partners because he'd wanted to.

I laughed. "Were you *jealous*?"

He inclined his head. "Of course not. I'd suspect that anyone here would love to dance with me. I am, if you haven't noticed, quite gorgeous. And I've just discovered: a fantastic dancer, too."

I rolled my eyes. "*Ugh.*"

He positioned one of my hands on his shoulder as his sank to my waist, our other hands clasped tightly together, and gave me a smile so radiant, it took my breath away. I had never seen him smile like that before, wide and genuine, and my heart pounded against my rib cage.

"So what's your idea, Daisy?" he asked.

I tried to reel in my treacherous heart. "Bring everyone onto the dance floor. Get them all moving. Lose the guards in the packed group of bodies."

His eyes sparkled. "Create some chaos. I like it."

Oh dear. I wasn't sure which thought was worse—that he relished chaos, or that I was becoming more like him. Or, stranger yet, maybe that I was always the kind of girl who didn't belong trapped inside garden walls.

We spun away from each other, each of us grabbing a new partner in the onlooking crowd. I went for a young child—maybe twelve—and he picked an old woman with a toothless smile. We danced around the bonfire, twirling away from our partners, gathering more people into the mix, and then they went to fetch their own partners, and then they found new partners after that, until the dance floor spun like a colorful hurricane.

And then—I dared to take hold of the hand of one of the guards. She was tall, her hair cut short, a scar on her lip. She wasn't willing at first, but then she joined in the madness. Her partner quickly followed, and soon they were both swept up.

Everyone was dancing now, and that's when I felt someone snag my hand and whirl me around. Fox grinned as he caught my other hand and placed it on his shoulder, his on my waist.

"Well, this is *chaos*," he said.

I glanced around at all the people laughing and dancing—something that we'd started, but within which we were now anonymous. Which was exactly what I'd hoped. "Good. We should leave before the guards wonder where we are."

"Must we?" Fox asked.

Time was of the essence, but he held on to me so tightly, and I couldn't remember the last time I'd felt . . . seen. Like this.

"Okay," I relented. "One more dance."

We followed the flow of the dancers around the bonfire

again. The waltzes at the castle in Aloriya were not like this. Those were stuffy and regal, and the dignitaries rarely looked to the edge of the garden, where I stood. But here I was dancing with a boy who was handsome in a way only wild things could be, as if he wanted to be bigger than his skin instead of wanting to fit inside it.

As the song ended, we held each other close. I wanted to let go—really, I did—but I couldn't bring myself to. I didn't want the moment to end, because at that moment, I didn't feel like a girl who lived inside a walled garden.

There were no walls here.

And that frightened me, because this was fleeting. This was not permanent. Like a match flaring in the dark, this was only a flash, here and soon gone. I wanted to hang on to it. This feeling. He was a fox, and I was a gardener's daughter, and there were no stories for enchantments such as us.

He leaned into me, pulling me gently against him, and I let him, my fingers falling into the curls of hair behind his ears. He was going to kiss me. I'd never been kissed before. I closed my eyes and waited for his lips to find mine.

28

THE FOREST OF THE FORGOTTEN

Fox

"WE . . . SHOULD PROBABLY get going," I said, pulling away from Daisy. Her eyes flew open. At first she looked confused; then something flickered in her eyes, and she looked away.

I had . . . almost *kissed* her.

She blinked rapidly and glanced around for the guards. They were caught up in the next song. "Right," she agreed, but her voice was distant.

I'm sorry, I wanted to say, though I wasn't sure what I was sorry for. That I hadn't kissed her? She had to know that we couldn't. That it would change everything. She was who she was, and I was . . . someone who would not last. I was a fox. Not a person.

The orchestra struck up another song, and the people

around me jumped into motion again, but it was as if I didn't remember the steps anymore. It was too loud, and the bonfire too bright. My skin tingled as if little tiny ants raced up my body—my bones jittery. I knew the feeling—it was like I was being hunted. My heart thundered in my ears.

Making sure that the guards were still occupied and that the Grandmaster remained in her wooden chair chatting with one of the brides, Daisy and I sneaked out of the night market and made our way back up the city silently. We didn't share words, and I really wasn't sure what we could say to each other now, anyway.

Daisy said she was sure the crown was still in the Grandmaster's study. There would probably be some guards to take care of once we got to the castle, but I figured I could deal with them.

We underestimated how difficult it would be to climb back up the stairway we had come down earlier, though, and by the top I was practically crawling. I wanted to sink down into a puddle and not move for days. Daisy leaned against a wall, trying to catch her breath. At the top, there was a small courtyard that led to the front doors of the fortress, where we'd left from, and Daisy said she knew how to get in.

There were no guards at the front. I hoped that meant we'd just gotten lucky. Daisy must have felt the same, and we slipped through the front door and into the foyer. The layout of the fortress was rather straightforward—with a grand entry hall and stairs leading up to the Grandmaster's offices. There were halls that branched out to the east and west, one way the kitchen, the other our own rooms. The great hall was dark, though, the candles burning low in their sconces.

Daisy and I were sneaking up the main staircase when we heard footsteps. We quickly ducked behind a pillar as a guard stepped out of the Grandmaster's office, face shadowed, as he tucked something into his uniform and quickly pressed on down the stairs.

That was much too close for comfort. We slipped through the curtain and into the room after him.

The Grandmaster's office was a simple large stone room with an intricate wooden desk in the middle that was covered with stacks of paper. There were bookshelves that lined the back wall and a door near the rear that led into her own private quarters. The moonlight was let in through a raven-shaped skylight above us, illuminating the desk itself. As Daisy hurried over to search it, I made sure the door was closed, and I kept an ear out for footsteps. The guard who had come out must've been part of a patrol. Another had to be coming by at some point soon.

Daisy riffled through the drawers. "It must be here some-where," she muttered, digging through the papers and objects in the drawers.

A dark shape caught my eye on the ground by my foot, and I picked it up. A lavender flower. I hadn't seen any of those in the city since I'd been here. It reminded me of a kind that, to my knowledge, only grew on the sides of the Sundermount.

Daisy closed the last drawer and cursed. "It's not here, Fox."

I tucked the flower into my trouser pocket and nudged my head toward the rear doors. "Let's look back there, then."

"She can't have it *on* her, can she?"

"No. She wouldn't be able to carry it for that long without putting it on," I replied.

"How do you know?"

I . . . didn't know, honestly. "It stands to reason," I said. "You felt the temptation before you learned better. And most creatures can hear its call."

"Wait—does that mean you can hear it?"

I cocked my head and listened in the quiet, but since being woodcursed and Daisy curing me, I hadn't been quite my fox self. I couldn't see the magnetic fields north anymore, either. I was sad, but not surprised, to find that I couldn't hear the crown. I shook my head, to her dismay. "I'm sorry."

"It must be here," she said, moving on so that I wouldn't feel embarrassed.

We moved toward the back of the office, where the door was left slightly ajar. Inside was the Grandmaster's private study. I peeked my head in first.

"I feel like this is trespassing," Daisy murmured.

"*Now* you're worried?"

"I just—we aren't supposed to be here."

"I say she gave up her right to privacy when she took the crown from you," I replied, irritated, and slipped inside. She followed me, wringing her hands together as if this was the first time she'd ever sneaked around—which I knew was a lie. She and Wen sneaked around all the time behind the seneschal's back. She should be a professional by now.

In the middle of the room was a war table that showed the different areas of the wood, and what looked like the fog surrounding the city. While the Voryns were trapped here, it seemed that they did have guards whose job it was to patrol the wood to guard against any bone-eaters who might find their way through the fog to Voryn. It also showed where Aloriya and the Sundermount were. The distance didn't seem that great when viewed on a map like this, though it had taken us four days to travel here. The walls were lined with a bunch of dusty old books I had absolutely no interest in, but something on the wall caught Daisy's eye.

She caught me by the back of my shirt. "Fox."

I glanced over my shoulder at her. Daisy let go of my shirt and grabbed ahold of the curtain. I thought it blocked a rather large window, but when she pulled it back, her eyes grew wide with surprise.

29

THE LIES OF MOUNT SUNDER

Cerys

IT WAS A painting, stretching from one side of the study to the other. The canvas was old and sagging, and the paint had faded, but I could see the story it told, nonetheless. There was one hanging in the throne room of the castle of Aloriya, too, telling of King Sunder's noble quest to save his people, and his triumphant return with the crown.

This painting, however, told a different story.

The Wildwood was on fire, the city of Voryn was burning, and there was a figure standing in the flames, untouched by them. Was it King Sunder? He commanded flames, like Anwen and the late prince could, like everyone else in his bloodline. And on the other side, past the razed forest, burned and blackened, animals fleeing from the destruction, was a woman.

241

She was brilliant and golden—not like fire, but bright like the sun—and standing with her were all the old gods of the Wildwood. A brilliant stag with branching antlers, a snake as large as an old oak tree, a giant white wolf, a broad hawk bigger than any horse I'd ever seen, and more. So many different creatures, grander than the normal animals that resembled them.

The old gods.

My fingers came to rest on a gray bear in the menagerie.

"Vala," Fox whispered.

I ran my fingers across her image. She'd stood with the Lady of the Wilds. She must have survived while the rest of them had been corrupted by the woodcurse. She had led us through the wood. She had shown us where Voryn was.

Then Fox asked, "Where's the crown?" He scanned the portrait. "As the story goes, the Lady gave King Sunder her crown, right? Shouldn't it be shown here?"

He was right. The crown was nowhere to be seen in this depiction of the story.

There was a sound to our left—a wet cough.

I quickly moved around to the other side of the war table and froze. The oversized piece of furniture had been hiding a guard. He was unclothed and nearly dead; he bled across the ornate rug, a gaping hole in his stomach.

From the wound spread the dark roots of the woodcurse.

I dropped to my knees beside him and began to unwind

my bandage. "Hold on," I told him. "You'll be okay."

"Daisy."

"I just need to undo my bandage, Fox. Can you get an envelope cutter? Or something sharp? Maybe—"

"*Daisy.*" Fox put a hand on my shoulder and gripped it tightly.

I paused for a moment, then watched as the guard took one last stunted breath—and stopped. His eyes were still open, his mouth caught between one breath and the next, but he was gone. I pushed myself away.

I had never seen anyone die before.

Fox squatted down beside me and picked up a flower that lay beside the body. A lavender. He twirled it around between his fingers before he handed it to me. "There was another one inside the office door."

My fingers were shaking as I picked the flower from him. A lavender . . . but to my knowledge, they were only found around the Sundermount. "You've spent more time in the wood than I have," I said to him. "Do they even grow around here?"

"I doubt it" was his reply.

I cursed under my breath. It couldn't be a bone-eater—we would have seen it. But . . . we had seen a guard leaving this office. And the only creature I knew of who could masquerade as a human was— "Seren."

ᴄ 30 ᴅ

THE FOOL AND THE FALL

Fox

"YOU TAKE THE east wing, I'll take the west!" I told Daisy as we raced out of the Grandmaster's office and down the stairs, looking for any sign of where Seren had gone. She nodded and quickly disappeared down the east wing hallway. I didn't have time to worry whether she'd be safe or not. I didn't have time to worry whether *I* would.

If only I'd killed that bastard back in the wood when I had the chance. I should have. Why hadn't I? That was a question I still didn't know the answer to. There were more questions than answers the longer I stayed a human, and the longer I stayed human the more of myself I forgot. I couldn't even sense the crown any longer, or else I would've sensed it on Seren when he passed us on the way out of the Grandmaster's office.

I couldn't even smell him anymore.

I checked every room—the kitchens, the larder, the weapons room, on and on into the west wing. The few guards I did find were hidden behind corners or underneath tables. They weren't dead at all—they were playing card games, sitting on the job. They glanced up when I passed them, asking what I was doing here.

"Exploring," I lied, and hurried on before they could abandon their card games and come after me.

I hoped I would find that walking carrier of death before Daisy did.

The west wing finally ended at the rampart overlooking the city, and out beyond it were the Wilds, and the mountains in the distance. To catch my breath, I leaned against the rampart. It faced the dark wood, and it beckoned like little else could. The wood was vast and terrifying, and there were no walls or fences or gates. It was wide and wild. If it had been a day—a week before, I would've dived into that forest. I would've run and never looked back, shoving the memories of the crown, and the ancients, and this city into some forgotten recess of my mind— the food, and the language, and the warmth of Daisy's fingers laced through mine as we danced, the sound of her laughter, how she looked up at me with her ever-changing hazel eyes. And the look in that guard's eyes as he died.

I wanted to forget it all. I missed being a fox. I missed the wood being a place I could roam, rather than a place to fear.

. . . But it was no longer home.

I just wished I knew what to do—

A bloom of pain lit just behind my eyes, and I massaged my temples to try to alleviate it—

"C'mon, I want to show you something!"

I glanced over, the pain so bright I could barely keep my eyes open. There were two hazy figures on the other side of the rampart, small looking, childlike. A boy who had just spoken, and a girl with a flower crown on her head.

The boy climbed up onto the ledge and glanced back to the girl, outstretching his hand to her. "C'mon! The sun's about to rise!"

The girl seemed nervous. "I don't think we're supposed to be up here. Papa said the towers were forbidden."

"But I'm a prince. If you get in trouble, I'll save you."

The girl hesitated. Their words were too loud in my ears, and I clamped my hands over them to try to keep the sounds out—until I realized they were inside my head. "Don't you trust me?"

The pain crawled through my head like a wildfire, and I had to lean against the side of the rampart to keep my knees from going out. "Kids, get away from there," I called weakly.

They ignored me.

"I trust you," the girl replied after some hesitation, and took him by the hand.

Were they going to stand on the edge of the rampart?

I reached out to try to stop them. "Wait—stop. Stop, it's dangerous!"

The girl turned back—honey hair and hazel eyes—and I stared at her in surprise.

Daisy?

"Wait, don't go." I reached out my hand as I fought against the searing pain in my head. Blackness ate the edges of my vision.

"C'mon," said the foolish boy, "we're about to miss the sunrise!" Then he stepped off the ledge, and she went with him.

"NO—*STOP!*" I caught myself before I tumbled over the side of the rampart after them, but there was no one at the bottom.

They had just . . . disappeared.

"This area is off-limits." A voice startled me out of my thoughts, and I glanced over my shoulder. A young woman with short raven-black hair stood, a hand on the dragon-headed hilt of her sword. Her wooden leg ticked against the stones as she came near. *Tick. Tick.* She narrowed her eyes suspiciously. "You're Lady Cerys's . . . *friend.*"

I turned to her, trying to shake off the vision. "Voryn's in trouble. There's a man—he's broken into the Grandmaster's chamber and—"

"You're the one who was woodcursed," she interrupted. The grip on her hilt tightened; her shoulders straightened. I didn't have to be a fox to recognize when I wasn't wanted somewhere. "You might be calling to them now."

"What? No—"

I heard the sing of her sword through the air, and I dodged to the left. The blade struck against the stone wall of the rampart, sparks hissing.

"Whoa, whoa, *whoa*!" I cried, throwing my hands up in surrender. "I'm not here to—"

"You should be dead!" she snarled. "Why are you out here? Where's your guard?"

I yipped as I barely dodged the next attack. "You have to listen to me! It's the crown—it's missing. But I didn't take it."

"Lies." She pointed the tip of her blade at me, and I slowly began to back away down the rampart, my hands still up in surrender. "The city walls have never been breached. You are the first outsiders to enter Voryn in ages. The first *wood-cursed*."

"Do I look woodcursed to you?" I retorted. "I'm human."

As soon as the words left my mouth, I realized what I had just said and put my fingers to my lips. *Human.* I was a human. I wasn't a wild thing that hid behind Daisy's legs.

I *was* human.

She sneered at that and raised her sword to attack again. I could either leap off the side of the rampart—into the city twenty feet below—or get skewered by a pretty sword. I had decided on the twenty-foot drop when a sharp voice came from behind me.

"Petra."

It was so cold it chilled me to the bone. Coming up the stairs to the rampart was the Grandmaster, still in her white ceremonial robe from the wedding in the night market. "Let him be."

"But, Grandmaster, he's—"

"As much as I dislike him, he's telling the truth. Someone has stolen the crown, and it isn't he," replied the old woman. Her gaze lingered on me long enough to tell me that she liked me about as much as she liked bone-eaters—probably less, to be honest. But I had come with Daisy, and that, for some reason, kept me safe.

The young woman—Petra—said to me, "You told me you knew who took the crown. Tell us. Now."

Still shaken from the headache, I said, "I'm glad you finally believe me. We saw him take the crown, but we lost him in the fortress. Daisy went one way, and I . . ." Fear lodged the words in my throat. Oh *no*. If I hadn't found him, then . . . "Daisy. We have to find her. *Now!*"

✦ 31 ✦

A GARDEN OF ASHES

Cerys

WHEN I FOUND the first guard in the east wing, I thought he was dead—but he was just unconscious. He wasn't even woodcursed. It seemed like Seren hadn't had time to plant a seed in his escape. This also meant he was getting farther away with the crown the longer I lingered on each guard to check to see if they were alive.

They became like a bread trail to follow, out of the east wing of the fortress and into a garden that reminded me too much of the royal garden of Aloriya. Honeysuckles crawled up the walls, reaching out to willow trees that grew against the edges. There were wildflowers in pots and, spread across the ground, fat orchids and endover lilies and other flora I'd only seen in one other place before: the corner of Papa's garden, where my mother had planted the strange Wildwood seeds.

And that's where I found him. At the far side of the garden, his back to me, he was judging the wall to see if he could scale it.

"Seren," I called.

He spun around, surprised I'd said his name. In his grip was the crown. His hands shook as he held it, his eyes wide—as if he was scared. Of me? "Why can't you just give *up*?" he snapped. "You're so much more annoying than you were back then."

That made me pause. So he did remember. I put my hands up slowly, in a calming motion, to show him I wasn't armed—I wasn't someone he should be afraid of. I'd seen Papa do it to our horse, Gilda, when something spooked her.

"Seren"—I repeated his name because it seemed to draw his attention to me—"you know you don't want to do this."

His eyes narrowed. "I've little choice. The wood demands it. You . . . you can't understand."

Demands? "But why does it want the crown so badly?"

"Because it wants to do to you what your kingdom did to her."

Her? The Lady? I didn't understand—but I knew that if he wore the crown, something terrible would happen. He couldn't wear it—like I couldn't. I hesitantly offered my hand, taking a step closer. "Seren, please. You can explain it all to me. Just—just give me the crown. . . ."

"And what do you think'll happen when I do?" he asked,

backing up against the garden wall. "Will you grow some more *flowers* on me? Turn me into a pretty bouquet?" He motioned to the flowers sprouting from his shoulder. They bled down half of his chest, swirling with green moss and leaves. The wound Fox had inflicted back at the cottage. "I have to do what the wood asks. I must. Because you left me in the wood to die in the first place."

"Do . . . do you think I didn't want to look for you?" My voice wavered, because hadn't that been the same thought that rebounded in my head for years? "Did you think I didn't lie awake every night hating myself for surviving when you and my mother and Lorne—when you all *died*?"

"You still don't know, do you." It wasn't a question, but then he shook his head anyway, dismissing the thought. "It doesn't matter."

He raised the crown to his head, his hands shaking.

"Seren—*no!*"

But it was too late.

A strange ripple passed through the garden, like a pebble tossed into a river—a wave of magic that distorted everything around us. The flowers turned their heads toward him. The trees leaned in.

I stared in horror as the flowers on his chest began to wither, turning brown and then black with rot. They shriveled, the edges of their petals turning orange as if they were—*burning.* As if *he* were burning, from the inside out. It was like watching whatever was left of his life being sucked out of him.

And through it all, Seren was screaming.

I felt the ground shift beneath my feet, and roots sprang up and twined around my legs so I couldn't move. I cursed, trying to rip the roots away, but every time I did, more came, faster and faster, twisting up my legs. One sliced the back of my uninjured hand, and I quickly covered it so I wouldn't feed the dark plants my blood.

"Seren!" I cried above the strange roar of the magic. "Take it off! Take it off before you die!"

He looked at me with eyes that were as white as clouds, wide and pain stricken and terrified. *"They are coming, and no one can stop them—"*

Suddenly, a blur of gray rushed through the garden and tackled Seren to the ground. Vala pulled the crown off him, baring her teeth.

The garden quieted.

I tore the roots from my feet and ran toward them. Behind me, Fox shouted my name, rushing into the garden with a cadre of guards, but I was already dropping to kneel beside Seren. I ran my fingers along the rotted wildflowers on his shoulder. He truly looked like a corpse, broken and pale and forgotten, and I could finally see the extent of the woodcurse in him. It was visible beneath his paper-thin skin, deeper than the wound he'd gotten all those years ago in the wood. He must have been woodcursed before he died. The curse suspended him somewhere between life and death, controlling him, biding its time until the king had died, and then the wood sent Seren into the Village-in-the-Valley.

But if my blood could heal the woodcurse . . .

"Daisy! Get away from him!" I heard Fox cry as he raced across the garden to me.

The flowers and moss that had been growing from Seren's wound hadn't been hurting him—they had been bringing him back, fighting the curse. Saving his life.

Quickly, I pressed the back of my bleeding hand against Seren's once-flowered shoulder. Little sprigs of green peeked out from his charred wound, growing into bloom once again. It spread like moss over a stone across part of his chest and burrowed deep. The wood had taken so many things.

I didn't want it to take him, too.

I curled my fingers into the moss and willed harder, because I knew Seren. Not this Seren, corpse dry and twisted, but the Seren before. The Seren who wanted to become a knight, who walked me home from the castle every evening, who taught Anwen how to ride a horse, who ran into the cursed wood after his charge, knowing he might die.

He had to be there still—somewhere—under all this rot.

The truth was: If he had wanted to kill me back at the cottage, he could have. He had seen us. And again when he and Fox met in the wood. He could have killed Fox. He could have killed me here.

He didn't—and I refused to let him leave again.

White flowers bloomed across his shoulder, opening wide with bright yellow hearts. His body jerked. His eyes flew open wide—and he gasped, his strange white eyes focusing on me. "*Why?*" he wheezed, and then winced, bringing a hand to his chest where my flowers grew.

"Because we all have a promise to keep," I replied, and stood, letting the guards come and draw Seren to his feet. As they handcuffed him, Vala came over to me and planted her head against my chest, as if to tell me I'd done a good job.

I thanked her quietly and took the crown from her mouth. It was still warm, and it pulsed gently, enthralling.

Fox ran up to me, and before I could tell what he was doing, he pulled me into a hug. "Fox—you're squishing me!"

"I was so worried," he replied, releasing me and holding me at arm's length. "You aren't hurt, are you? That diseased sack of bones didn't do anything?" And when I shook my head, he gave a visible sigh. "I should've gone with you."

"You didn't know," I replied, and caught sight of the Grandmaster standing at the entrance to the garden, stone-faced and rigid. It was clear through Seren that the crown had something to do with the curse—with *Her.* The Lady. I wasn't going to be played for a fool anymore. I held up the crown and said, "I know you're keeping something from me. Tell me everything you know about the crown." She took a deep breath. "And the curse."

Because I was no longer that scared girl on the edge of the Wildwood, unable to save her friends.

I would save them this time.

The Grandmaster inclined her head. "I have told you all that I know—"

"*Liar*," I snapped.

At my venom, Petra, who stood beside the Grandmaster, reached for her sword at her hip, but the Grandmaster held up her hand. Petra stood down.

"I saw the tapestry in your office," I went on. "I saw the maps. I know you know more than you're letting on."

"So you were snooping about? After I gave you food and shelter?"

"You *lied* to me!"

"You didn't ask the right questions," the Grandmaster replied sharply. "And why should we tell you anything? Your entire kingdom left us to rot. Shouldn't we leave your kingdom to the same fate?"

"Don't you *want* to end the curse?" I snarled in reply, clenching my fists together. "I know my kingdom left you. I know I perpetuated the same stories, lived in the same golden glow of the crown—never asking questions. I *know*. And I want to fix it. I want to try. Just help us end this curse. *Please*, Grandmaster."

Because for so long I'd thought that the crown only protected Aloriya from the ancients and the bone-eaters and the woodcurse, but now I was beginning to suspect that the crown had something to do with it. Why else would the wood command Seren to take the crown? Why would the ancient magic of the Wildwood need the crown in the first place?

And why was there never talk of the woodcurse before the crown?

They were questions I should've been asking before, but my ears had been filled with stories that were lies.

The Grandmaster inclined her head, and then she motioned for me to follow her. She turned and went into the fortress again, but as I started to follow her, Fox stopped me.

"Daisy, I don't like this. How do you know she'll tell the truth now?"

I hesitated. "Because if she doesn't, she's dooming her own city. Because Seren failed, the wood will send more monsters. Bone-eaters. Ancients. I know she knows that. These walls have only held because the fog kept the curse away."

Fox pursed his lips, because he still didn't like my answer.

I kissed Fox on the cheek. "Thank you for worrying about me."

He let go of me in surprise. "I—um—yeah, of course." He rubbed the back of his neck, a blush creeping across his cheeks. "Just—be careful, Daisy."

"Always." I smiled at him, and his cheeks seemed to get even redder, and he looked away in embarrassment.

I left Vala to look after Fox in the garden, and I followed the Grandmaster into the fortress and down the long and dizzying halls back to her office again. She let me inside first and closed the door behind her. I didn't realize we were alone until I turned back to her, and she closed the door. I tightened my grip on the crown.

Slowly, she circled around me, toward her desk, and began in a matter-of-fact tone, "When the Lady of the Wilds ruled the wood, there was no crown. Your King Sunder razed his path to the heart of the wood, where the Lady held her court, and when he returned, he had a glorious golden crown and the Lady was gone. As he left, a great fog settled over Voryn. The roots of the wood turned bitter, the flowers poisonous, and the old gods rotted. We hadn't protected our Lady, and so the forest would. The only way it could—with a curse."

I stared at her in disbelief. "The Lady of the Wilds is *gone*?"

"Gone. For three hundred years." The Grandmaster leaned back on the front of her desk, looking older than she had just a few hours before. "So—what do you think I thought when you came into my city with the last of our Lady's old gods, King Sunder's crown, and blood that could break the woodcurse? The last visitor we had destroyed our lives and left us here to die. I didn't trust you at all—but now I see I don't have a choice. That *thing*—"

"Seren," I corrected.

She glowered at me. "Came from the wood. It found its way through the fog. Over the wall. Into my office, and if I wanted to be thick, I would ask why you and he were here at the exact same time, but you wouldn't have risked your life to stop him if you were working together. And you did risk your life for this city—whether or not that was your intention." She pushed off the edge of her desk and rounded it, opening one of the drawers. She took out a yellowed piece of parchment and presented it on the desk. It was a map—old and gnarled. "You were correct in your assumptions; I haven't been honest with you."

I came closer, looking down at a strangely detailed map. It showed mountains and rivers and valleys, but it also showed areas where ancients prowled, and near the center of the forest, just past Voryn, was a clearing drawn in a perfect circle.

The Grandmaster tapped her forefinger on it. "It stands to reason that returning the crown from whence it came will reverse the curse—by taking it to the heart of the wood, where the Lady once held her court, perhaps you'll find where she went. But you aren't the first one to try to break the woodcurse. My daughter once set out, and she failed." The old woman paused and shook her head. "It is dangerous. Impossible, even. And only a Grandmaster or their apprentice knows the way, and I swore to myself I would never send another of mine out on this fool's errand—"

"But I'm no fool, Grandmaster" came the voice of Petra from the door. I glanced back, surprised she'd come in so quietly. She closed the door behind her and gave a small bow. "Let me lead her to the heart of the wood. I know the way."

The Grandmaster's lips pursed into a thin line. "Absolutely *not*."

"Then I'll go without your permission," Petra replied. "You saw that monster in the garden, Grandmaster. More will be coming. The fog is weakening."

"Or the wood is growing stronger," I whispered, my fingers curling tighter around the crown. I knew this was the kind of sacrifice I shouldn't be letting her make, but I didn't know the way to the heart of the wood. "Thank you," I said softly.

Petra gave a simple nod. "We didn't believe you at first. That was our mistake."

"You go and you will die, Petra," the Grandmaster said through clenched teeth.

"We shall see," replied her apprentice, before turning and leaving the office once more. The Grandmaster stood there, visibly shaking, her fingers curled into fists. I didn't know whether to be relieved or frightened. We finally had a set course—somewhere to go, a light at the end of this long tunnel. But to get there, we had to return to the wood, something I wasn't very keen on.

As I left, the Grandmaster said, "You remind me so much of my daughter. I pray this fool's errand breaks the curse."

I did, too.

I tried to sort myself out before I met up with Fox again. This was for the best, I told myself.

This was the only way it could be. Our only hope.

Even if it killed me.

32

A TASTE FOR A TRUTH

Fox

AS THE GUARDS led Seren to the prisons and Daisy left with the Grandmaster, I had to find something to do, so I went to the kitchens. My heart was still racing. It wasn't like I could just go to sleep now, not after Daisy had almost died—*again.*

As I'd run through the halls with the Grandmaster and her guards, I had convinced myself that I was too late, and I was. Vala had gotten there in time, though. She had knocked the crown from his head this time, like I had done for Daisy back at the castle.

If only I'd chosen the east wing instead, Daisy wouldn't have had to even face that corpse. I should've killed him back at the river. I should've snapped his neck and torn him into a dozen pieces, so even if he couldn't die, he'd spend at least a decade trying to put himself back together.

But I hadn't, and it still bothered me that I couldn't understand why. It couldn't have been that I'd been tempted by his offer . . . could it?

There was no one in the kitchens this late at night—the kitchen staff all asleep—so there was no one to shoo me out. Maybe staying a human wouldn't be so bad.

Don't even entertain it, I told myself.

Absently, I stocked a tray with leftovers from the pantry: coffee cake, carrot cake, and some sort of strudel, which also called for a hot pot of tea. As I plated some more pastries, my mind was off elsewhere. Why did Seren seemed so familiar? And why did he think he knew me? Had I bitten him in my previous life? Had I come upon him in the wood after he was lost? He was someone Daisy had once known, so maybe I'd met him, too?

I found a kettle in a cabinet and filled it with water from a pump that must've led to whatever water source the fountains in the city fed from, and set the kettle on the stove. I waved my hand over the stove, and fire sparked in the burner—

I glanced down at it with a start.

Did I just . . . ?

No. I couldn't have.

I *definitely* didn't know magic.

I stared at my hand for a moment and did the same motion—and fire burst onto my fingertips.

My hand began to shake.

"C'mon, this way!"

A voice startled me from my thoughts, and I jerked my head around toward it. It was that kid again—the one who'd pulled Daisy off the rampart earlier. He came into the kitchen, his hair golden, dressed in dark leathers that itched at the collar. How did I know they itched? He was followed by a tall, broad-shouldered man.

The world tilted, and I stumbled and caught myself against the stove. My head spun like it had on the rampart. I blinked the black dots out of my eyes, but the voices were still there.

"Patience, son, I'm coming as fast as I can." The man laughed. He had the same fair hair and tan skin as the boy, and a thick beard.

He wore the crown on his head.

I took a step toward him.

The boy sighed, rounding the other side of the counter. "You're so slow!"

"Well, the crown's heavy."

But it wasn't. The crown was light. It was the magic that was heavy. I smelled it where I stood—like poppies and burning wood. It drew at him from the inside out, hollowing him, and the boy was afraid that someday when he took the crown, he would be hollowed out, too—

"Stop it," I growled, pressing the palm of my hand into my

263

eye. The headache was returning—that sharp, needle-point throb at the back of my head.

"What do you want to show me in a hurry, anyway?" the man asked.

"I need your help. There's a fox caught in the barn."

"And why couldn't you get Seren to help? Or one of the other guards?"

The child looked embarrassed. "Seren likes hunting. He'd kill it. And I don't want him to. It's just a fox. I like foxes."

"Do you now?"

"STOP IT!" I snarled at the illusion, throwing my hand out toward it. A blade of flames shot out of my hand and disintegrated into the air. The pots and pans hanging on the racks swung with the force of the heat.

A moment later, a guard swept into the kitchen, pushing back her helmet. "What in kingsteeth . . . you!" she said when she spotted me. "You're not supposed to be in the kitchens at night."

I leaned back against the counter. The illusion was gone, and I felt like I'd just run clear across the fortress. I tried to catch my breath. "Right, yeah, just—getting a midnight snack."

"You better be gone before I get back," she warned, eyeing the swinging pots and pans. She left the kitchen.

I rubbed my face with my shaking hands.

What was happening to me?

With a high-pitched squeal, the kettle began boiling, and it startled me out of my thoughts. I fixed Daisy a cup of chamomile tea and returned to the third floor, where our rooms were, expecting the tray to catch fire, but it never did. Her room was at the end, and I pushed the door open. "Daisy, a weird thing just happened in the . . ."

She glanced up, her eyes rimmed red.

The thought of magic quickly flew from my mind. I set the tray down on the nightstand. "Are you okay?"

She nodded unconvincingly.

I sat on the edge of the bed beside her and handed her the cup of tea. She took it to warm her hands and sipped it cautiously. Her eyebrows shot up in surprise. "You made this?"

"Is it good?"

"It's good."

"Then absolutely, I made it."

That made her laugh a little—but what had she been crying about? I opened my mouth to ask when her eyes fell on the food tray. "Raided the pantry, did you?"

I shrugged. "The food was just lying around, so I figured, why not?"

She pursed her lips, but the sides of her mouth quirked up a little—as if she was trying not to laugh. "Someday all this thieving's going to catch up with you."

To that, I grinned. "It hasn't yet." I took a bite of the carrot cake and poked around at whatever else I'd managed to grab, until she suddenly said—

"Thank you. For . . . for everything. I mischaracterized you in the wood, I realize."

I paused as I picked up a fork and then set it down again. Her sad, tired eyes had dropped to my wrist—the one with the foothold trap scar. It was cruel and jagged, like a lightning bolt, the skin lighter and tougher than the rest. It was a constant reminder of how we'd met. The memories were hazy, but they were still there, like a story told to me. I'd wandered onto Gregor's farm and gotten caught in his foothold trap. It had nearly crushed my paw. I would've been made into a nice hat if Daisy hadn't come through the fields. She had been gathering wildflowers for something. I couldn't remember what, but I did remember that she had daisies in her hair. She pried the trap open and took me home. How long ago was that?

Time was strange in my head. It felt like yesterday and another lifetime ago at once.

I had thought she was going to kill me after she freed me from the trap, but she hadn't. I had been wrong about her then. And other times since.

"Well," I said, rolling the word around on my tongue, "that makes two of us, then. But, despite everything, I'm glad I went through the wood with you. I'm also really glad we didn't die. And I'm glad Seren didn't kill us, either," I added.

She drew her knees up to her chest. "I just keep thinking I should've died instead—instead of Seren, instead of the prince. It should've been me." Her voice wobbled. "The whole kingdom missed them; they still miss them. The king was never the same after he lost his son; some say he would still be alive today if the prince hadn't been killed. But me—"

"I would miss you," I interrupted.

She pushed her palm against one of her eyes to wipe away the coming tears. "We wouldn't have met."

"Then there would be a hole where you should have been, and I would miss whatever was supposed to fill it."

She buried her face into her knees to hide. "None of this would've happened if it had been me. The wood wouldn't have come. Anwen wouldn't have turned. Papa would still be safe—it's all my fault. It's all—"

I couldn't stand it anymore. I set her tea on the tray between us so she wouldn't spill it and took her face in my hands. "If you had died, then there would be no one to save Aloriya. The wood would have come for the crown no matter what anyone did, whether it was now or later—it was only a matter of time before it came knocking. You're the bravest, smartest, most stubborn person I've ever met, and if anyone can break a curse, I know it's you."

She hiccupped a sob, shaking her head. "And what if I fail? What if—"

"We'll find a way. I'm with you, Daisy. To the very end. I go wherever you go, because when I'm with you, I forget I don't want to be human."

She turned her gaze back to me, eyes wide.

Oh, kingsteeth—what did I say? I let go of the sides of her face, reeling, because I had definitely just said that. And I'd meant it. I opened my mouth, gobbling for words. "I meant— what I said was—when I'm with you—"

And then she leaned forward and kissed me.

Her lips were soft, and at first I wasn't quite sure what to do. I'd seen humans kiss before, but I had never paid much attention to it. It just looked like two people ramming their mouths together. But that was before. She began to pull away, realizing that I wasn't kissing her back, but then I followed her lips in response, and she tasted like chamomile and daisies.

"Do you like me more than meat pies?" she whispered.

"Well, I wouldn't go that far," I replied against her mouth, "but we're still getting to know each other."

She drew away, and the distance between us felt hollow, and I just wanted to fill that space again. She smiled in that endearing, stubborn way. "I like you, too."

"Even though I'm trouble?"

"*Especially* because you're trouble," she said, weaving her fingers through mine, and the fox part of me feared that I didn't want to break the curse at all.

∽ 33 ∾

SAVE THE OUTCASTS

Cerys

I WOKE UP curled beside Fox, his fingers loose in my hair. Our faces were so close I could count the faded freckles across the bridge of his nose. Gray light poured in through the window, and I blinked the bleariness out of my eyes. Fox was still fast asleep, his breath soft and deep, and I watched him sleep for a few minutes, thinking how familiar he felt, how familiar he looked to me now, and even though we'd only really known each other a few days, all I wanted to do was run my fingers down his cheek like I'd known him for years.

Maybe he just looked familiar because he was my fox, and he sometimes slept at the foot of my bed, and he kept me company during the long hours in the shop when I was alone. He no longer took up just a little corner of my bed but half of it, because he was tall and broad shouldered, existing in a body he didn't have before. And for a moment, as I reached to brush the hair out of his face, I forgot that he had been a fox at all, that he wanted to be a fox again.

And with that I quickly retracted my hand. Because once we broke the curse, whether he wanted to be human or not, he would become a fox again.

I was walking a dangerous tightrope where I knew no one would catch me when I fell.

I moved to ease myself off the bed, his fingers falling out of my hair, when he pursed his lips together in his sleep. He grabbed at the pillow I had been lying on and curled it to his chest and pressed it against him, burrowing his face into it. I waited to make sure he was still asleep before I slipped the rest of the way off the bed, put on my shoes and my coat, and left the room.

I needed some space to clear my head. I needed to forget his fingers twining into my hair, how warm he felt against me, how he smelled like lavender and sandalwood—and most of all, I needed to remember that whatever I felt, it wouldn't last.

None of this would last.

Even as Fox professed that I should not have died in the wood all those years ago, it was still coming for me. I didn't have time for these kinds of feelings. They were better left for long summer days and lazy winter nights in the flower shop. They were better left for girls who did not hide behind garden walls.

For princesses, not cursed gardeners' daughters.

And what awaited us in the Wildwood.

I was thankful for the quiet of the fortress as I traveled along hallway after hallway, making my way toward the heart of the fortress. It was then that someone crossed down the hall in front of me, white ribbons in her short hair. She was alone, carrying a jar under her arm.

Petra.

Against my better judgment, I crept after her. She climbed the stairs, higher and higher in the fortress, until she opened a door onto the rooftop. It was a garden of sorts, with flower beds of dark green plants and soft white daisies bending in the morning wind. Dawn was fast approaching, the gray bleeding with pinks and oranges across the horizon, and it made the Wildwood below look as though it were on fire.

The wind from the east played with the long ribbons in her hair. I watched silently as Petra muttered over the jar she was holding. Then she tipped it over, and out poured flower petals, whites and violets and blues and yellows and reds and oranges, all the colors I'd seen in the fortress's garden. The wind caught them and took them far into the Wilds. Petra murmured a prayer I could barely hear, to keep Voryn safe, and its people fed, and the mists deep and vast. I wondered if the prayer worked. If it reached the Lady.

Perhaps if I had prayed and offered up petals of roses and daisies and bluebells, then my mother would still be alive, too. No, I doubt that would've made a difference.

When the jar was empty, Petra finally glanced over her shoulder at me. She knew I had been there, watching, though she didn't seem angry.

"How do you do it?" she asked, motioning to my wounded hand. There was blood still under my nails. I didn't think I'd ever get it out. "Is it some dark magic? Did you sell your soul to some ancient? A pact with an old god? That bear of yours?"

"I don't know," I replied.

"How do you not *know*?"

In reply, all I could do was unbandage my hand and pick off a small scab. A tinge of blood beaded on my palm, and I took one of the white flowers from my hair and wiped the blood on one of the petals. The flower began to grow, multiply, building up in my cupped hands, until I set the bouquet free into the wind.

Petra watched, astonishment overpowering her anger.

I explained shakily, "I was supposed to be woodcursed, but my mother sacrificed her life for me. I've always thought . . . maybe her love for me transformed the woodcurse into this, and I survived. This curse is the last bit of her I have left, and so when the curse breaks—I guess my magic will go, too. I know it's silly to hold on to that. My mother wouldn't really approve.

272

She said that the people who die never really leave. That we carry them with every breath we take, until the wind itself is gone."

"The Grandmaster's daughter used to say that, too," Petra replied quietly. "She said that if the Lady of the Wilds is dead, we carry her with us in every breath. We breathe her in. We become her."

"It's a good thought."

"But I don't think she's dead." Petra turned to me, and against the backdrop of the gray morning light she looked almost ethereal. "If she were, then how do you have your magic, Cerys? How is the fog still here? How are the ancients still living? How is the curse still set?"

I didn't know—I'd just assumed that curses and magic lingered after the magic bearer died. But if that was the case, then why did the crown feast off the people whose brow it sat upon? Because I remembered the power from the crown, the way it felt to be stripped of it, like someone ripping a second skin from my body. I hugged myself tightly against the chill of the morning. The painting in the Grandmaster's private rooms haunted me, King Sunder painted as a demon, the wood on fire.

When I didn't say anything, Petra went on. "You aren't like the Aloriyans I imagined. You trekked among the beasts and briars, and the deep heart led you all the way to Voryn."

"The deep heart?"

A small spread across her lips. "It's what we call that feeling

273

inside you, the part that leads you, draws you forward—toward some great purpose."

"Ah."

I didn't feel like I had been drawn anywhere, only dragged and pushed and shoved—but I liked the thought of it. I wondered if my mother had a deep heart guiding her, too. If that was how she found us in the wood all those years ago.

Petra bowed. "I'll excuse myself. I have a long day ahead of me. The Grandmaster will have me escorting you first thing this morning."

But then she paused and said before she left, "Please be careful of the Grandmaster. Her sole duty is to protect this city, and in her eyes you aren't a part of it."

"Thanks for the warning," I replied.

When she left, I sat down on the edge of the building to watch the sunrise, tracing my thumb across the wound on my hand. *You trekked among the beasts and briars*, Petra had said, and once I returned the crown, I wouldn't even do that. I would be no one again—no one spectacular, anyway, and the last bit of my mother would be gone.

Fox would be gone, too.

He had said he didn't want to become a fox again—but I didn't see another choice. We were almost there, almost at the end. We just had to return the crown to the heart of the wood and break the curse and save the kingdom. But things were so much more complicated than that.

There wasn't another way to break the curse on the wood without both Fox and me giving up what we wanted. Without my power, Fox couldn't be human—as far as I knew—and without the curse in the wood, would have my power. If only I could cure every bone-eater like I had Fox—

That's when I noticed a shadow at the gates of the city. It was tall and spindly, and although it was so far away, I knew the shape of it too well.

An ancient had broken through the fog, and it stood at the gates of Voryn.

34

THE COWARDLY TRUTH

Fox

I WOKE UP with a pillow curled to my chest and Daisy nowhere in sight—which immediately catapulted me into full-on panic. I quickly sat up, wondering where she'd gone, when I realized I wasn't alone in the room. A figure riffled through the wardrobe. I tensed, curling my fingers into fists. I no longer had claws, and I couldn't make out the person's face.

I rose swiftly into a crouch, flicking my wrist. It was second nature, like breathing. A spark of fire bloomed onto my fingers. I threw it at the intruder, who ducked. It burst into sparks on the wall behind them. "You better have a good reason to be—*wait!*" I called as the shadow darted out of the room.

I tried to go after them, but my legs tangled in the sheets. I pried them off and lurched for the door, but by the time I got into the hallway, whoever it was had vanished.

I snapped my teeth together agitatedly. Who was that? And where was Daisy?

Returning to the room, I nosed into the wardrobe the intruder had been riffling through and found Daisy's old sash that she had tied the crown to, along with our old clothes. It didn't take a mastermind to figure out what they were looking for—the crown. Too bad they wouldn't find it.

I glanced up at the burn mark on the wall.

And that made me think of a question that I wanted an answer to—one that Daisy couldn't provide, but luckily I knew someone else who could, and I knew exactly where he'd be.

Seren looked up when I came within a few feet of his cell. His hands were bound, and he sat cross-legged in the middle of the damp stones. The flowers had bloomed again over his shoulder, mostly lavender from the Sundermount, and they were striking against his torn dark tunic. He didn't seem all that surprised to see me.

"Let me guess," the corpse said with a tired sigh. "You have questions."

There was a handful of guards patrolling the area, so we had to be quiet if I wanted to ask him what I needed to know. I crouched down by the cell bars and curled my finger, silently mouthing, *Come here.*

With a roll of his eyes, he shimmied toward me. Closer, a little closer—when he was within arm's reach, I grabbed him by the collar of his tunic and forced him against the cell bars. He hissed in discomfort. I didn't care; he'd almost killed Daisy.

But the moment I grabbed him, I knew something was . . . off. It wasn't the way he smelled, or the pallor of his face. It was something I couldn't place. A strange energy or magnetism. And what was more . . . "Kingsteeth, you aren't woodcursed anymore."

"I'm so glad you have eyes," he replied calmly.

"How?"

"Same way she cured you, I'd imagine."

"I wasn't dead for eight years."

"Oh, I assure you I am still very much dead—"

I shook him one good time, and a flower broke off his shoulder and fell between us.

"Fine! *Fine*," he relented. "Her magic, I would assume, is keeping me alive now, just like it's keeping you human. But I can't be sure because I'm no longer connected to the wood, and once you break the curse, I *am* going to die and you'll be a fox again. Just like you wanted. You always liked running away from things."

"You don't know me."

To that, he smiled, flashing sharp shark-like teeth. "Don't I, Lorne?"

Lorne?

Where had I heard that name bef—

A needle of pain flared to life behind my eyes. *Not again.* With a wince, I let go of him and pressed my palm against my eye, watching the colors bloom under my eyelid, wishing that this wouldn't happen *now*, of all times—

"You're not supposed to be in here!" someone said from the entrance to the prison. The guards? Not *now.*

I could barely hear them over the high-pitched screech in my head.

Seren leaned against the cell bars. "I would suggest you run. They're coming, you know. And everyone's going to blame you." Even his voice sounded too loud, knocking against the inside of my brain like a sledgehammer.

"Blame me—f-for what?"

As the guards came closer, the corpse repeated, "I honestly suggest you *run.*"

I didn't know what he was talking about, but I fought to push myself to my feet. I could barely see straight anymore. I doubled over, my hand covering my face. It felt like a hot poker had been shoved into my eyes. My head hurt so much I wanted to vomit.

Then there were images again. Memories, I now knew. They folded together like Daisy braiding her hair in the mornings, tastes and sounds and smells. A castle—the Sundermount? The tallest spire. A girl with golden hair—Anwen.

My—

My sister.

My father, gray beard and swept-back hair, handing me my first sword. A town—no, the village. The Village-in-the-Valley. Pressing my face against the flower shop window, seeing a girl with honey-colored hair and freckles across the bridge of her nose, smiling at me with a gap where she's lost three teeth. Daisy. A lanky young man behind me—black hair and dark eyes, always smelling of horses and complaining of boredom. Playing in the wheat fields, studying with a gray-haired seneschal, an itchy purple uniform and a heavy circlet, looking into the mirror at—

At *me*.

I was—

I was back in the wood, hiding in a hollowed-out log. Thick, heavy mist hung in the forest. I was trembling. My trousers were dirty from crawling through the underbrush, my fingernails caked in mud.

"Where are you?" I heard Seren cry. He tore through the wood, his footsteps crinkling the fall leaves. "Princeling! You're going to get me in so much trouble! Come out!"

I began to shout back—when I saw it again. The ancient. Moss-covered limbs and vine-strewn horns, creeping through the wood, hunting. I knew I should've told Seren to run, but I was too scared to move. If I warned him, then the ancient would find me—and I didn't want it to find me.

"Hey! C'mon, where are you? We should leave before . . ."

I watched as his boots turned around and slowed to a stop to face the ancient. Then I couldn't watch anymore. I buried my head in my arms, but I couldn't block out Seren's screams. I heard him fight and beg, and I stayed safely in my hiding hole, cowering. I didn't even try to help. I just lay there, praying to every old god I knew, hoping the ancient wouldn't find me, trying to block out my best friend's voice.

I was a coward. I didn't deserve to be a prince. I didn't deserve to be human.

They were the words that kept repeating in my head, over and over again, as Seren screamed and fought—I was a coward. I didn't deserve to be a prince. I didn't deserve to be human.

I don't deserve to be human.

I curled my fingers into my hair, my eyes burning with tears, and I tried to keep myself quiet as the ancient lifted Seren off the ground. Blood splattered across the leaves where his feet had been. I tried to keep my sobs in my chest.

I didn't know how long I cowered there. It might have been minutes. Hours. An eternity.

I didn't notice the fur sprouting from my skin, my nails blackening to claws, my teeth sharpening to points, until it was too late.

And by then, I didn't remember my name at all.

But—I remembered it now, as I looked up at the flowering corpse, his long black hair tangled and wild, his leathers barely recognizable, ripped and punctured and too soft to protect him at all. He stared through the cell bars at me, waiting for me to see him—finally see him.

And I did.

"Seren."

Something odd flickered across his face. Relief? Worry? "You . . . remember."

Yes. I did.

The wood changed me. It turned me into a fox.

It protected me.

"You there! Turn around!" the guards cried behind me.

My hands tightened into fists, magic crackling at my fingertips. I swayed dizzily, but my head no longer hurt. It felt full and strange, memories lighting up in the dark parts of my head where I'd thought there was nothing. They came back to me slowly, like water through a siphon.

Seren leaned toward me, his eyes dark and gleaming. "Listen to me: Ancients are tearing through the gates. They'll kill everyone—or turn them. You need to run."

"But—Cerys—*Daisy*—"

Which was her name? Did I even deserve to call her anything?

"You couldn't even save me—how do you think you'll save her? *Run.* You're best at that."

Run.

He was right.

I pushed myself to my feet and stumbled down the corridor of prison cells. She would hate me—I hated myself.

I had to get out of here. I had to leave—

The guards followed me.

"Run, little princeling," Seren's voice echoed after me long after I'd torn into a sprint. I was faster than I'd been as a child, my legs longer, my body stronger—but I still felt like I couldn't run fast enough.

‿ 35 ‿

SIEGE OF THE ANCIENTS

Cerys

A SIREN SCREECHED across the city, followed by another and another. I watched as lights flared on in the windows of Voryn, families and children poking their heads out of their doors, as guards rushed down the many stairways toward the entrance.

There wasn't just one ancient—there were many of them. All twisted forms of the old gods—a horse-sized hawk with bone wings, a wolf with poison ivy in its fur, all dark and twisted creatures that weren't gods anymore, but monsters. And with them came bone-eaters that scaled the sides of the ramparts. Screams came from all over the city; I heard them from the top of the Grandmaster's fortress. The creatures swarmed in like ants, and there was no stopping them. A black seed drifted down from the night sky and landed on the back of my hand. It shriveled and turned to ash.

The woodcurse. I could smell the seeds in the air—the bitterness like biting into an apple seed.

I stumbled to my feet.

"*Petra!*" I cried, racing off the rooftop and down into the fortress proper again. I found her in the next hallway, and she caught me quickly by the shoulders.

"Why are the sirens going?" she asked, fear furrowing her brow.

"Ancients—they're at the gates. I think when Seren put on the crown, he called them," I said, now realizing what he meant when he said *they* were coming.

They weren't guards or Fox or the Grandmaster.

They were the nightmares.

Petra's shoulders stiffened, and her hand went quickly to the dragon-hilted sword at her belt. "Do you know where it is?"

I nodded.

"Is it safe?"

"I think so—but I need to find Fox," I added, and she followed me back to my room. The fortress had erupted into chaos, servants rushing toward a safe vault. Petra met Briath in the stairwell. She was crying.

"Bone-eaters are in the fortress!" the girl cried. "They're going to kill us! One tried to—one came into my room! It—it tried to—it—"

"Shh, shh, you're safe now," Petra consoled her. She couldn't both help me find Fox and get out of the city and protect her sister, and I didn't want her to have to choose.

I fisted my hands and made the decision for her. "Go with her and make sure she's safe—protect everyone else. I'll go find Fox. And whatever you do, if you see black seeds, do not let them touch you."

"Are you sure you can . . . ?" She hesitated.

I pulled a smile over my lips. "I'll be fine."

She didn't look convinced at first, but then she nodded, took her sister by the hand, and followed the other evacuees. There was a stone door toward the back of the fortress—the kind that you trapped yourself behind when you had no other choice. They would be safe there. I had to find Fox, and we would get the crown and Vala and leave—and hopefully draw the ancients away with us.

I flew down the next flight of stairs and rushed back to my room, stumbling through the curtain, gasping for breath. "Fox! We need to get the crown and leave! The ancients—" My voice stopped in my throat. I stared around at the empty room. ". . . Fox?"

But he wasn't here. His coat was gone, as were his shoes.

Oh, *no*.

I inched toward the bed and pulled up the edge of the mattress. The firelight caught the golden leaves of the crown. The anxiety wound tight in my middle loosened. It was still there, thank the old gods.

I took my old sash from the bottom of the wardrobe, tied it around my waist with the crown, like I had done in the wood, and ran out of my room. Fox wouldn't have left without a reason—good or bad.

But I had a feeling I knew where he might have gone.

"Where is he?" I asked as I rounded the stairs down into the prison.

There were no guards anywhere in sight, but Seren was waiting in his cell. Dark eyes and long face and sunken cheekbones, pale skin accented with his midnight hair. He sat leaning against the bars, his hands still bound behind his back. "Why would I know?" he asked, but then his eyes strayed to my sash. "You brought the *crown*? Do you have a death wish? All the ancients will be coming for it!"

"Then you'd better talk fast, I guess," I replied patiently. It still made me shiver how much he hadn't changed since he'd disappeared in the wood. It was like time had stopped for him. "I know he came down here—he must have."

"He did. And then he left."

I breathed out through my nose and pressed my forehead against the bars of the cell. If he wasn't here, then where *was* he? *Think, Cerys.* The ancients had already infiltrated the city. We had to stop them, but to do that I had to leave with the crown, but I didn't want to leave without *him.* "Damn it, Fox," I muttered under my breath.

Seren studied me for a moment before he said, "You've changed, you know. When you were a little girl, you'd never do anything remotely dangerous. Now you've traveled through the entire wood, cursed beasties on your trail, and you never looked back."

"Well, you haven't changed at all."

He shrugged. "I'm dead. I'm not supposed to. And your fox is gone. He's not coming back, and you're better off without him."

That took me by surprise. "Why would you say that?"

He grinned, shark teeth bright and white. "The wood makes monsters of all of us, Cerys, whether or not we have the curse." He shrugged. "Or maybe I'm just bitter now, and maybe you're better on your own."

"You're wrong. You don't know him."

He rolled his eyes. "Don't I? Don't you? C'mon, Cerys, the wood never just *takes.* It changes."

"I don't understand what you're getting at," I replied exhaustedly—

A screech rushed across the cobblestones.

Seren prickled with panic, the thorns on his shoulders spreading up to his neck, like fur bristling. "You have to get me out of here, Cerys. *Now.*" He nudged his head toward the desk at the other end of the prison. "There should be a set of keys in one of those drawers. On a key ring. Lots of them—"

"Why?" I asked. "They're not after you."

"Oh, but they are, because the wood couldn't keep me," he replied nervously, and shifted onto his knees. "Cerys, *please*. I don't want those monsters to catch me again. Let me help you. Let me do something right, for once. Please. Don't leave me."

I was going to regret this.

I hoped I wouldn't, but I had a feeling that I would.

But I went to the desk at the front of the prison and was riffling through the drawers when I first heard footsteps on the stairs. They were large, heavy. Not human.

The torches from the stairwell threw a bone-eater's shadow across the prison's damp stones, hulking, massive, sharp. It prowled in the graceful way I'd seen before, on all fours, a predator stalking after prey. It knew someone was down here.

I had to hurry.

I grabbed the key ring and hurried back to Seren. He pointed to one of the rusty keys, and I tried it, but no luck. Then the next, and the next. My hands were beginning to shake so badly I could hardly insert the stupid key. But it still wasn't the right one. So I tried the next. Then the next.

"Open the door . . . ," Seren begged.

"I'm trying," I hissed. Another key down. Why were there so many? Who could ever keep them straight?

"Not hard enough, apparently," he nervously singsonged.

"Do you *want* me to leave you?" Finally, a key turned, and the lock popped free. I pushed the door open, but Seren quickly shoved it closed again.

His eyes were wide, face pale. He shook his head and whispered, "I think I'll take my chances in here, actually."

A voice hissed, slithery like the first chill of winter. *"Cccerrysssss."*

Behind me, something low and rumbling echoed down the prison corridor.

I glanced over my shoulder at the creature with us, and my heart sank down to the bottom of the sea. The bone-eater's golden hair shimmered in the orange light from the sconces. She inclined her head, the skin on her face having peeled back to skull, eyes sunken to red pits.

It was Wen.

She curled her lips back from her unnaturally wide mouth, flashing jagged and sharp teeth. What was left of her coronation dress was gone, the seed of the woodcurse pulsing like a heartbeat in her neck. Thorns prickled out from her flesh like splinters, covering her torso, as a long ridge of briars swirled down from the nape of her neck to the small of her back. Black roots shifted just beneath her skin and broke out in places where her flesh had been cut or stripped or burst, weaving down along her arms and legs like strange braids of armor. She crouched, her long black tongue slithering hungrily over her teeth.

There was nothing left of my best friend. Nothing at all.

Anwen opened her terrifying mouth and lunged. I pushed myself off the cell bars and ducked beneath her as she crashed against them. Seren leaped back, hiding himself in the dark corner of his cell. A candle tumbled out of a sconce, spraying orange embers across the ground.

Wen let out a low, guttural growl and turned to me. I grabbed the sconce and went to slice open my palm.

"*No!*" Seren cried, making me pause. "She won't turn back. The curse runs too deep."

"Then how come *you* did? And Fox?"

"Because that idiot wasn't fully turned yet, and I was basically a corpse puppet until you stuck *these* in me." He wiggled his shoulder covered in flowers. "Now I'm a walking terrarium!"

"You're telling me my blood won't do anything to her?"

"I'm telling you she's going to die. Like the ancient by the river."

Anwen slowly stood again, baring her terrifying teeth. She gnashed them hungrily. The sconce shook in my palm. He had to be lying—he must not want me to cure Anwen yet. He wanted to use her. But . . . he wasn't woodcursed anymore. He couldn't command bone-eaters. And he could only know about the ancient by the river if he had seen it, but if he had been tracking us for that long, then why hadn't he sprung a trap?

And before that, in the cottage. I knew he had seen me, but he didn't sic the bone-eaters after us then. . . .

I didn't know what to think of Seren anymore.

"I carried a lot of anger with me for a long time, Cerys," he said, as if he could sense the question in my mind. "The wood used it to control me after I died. But I'm not evil."

Wen gave another howl and lunged again, smashing into the wall I had been leaning against a second before, her claws sinking into the stone like it was putty. She flicked out her black tongue.

"*Cccccerrrysssss*," she hissed.

I dropped the sconce and stumbled back into a corner. I had trapped myself. The bone-eater seemed to relish my horror. Her lips drew back from her terrifying teeth again, and she shrieked.

In it I could hear words—*her* words. "*You abandoned me!*"

I froze.

"*You left!*"

She took a step closer. Then another.

"*You ran!*"

She was so close now; I could smell the wood rot on her— as fresh as it had been on the ancient. The scent of rot and fresh spring grass together in a revolting concoction I remembered too well from when my mother came back. When she tried to kill me. The look in Anwen's eyes was the same as the look in my mother's. I could see the holes in her skin where centipedes crawled, from one tunnel to another, as if she was hollow on the inside.

There was nothing I could use in this prison to help me. In the forest, everything was ripe for my blood—but here, there were only stones and dampness. There was nothing.

The curse would claim me after all.

Suddenly, there was a loud bang. Wen jerked toward the sound, a snarl ripping at her throat.

Seren slammed against the cell bars again. "Forget about me?" he called.

The bone-eater lowered herself down on all fours and prowled toward him.

"Run!" he cried to me. "Get out of here—take the crown and leave!"

What in kingsteeth was he doing? I couldn't tell whose side he was on anymore, what he was trying to do. But I didn't have time to think about it. Now was my chance to leave while he had her distracted. I turned, ready to bolt up the stairs, but—

No. I couldn't.

"*Seren*," the bone-eater hissed. Instead of drawing back from the cell door, he threw it wide. The prison keys fell out of the lock and clattered onto the floor.

"I'm here," he replied quietly. Like he had all those years ago, when Wen and the prince had once been his charges. I turned toward them both, drawing the iron knife out of my pocket. I had kept it close since we'd arrived in Voryn. It wouldn't kill a bone-eater—but it didn't need to.

I wouldn't leave him again. If I had promised myself anything, it was that. No one was left. No one was forgotten.

Not again.

"I'm here," he repeated as Anwen eased into his cell and picked herself up onto two legs.

I was quiet until the last possible moment as I crept toward the cell, my breath painfully loud in my ears. Then I raised my iron blade. I struck, sinking it deep into her back. She gave a cry and tried to grab for me, but I'd already let go of the knife. She screeched, trying to grab it out of her back, stumbling farther into the cell.

I didn't waste time. I grabbed Seren by the arm and pulled him out of the cell with me, then slammed the door closed, trapping her inside.

∽ 36 ∼

THE SHADOWS OF THE HEART

Fox

THE ANCIENTS HAD breached the gates, and the guards were barricading the fortress doors, not that it would stop them. Nothing would. Moss had found its way underneath the door, spreading across the marble floor, and with it came the Wilds. The ancients would find their way in however they could, no matter what the Grandmaster did to stop them. I sneaked out through a side gate that a bone-eater had broken through. The sooner I got out of here, the better off I'd be.

I knew the Wilds too well. I *remembered* the Wilds too well.

I remembered everything now. Though I wished I didn't.

The wood was dark and smelled like freshly upturned earth, and I took a deep breath. I wasn't one for fighting, anyway. I just had to ignore the screams of Voryn, ignore the fact that Daisy was still in there, somewhere.

I would only make things worse. I was a coward, a danger to everyone I cared about. She was better off without me. Tugging at the pack on my shoulder, I glanced behind me one last time, seeing only the top of the spoiled cake that was Voryn, when I heard a snarl in front of me—

And came face-to-face with an angry gray bear.

I swallowed the lump in my throat. "Uh, hello there . . . friend?"

Vala pulled back her lips to show me her very nice, very sharp teeth. I took a step back. *No friend of mine.*

"Now, I know what you're thinking," I began, "but it's not—"

She snarled. *You left her.*

"It's not like that."

You left her, the bear repeated. She looked very angry, and that anger was directed at me, obviously for a multitude of reasons. *You left her, and you are running away.*

I set my jaw. "What else am I supposed to do? And if you care so much, why aren't *you* in there helping her?" I stepped around her to keep on my forward trajectory out of imminent danger. "You go be her hero, bear. I can't," I said over my shoulder. "I don't deserve it."

She doesn't need a hero, Lorne.

The sound of that name again stopped me in my tracks. I

hadn't heard it in so many years; that life felt like an odd half dream I'd almost lived.

She needs people who believe that she *can be the hero.*

"I'm not that person."

Aren't you?

I curled my fingers tightly into a fist. The wood had held the memory of what I'd done for eight years, and for eight years I'd evaded it by not being *me*. Prince Lorne died—he deserved nothing else. *I* deserved nothing else. I could still hear Seren screaming, and the ancient as it prowled around the hollowed-out log, and the sound of my fearful sobs in my throat, and I didn't want to remember.

For years I had been oblivious. I hadn't cared. I hadn't known. I had watched Daisy live with the trauma of her memory, crying in the quiet of her room, missing her mother and . . . and *me*. And I had been right there the whole time.

I had been there, but gone. Because I had wanted to go.

I hurt her so badly that it hurt me in a place I didn't know heartache could reach. I wanted to rip my heart out, I wanted to tear away my flesh, and I wanted to forget again. Things were so much easier, so much less painful, when I was forgotten, when I had forgot.

I couldn't save anyone—not Seren, not my sister.

Not even Daisy.

But . . .

I did not lead you and the briar daughter here so that you could run away, Vala said, her fur bristling. *I led her here to save us. And I led you here to help her.*

There was a noise in the underbrush, and I ducked behind a tree and waited for whatever it was to pass. Vala hunkered down next to me. It sounded lighter than most ancients, so I peeked around the trunk of the tree to get a better look.

I wished I hadn't. The bone-eater that was once a man was deathly pale, his gray hair matted with twigs and dirt, his clothes in shreds. A centipede crawled out of his ear and dived into a hole in his cheek. Even woodcursed, I recognized him. I recognized him because he looked so much like Daisy. He paused, as if he could sense me, and turned his head in my direction. I bristled. His eyes were gone, replaced by dark pits, red pinpricks at the center.

I quickly pulled myself behind the tree and pressed my back against it, praying he hadn't seen me.

But he had.

I could hear him move with that that slow, prowling gait of predators. I knew it too well.

Shit. If I ran, the old man would run after me. If I was still a fox, I could slip through the underbrush and get lost, but I was too big for that, and too slow. *Kingsteeth, think—*

I squeezed my eyes closed.

Think, think.

Magic crackled again at my fingertips—

"Easy on the flames, son!" I heard my father laugh. We

were on the training grounds aside from the barracks, two smoking dummies twenty feet in front of me. I had singed the tips of my fingers, and stuck them into my mouth to alleviate the pain. "Be gentle. Your magic is an extension of you—it can hurt you as well as help you, and if you use it all up, you'll have nothing left for the crown."

I gave a start. "The crown takes our magic? Why would I ever put it on, then?"

Father placed a hand on my head and said, as if it was a secret only for the two of us, "Because it's the price we pay. The crown is alive. It needs nourishment like the rest of us, so we provide it with our magic. That's why only we can wear the crown."

"And if someone else does?"

"It will take them instead." He had smiled, but it was tinged with sadness. All my life, I'd known him with circles under his eyes. He knelt down to me then, his hands tight on my shoulders. "We took something very precious from the Lady, and so we have to repay it with ourselves. A life for a life."

A life for a life.

Oh, kingsteeth, why did his cryptic talks only make sense *now*? I pressed my back against the bark of the tree, relishing the thought of escaping. Of leaving. Of running as far as I could. But I couldn't.

I licked my first two fingers, spun out from behind the

tree, and snapped. A burst of flames spread in a wall across the forest floor between Daisy's father and me. The fire was hot, first burning blue, then orange as it ate at the underbrush. The bone-eater reared back, hissing.

I didn't stick around to figure out what he'd do. I shook my hand to put out the fire at the tip of my fingers and turned to the bear to ask the one question I had been afraid to.

"Vala, the Lady isn't dead, is she?"

No.

"Then where did she go?"

She never left.

I took a deep breath, turned back toward the sieged city. "Okay. Then where is she?"

37

THE TIES THAT BIND

Cerys

"YOU WERE RECKLESS," Seren accused me as we raced up the stairs to the main floor of the fortress, rubbing his wrists where the ropes had been. "We could've been killed! Well, you could have been killed, but I could have been *almost* killed!"

"I saved you, didn't I?"

"I didn't ask you to!"

"Liar!" At the top of the stairs, we took a left and headed back toward my room. "We can't let those ancients take the crown. *Stupid fox*," I added under my breath. I didn't know where he'd gone, but I hoped wherever he was, he had a plan.

A good one.

Seren caught my hand and made me stop. "Your fox isn't coming back. He ran last time, and he ran this time."

I wrenched my hand out of his grip. "I know what hap-pened by the river," she snapped. "You need not remind me."

"No, before that. In the wood eight years ago—"

I heard the guards before I saw them—at least a dozen, brandishing their swords before us. Seren and I backpedaled, but three more came up from behind.

We were trapped.

"I hoped I could trust you, but I was wrong," I heard the Grandmaster say, and the guards parted for her. She wore dark leather armor and carried a sword at her waist, much like the one Petra had—no, it *was* Petra's sword; I could tell from the red ribbon tied around the dragon-headed hilt.

Where was Petra?

The guards shoved us to our knees and bound our hands behind our backs with rope. I struggled against them, but they were too many. The Grandmaster inclined her head toward Seren. She had a new cut on her forehead, a nasty slice. "You *are* in league with the wood."

"No—it's not like that. He's a friend," I tried, but the Grandmaster made a motion, and the guards brought us to our feet again. "What are you doing? We're trying to help!"

"And you will," she replied. Her eyes were flat and gray. I didn't like it at all. "Your blood cured that companion of yours—it will cure my city."

A cold chill curled down my spine. "I don't have enough blood for your entire city."

The Grandmaster shook her head, and I realized just how desperate and disillusioned she was. She wanted to save her city—but this *wasn't* the way to do it. The bone-eaters would keep coming, and the ancients would keep attacking until they found the crown. I struggled against the guards, but even as I did, I knew she wouldn't listen to me.

In her mind, I was her only salvation.

My blood was.

She came up to me, her face quietly concealing rage, and curled her fingers around the crown. She untied my sash and took it. I tensed. "No, wait. You're making a mistake—the crown isn't—"

"Take them to the main hall," the Grandmaster ordered, and without even a final glance she turned and left down the hall. "And bring me a sharp knife."

38

BRAVE

Fox

A GROUP OF guards held Daisy and Seren in the main hall. I leaned away from the doorway and pressed my back against the wall. My hair was stuck to my neck with sweat, and I tied it up into a ponytail with a bit of thread I unraveled from the hem of my shirt. Getting into the city the second time had been a lot harder than leaving, which just felt like tragic irony. Not only had I had to combat guards who seemed intent on thinking that I was woodcursed, I'd also had to deal with bone-eaters and at least two ancients. I'd lit so many fires with my fingers that they were blackened at the tips.

Beside me, Vala gave a grunt, but it was just the normal kind and not the scolding kind.

"I'm blaming you if I die," I told her.

She didn't seem to mind. We took a peek around the corner, careful so that no one saw us.

The Grandmaster grabbed Daisy by the hair and shoved her to her knees. On the other side of the main hall, half a dozen guards held down one bone-eater. The monster looked newly transformed, its face not yet unhinged. There were white ribbons in its dark hair—ribbons I recognized. It was Petra.

"You will change her back," snapped the Grandmaster to Daisy, and she winced as the bone-eater snapped and pulled against its chains. The city was under siege, and this old woman thought that she could bleed Daisy dry and save her people one by one. She was desperate, and that had made her dangerous.

The bone-eater snapped at Daisy, and she flinched away.

"Save her!" the Grandmaster commanded, as if that were how it worked. "Save her. I know you can."

"I—I *can't*. If the bone-eaters are already fully turned, I'll kill them— "

"*Lies!*" the Grandmaster snapped, and grabbed a chunk of her hair. She shoved Daisy closer to the bone-eater. "She isn't gone yet!"

Oh, but Petra was. She was all teeth and claws and hunger. It had taken her faster than it had me—probably because I had been under the protection of the wood; but Petra had no such shields. The seed had burrowed into her skin and dug through her muscles and sinew, and her eyes were pitch-black with red dots—like pinpoints of light. They flicked toward Daisy, and

305

then to the Grandmaster, as the creature gnashed its jagged teeth.

"I'll kill her!" Daisy cried, pushing back against the woman. "I don't want to—I don't want to kill anyone."

"Fine," said the Grandmaster, releasing her, and moved back behind Seren. She took him by his hair and forced his head back, pressing the blade of her sword against his throat. "Then if you don't help her, I'll kill your friend."

Seren sighed at the turn of events and looked over at the Grandmaster dolefully. The blade sank a little deeper into his throat flesh. "Oh, *please*, end my misery if you can."

The Grandmaster jerked her blade back, startled. "What are you?"

"A nightmare," replied the corpse.

I curled my fingers into fists. If I went charging in there, there was no way I would come out unscathed—but maybe that was the point.

"Bear, I've got an idea," I said hesitantly, leaning in to whisper into Vala's ear as I told her the plan. She *harrumph*ed in agreement and said, *I will assist you. Be careful.*

"What's careful to a fox?" I asked, flashing her a grin, though I didn't feel very confident at all—I was frightened out of my wits, so much so that I clenched my hands to keep them from shaking.

It was my turn to choose now: Daisy or the Wilds.

But to be honest, I'd made that choice a long time ago.

As the bone-eater snapped at Cerys again, taking bits of her hair in its mouth, I screwed my courage to the sticking place, remembering that day in the wood years ago when I had chosen to hide.

I couldn't rewrite the past, but I could, perhaps, amend it.

I licked my fingers so I wouldn't burn them again, then spun out from behind the entrance to the great hall and snapped them. "I'm sorry," I said loudly as the roaring fire curled through the hall, splitting the guards from the rest of us, "but I believe that crown is mine."

The Grandmaster shielded her face from my flames. "*You*."

"Me," I agreed above the roar of my flames. "Let Daisy go and give me the crown, or I'll roast all your guards."

"But the fire . . ." She watched the flames crawl through the great hall like a snake weaving through the tall grass as realization dawned on her. "You—you're bloodkin to the old king."

Daisy stared at me as if she had never seen me before. ". . . Fox?"

My gaze flicked to her, and I wished I could say everything that I wanted—that I was sorry I had been such a fool. I was sorry for leaving. I was sorry for being a coward. I was sorry for causing her so much pain, and hurt, and terror. I was sorry for forgetting who I was.

I was the boy who had run into the wood, and everyone else had only followed. If I had never gone in, Daisy's mother would be alive. Seren would be alive.

And I . . . I would never have had to put such a terrible burden on my sister.

The Grandmaster was never going to hand over the crown willingly. She was never going to let Daisy go. I knew that because I knew people like the Grandmaster, and I knew how the crown called. It screeched, it cried, it begged to be placed onto the brow of some unsuspecting prey. It promised what none of us could resist in a world where curses lurked in the wood and where power turned us against one another: safety. We would do anything for it. The Grandmaster was no different. I knew that even before she sneered at me and began to lift the crown above her.

And that's why my plan was not about getting her to hand over the crown. I just wanted her to look at me long enough for Vala to sneak by.

I braced myself.

The Grandmaster placed the crown on her head.

A wave of magic rippled from the old woman. Her bones cracked, straightening, her chin was raised high, and she began to scream. She screamed like Daisy had screamed, like Seren, loud and terrifying and painful. She clawed at her skin and jerked, and for a moment I think she realized her folly, but by then it was too late. And when she opened her eyes, they were no eyes at all, but sockets of burning gold, as if she were burning from the inside out.

"*I see what you truly are, blood of Sunder,*" the Grandmaster intoned in a voice that was hers and the sound of trees swaying in a gentle breeze, "*and I was mistaken. You are no monster.*"

Then she raised her finger and pointed it at me. I couldn't move.

"*You are a cowardly little thing.*"

Magic crackled across my skin, curling up my arms, around my shoulders, over my chest and face, and the feeling was familiar, like getting lost in a long sleep. *No!* Panic raced through me as I tried to push the magic from me, hold on to myself. I had to. But I couldn't, I wouldn't, I—

I didn't.

Fur sprouted from my skin, my fingers curling into paws, teeth lengthening.

The last I remembered, I thought about all the things I would never get a chance to do with Daisy, and it was a well of sorrow so deep I couldn't see the bottom—and then that sorrow vanished, too.

One moment I was there. And then I was gone again, and all that remained was a fox burrowed in human clothes.

⟋ 39 ⟍

ALL THAT ONCE WAS LOST

Cerys

"FOX!" I CRIED in horror.

The fire he had unleashed across the hall flickered to embers, and then to smoke as they disappeared, too. The guards raced through the wall of smoke, only to see their Grandmaster possessed by the crown. Her skin cracked around her eyes, peeling away to red muscle and bone. Her hair burned at the ends. Her tongue blackened in her mouth.

She was there, but she was no longer alive, as if the crown had drawn all the life out of her and run her dry.

It was truly a horrifying sight.

The next thing I knew, a roar shattered the quiet, and Vala pounced on the bone-eater that was once Petra and threw her like a rag doll clear across the hall.

"*Kill the bear*," the Grandmaster commanded in a terrible crackling voice. She raised her hand again. The ground shook, and roots burst up from beneath the stones, swirling toward us with the intent to stab us through.

The bear faced the Grandmaster, teeth bared in a vicious snarl, and before I could stop her, she charged. "Vala! *No!*" Vala caught the roots in her mouth, tore them up from the floor, and tossed them back toward the Grandmaster, barring the way—making herself a shield for us.

Then Seren cried out in surprise, and I felt something nibbling at my wrists. I glanced back and—there was a fox, chewing through the ropes that bound me. The fur on one of his paws was in a jagged line, as though there was a scar underneath.

I recognized the creature with a tinge of heartache. "Fox."

He gnawed his way through the first binding and began to claw and scrape against the second, his tail flicking agitatedly. He finished with my bonds and then went over to free Seren as I began to unwind the bandage on my hand, glancing back up to find that Vala had fought her way through the onslaught of roots and vines and lunged for the Grandmaster.

The bear took a hold of her by the arm and pulled—a full-body pull. The force rippled through her body. It should've been enough to cleave the arm off the old woman, but the

Grandmaster barely budged. She pressed her hand to Vala's face, and the bear let go with a roar, her fur singed in the shape of a handprint.

"We have to help her," I said as I tried to get to my feet, but Seren caught me and pulled me back.

"I don't think we can," he replied softly.

I didn't understand—until I saw the jagged roots curling up around Vala and the Grandmaster like a den of briars, long and sharp like spears.

My heart sank.

Vala snarled, spittle drippling from her maw, and attacked again, this time sinking her teeth into the Grandmaster's shoulder, and the force tilted her crown sideways, making it slide off her head—

The roots shot inward, closing like a massive foot trap, impaling Vala through the middle a dozen times over.

"NO!" I screamed, wrenching my arm from Seren as I hurried over to the bear. Blood pooled around her, running in rivulets down the roots. Too much blood. I tried to pry her out of the trap, to pull the roots away, but she was already gone. Her blood soaked into my trousers; her skin was warm but her heart had stopped. Hot tears burned in my eyes as I turned to the Grandmaster, hollowed and wanting. "You didn't have to kill her!"

"The crown. Where is the crown?" the woman asked feebly. Her gray hair was singed and smoking, her eyes darkened to black pits. "Where is it? *Where?!*"

The crown had toppled off the Grandmaster's head and now sat where it had rolled, in the center of the great hall.

That's when there was a pounding on the door. Two loud knocks, and then the discreet, soft sound of scratching. Like teeth against wood. From between the cracks in the door wormed vines, and they burst through, swirling up over the door, and wrenched it open.

I stared as the bone-eater that was Anwen came in.

She had escaped the prison, but it must have cost her dearly. She was no longer recognizable at all; her face was still torn from a too-wide mouth inset with jagged teeth, but now antlers curved up from her scalp, twining with chains of poison flowers. And every inch of her looked like it was rotting. As she came in, her footsteps left black mold in her wake, and it spread across the floor like ink spilled on a tablecloth.

Against her neck, pulsing like a heartbeat, was the seed that had originally infected her with the woodcurse.

I couldn't take my eyes off her, but the Grandmaster had already turned away, looking for something else. "The crown! There it is!"

She stood to run for it—but she never reached it.

Wen had been a fast fighter as a human, but as a bone-eater she was something else entirely. She rushed into the room, the wood swirling in behind her, roots and brambles and thorns, and grabbed the Grandmaster by the face, dragging her close.

The old woman struggled, trying to free herself, but Wen's mouth yawned wide and she sank her teeth into the woman's throat. The Grandmaster gave a gurgling scream, jerking, clawing at Wen to let go, but it was too late. The bone-eater that was Anwen tore the woman's throat out, and she sank to the floor.

Then Anwen turned slowly to me. Blood dripped from her too-wide mouth.

The crown lay between us.

Until a bolt of orange—Fox—grabbed it up off the ground and ran away with it.

Anwen shrieked. As if called by her rage alone, bone-eaters swarmed into the main hall, scurrying toward me on all fours. Two ancients loomed behind them in the doorway, watching. They were all coming for me, teeth gnashing, claws clicking—

That's when I heard a yip and the crown clattered to the floor. I whirled toward the sound, and Fox was slowly struggling to his feet, a bone-eater towering over him, having knocked him to the ground. There was a deep gash in his shoulder. A bone-eater hissed at him, and he snarled in retaliation, the fur on his back bristling.

I didn't have time to think before I was running toward the fox. Stumbling, I pressed my bloodied hand against the floor, and briars immediately began to grow. Thick, thorny ones that curled around one another, creating a barrier between us. They grew, snarling themselves, weaving thick and prickly and dense—denser than any garden wall. They snagged the crown and wrapped it deep within.

I scooped up the fox in my arms.

A bone-eater launched itself toward me.

Kingsteeth.

I threw my free hand over my face. With a flash of a blade, Seren was there, batting the creature back. He shoved it away with his foot. "You go for the fox and not the *crown*?" he exclaimed.

"I'm sure I'll regret it later," I said, and forced a smile, despite everything.

He looked like he wanted to strangle me, but instead he pushed the bone-eater back and with the flat of his blade knocked another one away. "Get somewhere safe," he said. "I'll distract the monsters. You figure out how to stop Anwen."

"I can't kill her," I said.

"You might not have a choice."

He was wrong. If I'd learned anything in the wood, it was that there was always a choice, but sometimes the right one wasn't the easy one.

Suddenly, one of the bone-eaters caught Seren by surprise and knocked him back. His sword went spinning away, and the bone-eater tossed him against the wall like a rag doll. With a cry, I grabbed one of the growing briars with my bloodied hand, thorns pricking my skin, and tossed it at the bone-eater. It became embedded in the monster's skin and began to grow across it at a frightening rate, binding it.

With Fox tight in my arms, I backpedaled behind one of the pillars to collect myself. The briars were still spreading across the room, but they were slowing now, and the bone-eaters were almost through. The smell of blood was heavy in the air.

Anwen prowled back and forth on the other side of the wall of briars, searching for a way to the golden crown in the nest of thorns.

In my arms, Fox tried to wiggle free. He was the prince, and he'd come back to help me.

"You should've run," I whispered to him, because I didn't know how we'd survive this. Maybe we weren't supposed to.

I had spent so many years thinking that he and Seren were dead—I hadn't thought of the possibility of either of them being alive. Because in no version of the story were they. But Seren was here, and Fox had been with me all this time. They had never really been gone.

They were still here. But to what end?

Fox pressed his face against my cheek. I scratched him behind the ears, grateful and sad all at once. I reached for my iron knife to cut a slice in my other hand for more power, but then I stopped myself. No matter how much magic I had or how thick I grew the thorns and briars, it wouldn't bring Anwen back. She was too far gone, and I was too late, and we were too far from home.

"*Ceeeeeeeryssssss*," called Wen, and I shivered as she hissed my name. "*Let me—let me ssseeeee. Let me see your fangs.*"

She knew I wasn't as powerful as she was—that I wasn't good at fighting, that I couldn't face her head-on no matter what I tried.

"*Ceryssssss,*" Anwen went on. She grabbed a fistful of briars and tore them through. "*Comme outtttt.*"

Fox's cold nose pressed against my cheek softly, comfortingly.

I didn't know what to do.

In Aloriya's tale, the curse was always here. But in Voryn's tale, it had come from King Sunder stealing the crown from the Lady of the Wilds. And now the Lady was gone—vanished for three hundred years. If the wood had become cursed the second she gave her crown, why had she given it in the first place?

I don't think she's dead. Petra's voice whispered in my head, like a secret.

If it had been stolen, then wouldn't the Lady have come after it with her old gods? She knew where it was and how to get it. But if she was dead, if she was in the air we breathed, then the curse would be gone.

Unless . . .

I glanced out from behind the pillar at the golden circlet in the thicket of briars. I'd never understood why the Lady of the Wilds needed a crown to sway a forest, but that was because she didn't. In the Grandmaster's study, the tapestry didn't depict her with a crown. And ancients didn't need a crown to spread the woodcurse. Bone-eaters didn't need a crown. Nor did the animals, or the trees or flowers or the river. . . .

Humans needed crowns.

Wen had almost torn through the thicket. She reached through the briars, thorns scraping her skin off her bones, toward the golden crown. Fear swelled in my throat, making it hard to swallow. I didn't want to get any closer to this monster—but I had to.

I had to remember that my Anwen was still there somewhere beneath the poisoned roots of the woodcurse that had twisted into her heart. I knew she was still there, even though I couldn't see her anymore.

If I was going to save her—save this city, the wood, my *home*—I had to believe I still could.

I grabbed Seren's sword, which had landed close to where I crouched, and took it tightly in my bloodied hand. The briars that I had grown began to wilt and rot once Wen touched them and carved a hole big enough for her to step through to the other side. There were other bone-eaters lost in the thorns, and they raged and cried, trapped in their snarls. I stood out from behind the pillar and began moving toward the crown in the thicket. The vines and roots wove away from me, creating a tunnel of sorts, leading me straight to the crown—as if they knew what I was about to do.

Fox curled against my shoulders. I looked down at the

crown and all the curses it held, and all the ire. Fox had said that I had screamed when I'd put on the crown, and Seren had screamed, and the Grandmaster.

But it wasn't they who were screaming, not really.

The Lady had been trapped just as surely as we, and she had been suffering for such a long time.

There was no cure for the woodcurse. There was no way to break it. And as long as the crown existed, we would all be trapped.

I curled my fingers around the sword and raised it, and Fox pressed his head against my cheek. I didn't know what the world would be without the crown—who I would be, or Anwen, or Seren, or Fox, or the Wilds itself. But I knew what we were *with* the crown, and with the crown there were no happy endings.

Wen screamed, reaching for me, her voice a chorus of death.

With all my might, I slammed the sword against the crown. Cracks raced across the golden briars and gilded leaves. A light poured out of the cracks, soft at first, but it grew steadily brighter. Wen shrieked again, and the bone-eaters cried, reaching out their hands to the broken crown at my feet. I pressed my face into Fox's fur as the light bloomed brighter, and brighter and, like the coming of a sunrise, washed away the night.

❧ 40 ❧

FOR LORNE

Cerys

SIX MONTHS PASSED like a sigh through the trees, soft and brisk.

The Wildwood grew orange with autumn, then white and barren in winter, but now I could feel the first sun-kissed winds of spring again. Of change. It pecked my cheeks like pinpricks. I stepped lightly across the last crumbles of snow in our garden and crouched beside a small hole in the ground beside our storehouse.

Humming, I unwrapped a basket full of leftovers—bits of breads and meats that were about to go bad. I clicked my tongue, calling, and a wet nose poked out of the burrow, followed by beady black eyes and large orange ears.

"Good afternoon," I greeted the fox as he slunk out to take a bit of bread. I rubbed him behind the ears, and he tilted his face toward me, relishing it.

Behind him, three small kits eased out with their mother.

"Oh, they're growing so fast," I mused as they came up and ate their fill before returning into their burrow. "You'll have a family ready for exploring soon. Just don't go into the baker's yard," I added softly. "I have it on good information that he doesn't take too kindly to foxes——"

"Sprout?" Papa called from the house, and poked his head out of the back door. "C'mon, hurry up—we don't want to miss it!"

"Coming!" I left the basket for the foxes to pick through later. As I came back into the house, I shrugged out of the tartan shawl I'd wrapped around my shoulders, pulled my shoulder-length hair out of its bun, and shook it out. I'd cut it a few days after I broke the curse, since it'd been burned on the ends, and there were snarls of briars I couldn't possibly hope to untangle. I liked the new length, though, so I'd kept it.

Papa was on his fourth cup of coffee this afternoon. He didn't sleep well anymore, and sometimes I could hear him having nightmares from my room across the hall. Most of the people who had been turned into bone-eaters did. Papa said his felt like memories of things he'd surely done—of running through the wood, of tearing meat off a still-kicking rabbit, of a hunger scratching at his bones.

I never asked Wen. Not during our brief stay in Voryn after I broke the curse, nor during the week-long trek back to the Sundermount before the first snowfall, nor any time after. She clearly didn't want to talk about it, and I didn't want to know whether or not her nightmares were memories, too. I hoped they weren't.

With the crown's magic returned to the wood, the forest awoke in bits and pieces as spring came—a tree here, unfurling from its bone-white husk into a flowering dogwood, another bursting with strange pink flowers, while others still waited to thaw. I could smell it in the air, sharp like lavender. Most folks Papa's age were still apprehensive about the Wildwood—old habits die hard—but the rest of us felt like a wall that had been up for most of our childhoods was finally gone.

The trees were no longer forbidden, and the wood no longer cursed.

All my life I had thought that I would never flourish where my roots did not grow, but I think that was just a lie I told myself.

When I first returned to the village, it felt so small. The Village-in-the-Valley had been torn apart by what had happened at the castle. Family members turned into monsters, missing, or worse yet, they returned corrupted and wrong. The villagers who had not come to the coronation, who had evaded the woodcurse and kept to their homes, had erected barbed wire around the town when the wood had come for them. They'd protected themselves. They'd fought.

And when the curse broke, most of the people who had been cursed woke up on the edge of the wood. Some of them woke up with too-pointed teeth, others with too-long nails, scars across their arms from where something else had settled where their skin had been. They woke up with a ravaging hunger, some with the taste of blood in their mouths, and nothing settled back into the way it should have been until Wen returned to the castle, her teeth a little too sharp when she smiled.

Most of Aloriya didn't mind that we no longer possessed an enchanted crown, because we also didn't have a cursed wood anymore, either. Anwen returned to the Sundermount with her determination and her courage, and she picked up the pieces of her fallen kingdom, and the village began to heal. We began to find a way to live without the crown.

Without the magic.

Without the curse.

Barbed wire still encircled the town, but it grew with brambles and rusted to brown, and soon the village was the one I remembered—with its smoky chimneys and brightly covered rooftops and the clock in the town square ringing noon every day, the sweet smell of cinnamon rolls and high-rising breads from the bakery, the town musician on his fiddle. Kids played in the square again while old men gamed chess on benches outside the pub.

When I returned from Voryn, Papa was waiting for me at the flower shop. "I knew you'd come back," he said, and we hugged for a long time.

The garden in the backyard reflected our time away. The sunflowers, once bent low on their stalks, were dead on the ground, while the rosebushes grew in snarls, their flowers gone and leaves falling. The magnolias and crawling ivies and buttercups had withered in the coming frost. But the shovel was still propped against the shed where Papa had last put it the day before Anwen's coronation, and his gloves still hung from their book by the back door. Though now spiders had roosted in the fingers.

It was as though the garden had changed with us.

Everything that I grew up believing was a lie. The stories, the history, the magic. Aloriya was far from perfect. It held poison in its roots like an elderberry tree, where you thought all it offered was wine. And this house that stood in the over-grown ruins of the garden reminded me of the girl who used to drink the wine without questioning how it came to be.

As afternoon sunlight spilled into the quiet flower shop, I leaned my head against Papa's shoulder. All the vases were emptied, waiting for the spring thaw. "I think we should harvest your mother's flowers this spring," he finally said. "The ones in the corner. The ones that came from the wood."

"I think she'd like that." I lifted my head from his shoulder. "Can I ask you something? About her?"

"Of course."

"Did she . . . did she come from Voryn?"

He didn't seem surprised, but a little resigned. He scratched the side of his head and sighed. "Your mother was a secretive kind, Sprout. She never really said, but I did catch her, some nights, mumbling about a city in the wood. I thought it was just hogwash. But she said it was beautiful—is it?"

"Yes," I replied, and as I did, my heart filled with the kind of longing I couldn't describe. I'd felt it all winter, in this house that was small and simple and familiar. I always thought I would live here forever, but now I wasn't so sure I wanted to.

Papa gave me a quiet sidelong look and sipped his coffee. "This is going to be a long evening."

I groaned. "Don't remind me. I hate these things. I'd rather face the wood again than another coronation."

"Ah, but at least you've got a dance to look forward to tonight, eh?" he asked, elbowing me in the side, and winked.

A blush ate up my cheeks.

"*Aha!* Oh, I can't wait to see this," he crowed, smiling so wide he showed all his teeth—even the chipped one in the back that hadn't been chipped before the woodcurse. He didn't like showing it. It reminded him of things he preferred not to remember. "My little girl, dancing the night away!" He did a little jig as he went up the stairs to finish getting ready, and I wanted to bury my head under the dirt in mortification. "Now put on your dress! We've got a coronation to attend!"

My only proper dress was lost somewhere in an aban-doned cottage, so Wen had lent me one of hers. It had to be let out a little in the sides and hemmed on the bottom, but it was a pleasant rose color with embroidered vines curling across the hems and sleeves. I rather liked it, as far as dresses went.

Papa put on his old tweed suit and combed his gray hair over the balding spot on his head, and after I helped him fix his bow tie, we were ready to go.

"Oh! Almost forgot." I slipped back into the shop and took a crown of daisies off the counter. I had grown and laced them myself—the hard way, too. I couldn't make flowers bloom anymore. It was like a small part of me had been ripped away, leaving room for something else to take its place. I just wasn't sure what yet.

"Can't go to a coronation without a crown," he tsk-tsked as we left the shop.

"I don't think it's the crown that makes the ruler."

"No, but it sure is a nice one."

I had to agree.

Villagers emerged from their houses, carrying food and drink, starting the long hike up the King's Road to the white castle at the top. Some of the older folks hitched rides on the backs of wagons; kids ran along trailing streamers behind them as they curled up the mountain.

As Papa laced his arm in mine and we started up the road, I remembered what waited for me at the top—and I smiled.

I wasn't sure if the wood had changed me or if I had changed myself, but I felt it. Like a seed outgrowing its shell, a bloom unfurling from its bud. I was not the same girl I had been the last time I'd traveled up this road.

I knew better now. There were no perfect kingdoms without cost, and there were no stories that were completely true—or completely false.

Not even mine.

I always thought that gardeners' daughters couldn't thrive where our roots didn't grow. But maybe we were like dandelion tufts.

Maybe we were built to catch a warm spring wind and grow somewhere new.

Soon, the bakers next door joined us on our trek to the Sundermount, and the two old men who always played chess by the tavern, and the blacksmith's son even *winked* at me. Halfway up the mountain, Papa asked, "So how many kits do we have now in that burrow?"

"Three."

He guaffed. "*Three!* Three more pests in my garden!"

"You enjoy the pests," I teased, knowing that he fed them more than I ever did, in secret, when he thought I wasn't looking.

He lifted his chin regally. "At least they're not as bad as *your* fox."

I smiled at that. "*My* fox is one of a kind," I replied, and began to hum along to the baker's brood—their three kids and their two yapping hounds—as they sang some silly rhyme about a flower in the wood that could cure death itself.

The Sundermount slowly came into view, the forest unfurling like a flower, and then there was the castle where I had spent my childhood, and Papa looped my arm into his, and squeezed my hand tightly.

This was only the second coronation I'd ever seen, but if the first one was anything to go on, they weren't all they were cracked up to be.

Queen Anwen of Aloriya accepted her daisy crown with grace. She smiled down at me in the crowd, her teeth a little too pointed, and I smiled back at her because I knew a secret—she would do just fine without the magic of a golden crown. No, she would do *better* than fine.

I couldn't say the same for most of the townsfolk, though. When I told Anwen that inviting the entire village was a bad idea, she obviously didn't believe me, but not even an hour after the coronation itself, Papa was on his third drink and already recounting the tale of the Great Pig Race of the Summerside Year, and was it as riveting as it was the first two times he'd told it already?

I would've been a terrible daughter to say otherwise.

As the party wore on, I slipped away to a quiet area of

the garden and leaned against the wall by the archway I used to look in from, watching the people swirl and tumble about, laughing as the music drifted into the evening. Everything looked so much the same from the inside of the garden, I couldn't remember why I was so obsessed with it.

A laugh drew me away from my thoughts.

To the other side of the garden, where a boy with hair the color of marigolds and a smile that tugged up a little too much on one side, tricky and daring, laughed with a crowd of dignitaries. They fawned over him the longer he talked. He was very good at talking. He could make you fall in love with him with a single word.

Everyone said the newly returned crown prince of Aloriya was handsome.

He *was*—don't get me wrong—but he also had a stomach the size of an endless pit, made terrible puns, fled at the first sign of trouble, and if you gave him a choice between eating meat pie and ruling a kingdom, he'd choose the meat pie.

And I think I loved those things about him the most.

"Well, he looks quite content with himself," said a monotonous voice to my left, and I jumped, spilling my wine all over the front of my dress.

Seren leaned in the archway, his arms folded, feet crossed.

"*Kingsteeth*, don't sneak up on me like that!" I mumbled, frowning down at the growing stain over my chest. "Elderberry wine is almost impossible to get out, you know."

"Sorry," he replied, sounding earnest. He was in dark leather armor, although on the left side of his chest, bits of strange star-shaped buds sprouted up through his collar. The dark circles under his eyes were, somehow, impossibly deeper, and his hair was washed and neatly combed back, pinned at the base of his neck with a twist of briars. He eyed me suspiciously. "Why are you over here alone? And not—say—dancing with your *prince*?"

"Well, I'm not alone if you're here," I replied smartly.

"Mmh."

"Why don't you join the celebration?"

"Anwen asked, but . . ." He motioned to himself. "I doubt anyone would really like a corpse waltzing around her coronation. Especially the seneschal. You know how she is. Besides, I have a job to do, and I shouldn't stay long."

"From the Lady?"

"Who else? And that bothersome bear is waiting at the edge of the wood. I suppose she'll track me down if I don't return soon," he added with a sigh.

After I'd broken the curse and freed the Lady of the Wood, she had appointed him her liaison between the world of humans and the heart of the wood for eight years—the amount of time he had been under the control of the woodcurse. For eight years he would be her servant, and afterward . . . well, he didn't know. None of them did. "But quite honestly," he had added when we first discussed his predicament back in the winter, "I would rather be this than dead, which was the other option."

I really didn't want Seren dead either, though it was only the magic of the wood that kept him alive. But maybe in eight years we would be ready to say goodbye, and he would be ready to go. Eight years was a long time, though it didn't seem long at all.

Seren watched the dance for another song and then turned to leave.

"Aren't you going to at least stay to congratulate her?" I asked.

He inclined his head. "Oh, I wouldn't want to jinx anything." Then he ducked through the frozen honeysuckle vines and disappeared into the darkened line of trees, where a silver bear waited, her bones stitched together with ivy and honeysuckle vines.

Cryptic undead men were the worst.

I frowned down at the elderberry wine stain on the front of my dress, my dread growing because the more I scrubbed at the stain, the worse it got.

Seneschal Weiss was going to *kill* me.

As I licked my fingertips to try to perhaps scrub out the stain, a familiar voice asked, "So he's gone already?"

I jumped, startled. "Oh—Wen. Hi."

She was flanked by two bodyguards who kept an amiable distance. I'm sure the seneschal had told them to stay on

Wen all evening, especially after the *last* coronation. The daisy crown I'd made fit her head a lot better than any golden crown ever would. Wen glanced behind me to where Seren had been a few moments before, a frown curling across her soft pink lips. "He could have stayed," she added a little softer.

"I think he still feels guilty about—you know. Disrupting your last coronation."

She tilted her head slightly. "Yes, well, I'm sure we would've had a lot to talk about."

"With *that* corpse? He really hasn't changed much. Still the same tall, broody, smart-mouthed—"

"I still feel it sometimes." She lifted her eyes toward the wood beyond the wall, and I noticed her hands curling into fists.

"The woodcurse?" I asked in alarm.

"No— yes? No," she finally decided, and her fair eyes drifted toward the golden lights and the merriment and the music, as if they were on the other side of endless chasm. "It's different. Similar, but not quite the same. It's this itch that I can't scratch. Under my skin. This part of me that . . . that *remembers*. I remember succumbing to the curse, hunting you through the wood, trying to kill you. I remember feeling lost and broken and *alone*. I was so hungry and alone, and after a while I just . . . gave in to that. But you never gave up on me. Not once."

At that, I stepped in front of her so she could no longer see the people who didn't understand the forest's shadows, and I took her hands in mine and squeezed them tightly. "Anwen Sunder, you will always be my best friend. Forever."

She pressed her forehead against mine, a silent promise between us. "Forever."

The orchestra drifted into a softer waltz. Anwen pulled away from me, wiping a stray tear from her eye, and studied the deepening stain on my borrowed dress. "You should get that stain looked at. You know Seneschal Weiss is going to *kill* you if you hand it back like *that*."

"Maybe if I drown myself in a barrel of wine, she won't notice the dress is a different color?"

"Yes, but then she'll get at you for ruining the wine."

"I will never win," I lamented tragically, and we laughed, because even in the forest's shadows, we were still us, and things that were different weren't the ones that would tear us apart.

"Gossiping about Lord Aleran's nose again?" The prince materialized out of the crowd with Petra. Somehow, they had escaped the horde of dignitaries fawning over them. I quickly crossed my arms over my chest to try to hide the wine stain. I didn't need *everyone* knowing I was a disaster.

Wen raised her chin defiantly. "A queen never gossips, thank you."

"Mm-hm, I'm sure that's a lie."

"Says the king of liars."

"At your service." He gave a mock bow and introduced

the young woman beside him. "Wen, meet the Grandmaster of Voryn."

Petra was probably the most smartly dressed at the coronation, in comfortable-looking trousers and a simple button-down shirt. Her brown skin was soft in the orange lantern light, her short hair pulled back with balm. She had a pin on her collar in the shape of Voyrn's crest—the only signifier that she was nobility. "Your Majesty," she greeted her with a bow, "it's a pleasure to finally meet you in person. The penmanship in your letters is excellent."

"Wen, please! And thank you—yours is quite elegant as well." She offered her hand, but Petra, instead of shaking it, brought Wen's hand to her lips and kissed her knuckles. A blush quickly crawled across Wen's cheeks.

"I believe I promised you a dance in the letters," Petra said, not letting go.

Wen's eyes widened. "Oh—oh yes. And to discuss the treatries between Voryn and Aloriya, I believe."

"Why not both?"

As Petra pulled her toward the dance, Wen gave her brother a skeptical look, but he simply shrugged and she let Petra pull her out onto the dance floor. We waited until they were far enough away before I accused him, "You knew that would happen."

Lorne was trying very hard not to look too proud of

himself. "Call it my animal instincts." Then he dug for a kerchief in his waistcoat and presented it to me. "I would invest in pockets if I were you."

"This is your sister's dress," I replied, irritated that he'd noticed the stain, and took the kerchief to scrub at the spot. "I'm just borrowing it."

"I would keep it."

"Because I ruined it?"

"Because it looks impossibly beautiful on you," he replied with a grin. Tonight, he wore a bright blue jacket and dark trousers, and a circlet of daisies on his head. He'd cut his hair, and it was short, a strange orange-gold that wasn't quite one or the other anymore, now a little wild and unkempt no matter how much he tried to tame it. "Rose may even be my favorite color now."

I gasped to hide my blush and handed the kerchief back. "Prince Lorne giving the gardener's daughter a compliment? Oh, scandelous!"

His face pinched as he slid the kerchief into his pocket again. "Ugh, please don't. You know I hate that name."

"It's a good name."

"But it's not *me*."

No, it really wasn't. "Prince Lorne" reminded me of a timid boy who disappeared into the wood, chasing after a sound that was never there. He certainly wasn't a boy anymore, or remotely timid, and he never chased things if he didn't have to. And when he did, he didn't cower like that boy in the wood so long ago, or the fox he became. The wood changed us, but perhaps it changed him most of all.

I offered my hand to him. "Fox," I addressed him, and his eyebrows shot up at the name, "would you care to dance?"

A smile stretched across his lips. "Why, Daisy, I think that would 'break protocol,'" he said, mocking Seneschal Weiss's sharp accent. He slipped his hand into mine. "So of course I'd love to. I am a fantastic dance partner."

"Because you're dancing with me," I teased, and led him out into the middle of the royal garden, where all the people I had known my entire life danced and sang and laughed. Where Wen was falling for the Grandmaster of Voryn, and my father was recounting the Great Pig Race of the Summerside Year—*again*—by the wine barrels. The music was bright and happy, and Fox gathered my hand in his and placed my other hand on his waist, and we followed into the dance, swept away in the happiness of it all.

There was no curse, no dark clouds.

I had lived a fairy tale, where for a moment a royal gardener's daughter was no longer stuck behind garden walls, and foxes turned into princes, and I said without thinking, "I think I love you, Fox."

He stumbled on his feet. A blush ate up his cheeks. "Wh-what?"

"I think I love you."

He stared at me, and the part of his brain that he had sectioned off for dance had died, because we were just standing now in the middle of the crowd of people, and he had this awestruck look on his face. "You . . . you *what*?"

People were beginning to stare. "I mean, you don't have to make a *scene* if you don't feel the same—"

"You too," he quickly fumbled, and winced. My hopes began to rise like morning mists in the valley. "I mean I yes—no, that's not right. You think you love me—I love that you—what I mean is—"

I stood up on my tiptoes and pressed my lips to his to save him the embarrassment, and he melted into me, relieved that I understood what he meant. He smelled like fresh oak trees and spring rain, and as I curled my fingers into his hair he nibbled at my lip, exploring, tempting. My heart thumped in my chest like a jackrabbit, so bright and hopeful it hurt, and when we finally broke apart, he asked, breathless, "How do you feel about foxes?"

"I love foxes. Even the thieving, sly ones. How do you feel about gardeners?"

"I love one in particular," he replied, and twined his fingers into mine.

I grinned. "Do you want to go?"

"Where?"

"Anywhere. Everywhere."

He blinked in surprise. *"Now?"*

"Now," I whispered, and led him toward the archway draped in thawing honeysuckle vines, away from the garden I had always known. I glanced one last time at Papa, who watched me from the dessert table and raised his glass to me. *Wander*, he mouthed, and smiled the kind of goodbye that had good luck tucked into the corners.

The night was fresh, and the new spring winds blew warm and sweet, and like a dandelion tuft caught on a breeze, I let go of the girl I used to be and led Fox into the Wilds.

THE END

ACKNOWLEDGMENTS

When I wrote *Among the Beasts & Briars*, this story was only a seedling of an idea—a flower just for me. And I'm so thankful that I have the opportunity to share it with you.

I would like to thank Holly Root for believing in this strange story of mine, and for Kelsey Murphy for first seeing the spark of what it could be. But mostly, I want to thank Jordan Brown, who saw that spark, and saw what this book could become, and helped me create something wild and wonderful. I also want to thank my copy editor, Renée Cafiero, who I have worked with twice before, and every time I am just blown away by how she polishes my words into something that shines. Thank you all so, so much.

Thank you to Nicole Brinkley, who read an earlier draft and said, "This is only half a story, Ash," and to Ada Starino and Savvy Apperson and Shae McDaniel, who all read my last drafts and confirmed that yes, finally, it *is* a whole story!

I want to thank Katherine Locke and Kaitlyn Sage

Patterson, both for telling me this story is worthy and for never giving up on me when I felt like giving up on myself. Get yourself friends who will look your depression in the eye and tell it, "Not today."

And thank *you*, reader, for reading to the very last page, past THE END. These stories have always been for me, but I am so glad that I can share them with you.

Thank you.

Petra escorted the queen of Aloriya back to her chambers after the coronation, though there were still quite a few people dancing through the night. She didn't know how late—or early—it was, but the night felt endless. She didn't want it to end, especially now.

The queen paused in the doorway, as if remembering. "Oh, we never talked about the treaty!"

"I think we'll have time tomorrow . . . Wen." Every time she said the queen's name, it felt electric against her tongue. She dared not hope too much, because this was the queen of Aloriya, and she probably had plenty of suitors who didn't come from a once-cursed wood.

But as she began to leave, the queen caught her wrist. "Wait."

Petra's heart raced like a shooting star across the sky. She dared not hope as she turned around, and the girl with golden hair and a crown of daisies and teeth a little too sharp pecked her on the lips. Softly, sweetly, as if asking a question. And in reply, Petra took her gently—so gently—by the sides of her face and pressed their lips together again, and in the open doorway of Queen Anwen of Aloriya's chambers, they kissed in a sliver of moonlight.

Seren stepped into the heart of the wood and knelt down beside the Lady, his joints stiff from rigor mortis. "You summoned me?" he asked in a dry baritone.

The Lady was too bright to look at directly. He wasn't sure if she was on fire or simply shining with a brilliant sort of magic, but she bathed the entire grove in golden sunlight. Even in her brilliance, though, he did notice by the roots of her throne a young woman with dark hair and amber skin and peculiar violet eyes—a person from Nor. She watched Seren cautiously, curling her knees up toward her chest, drawing attention to her unmoving arm that was being turned, millimeter by millimeter, to stone.

A curse.

And stranger still—she wasn't frightened by his appearance, unlike everyone else he had come across.

The Lady said in a voice that sounded as though it came from the roots and the trees and the leaves and the flowers all around him, "This young woman has invoked the Rites of Debt. She wants the flower that cures death itself to save her. And you shall help her find it."